Kane's blue-gray eyes chilled her

As did his next words. "Maybe he's been captured, or maybe it's what he wants us to think. Either way, Lakesh is on his own."

Brigid stared at him unblinkingly. "You don't mean that, Kane."

"Every damn syllable."

She kept staring at him. "You can pack up and run, but I'm going after him."

He shook his head gravely. "That's where you're mistaken, Baptiste. You're not going after him."

"Who'll stop me?"

She heard a click, the faint, brief drone of a tiny electric motor, and the solid slap of the butt of the Sin Eater sliding into his palm.

Kane raised the big-bored handblaster. "Lakesh has put you in harm's way for the last time, Baptiste."

Other titles in this series:

Exile to Hell
Destiny Run
Savage Sun

JAMES AXLER

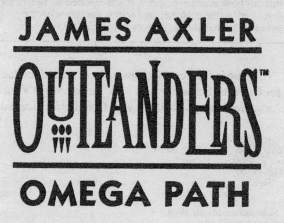

OUTLANDERS™

OMEGA PATH

A GOLD EAGLE BOOK FROM
WORLDWIDE®

TORONTO • NEW YORK • LONDON
AMSTERDAM • PARIS • SYDNEY • HAMBURG
STOCKHOLM • ATHENS • TOKYO • MILAN
MADRID • WARSAW • BUDAPEST • AUCKLAND

This one is for Terry Collins and our shared fondness for Old Man Schwump and Mrs. Mendelbright's bureau which was shipped all the way from Fort Lauderdale.

First edition March 1998
ISBN 0-373-63817-5

OMEGA PATH

Special thanks to Mark Ellis for his contribution to the Outlanders concept, developed for Gold Eagle Books.

A wanderer is man from his birth.
He was born in a ship
On the breast of the river of Time.
—Matthew Arnold

The Road to Outlands—
From Secret Government Files to the Future

Almost two hundred years after the global holocaust, Kane, a former Magistrate of Cobaltville, often thought the world had been lucky to survive at all after a nuclear device detonated in the Russian embassy in Washington, D.C. The aftermath—forever known as skydark—reshaped continents and turned civilization into ashes.

Nearly depopulated, America became the Deathlands—poisoned by radiation, home to chaos and mutated life forms. Feudal rule reappeared in the form of baronies, while remote outposts clung to a brutish existence.

What eventually helped shape this wasteland were the redoubts, the secret preholocaust military installations with stores of weapons, and the home of gateways, the locational matter-transfer facilities. Some of the redoubts hid clues that had once fed wild theories of government cover-ups and alien visitations.

Rearmed from redoubt stockpiles, the barons consolidated their power and reclaimed technology for the villes. Their power, supported by some invisible authority, extended beyond their fortified walls to what was now called the Outlands. It was here that the rootstock of humanity survived, living with hellzones and chemical storms, hounded by Magistrates.

In the villes, rigid laws were enforced—to atone for the sins of the past and prepare the way for a better future. That was the barons' public credo and their right-to-rule.

Kane, along with friend and fellow Magistrate Grant, had upheld that claim until a fateful Outlands expedition. A displaced piece of technology…a question to a keeper of the archives…a vague clue about alien masters—and their world shifted radically. Suddenly, Brigid

Baptiste, the archivist, faced summary execution, and Grant a quick termination. For Kane there was forgiveness if he pledged his unquestioning allegiance to Baron Cobalt and his unknown masters and abandoned his friends.

But that allegiance would make him support a mysterious and alien power and deny loyalty and friends. Then what else was there?

Kane had been brought up solely to serve the ville. Brigid's only link with her family was her mother's red-gold hair, green eyes and supple form. Grant's clues to his lineage were his ebony skin and powerful physique. But Domi, she of the white hair, was an Outlander pressed into sexual servitude in Cobaltville. She at least knew her roots and was a reminder to the exiles that the outcasts belonged in the human family.

Parents, friends, community—the very rootedness of humanity was denied. With no continuity, there was no forward momentum to the future. And that was the crux—when Kane began to wonder if there *was* a future.

For Kane, it wouldn't do. So the only way was out— way, way out.

After their escape, they found shelter at the forgotten Cerberus redoubt headed by Lakesh, a scientist, Cobaltville's head archivist, and secret opponent of the barons.

With their past turned into a lie, their future threatened, only one thing was left to give meaning to the outcasts. The hunger for freedom, the will to resist the hostile influences. And perhaps, by opposing, end them.

Chapter 1

Lakesh awoke, strapped to a bench, sweating and nauseous from the drug. From beyond the steel-riveted door came the sound of footsteps, faint voices, the odd scream.

He lay there for some time, staring at the damp ceiling, at its single lightbulb, wondering how bad things would get and how soon they would begin. He didn't have to wait long before the door scraped open.

Two men stepped in. Without surprise, he saw one of them was Salvo. The other was a stocky, blunt-featured Mag with a moon face. Because of the poor lighting and the residual of the drug creeping through his system, he had to grope for the man's name. Finally he recognized him as Pollard. Both of them were dressed in the pearl gray duty uniforms of Magistrates.

Salvo's teeth gleamed in the gloom. "How are we feeling?"

Lakesh said, as clearly as he could, "I'll only tell that to the baron."

Salvo chuckled. "If only it were as simple as that. However, if you could bring yourself to cooperate, I might open certain avenues that would offer you a way out."

"A way out of what?" Lakesh demanded.

"A death sentence for sedition."

"You've assaulted me, imprisoned me and you dare to speak of sedition?"

"My powers are broad," Salvo replied softly, "with plenty of room for interpretation."

He paused, pursing his lips. "I am going to ask you questions, some personal, others dealing with ideology."

"I will not answer any questions unless they are put to me by the baron."

Salvo made a spitting sound of impatience. "You're a difficult man to sympathize with. However, you are worth more than even the baron imagines."

Lakesh turned his face away, staring again at the ceiling, at the feebly glowing lightbulb.

Pollard said, "Why don't we make it easier for him to think it over?"

Salvo nodded. "Lakesh, you know as well as I there's an easy way and hard way of getting things done. Just for you, we'll dispense with the hard way."

Pollard leaned over him, inserting a key into the lock of the restraining straps. He opened them, flung them away and hauled Lakesh to his feet by the front of his coverall. He stood there, temples throbbing, belly lurching, heart thudding.

"Turn around," Pollard said. "Face the wall."

Slowly, unsteadily, Lakesh did as he was told. "And now?"

"This."

Pollard kicked him effortlessly in the base of the spine. There wasn't enough room in the cell for him to fall, and he slammed face-first into the wall. Blood ran in a rivulet from his nostrils, over his lips.

"Again," said Salvo pleasantly. "And again and again until he understands just how valuable he is."

Pushing himself away from the wall with one hand and mopping at the blood streaming from his nose with a sleeve, Lakesh demanded, "Even if I learn to understand my value, how can I answer your questions if I'm beaten senseless...or to death?"

Pollard, readying himself to launch another kick, hesitated, glancing over at Salvo. For a long, tense moment, no one moved or spoke in the cell, or even appeared to breathe. Finally Salvo chuckled.

"Perhaps you're right. I can always resort to less personal methods, certainly ones that are less messy and cause a great deal more pain than simply kicking you around. I'd hoped intimidation and the sight of your own blood would serve, since I'm on a tight schedule. Please get back on the bench and we'll proceed."

Lakesh didn't move, refusing to allow the fierce pain in his back to show on his face or the terror mounting within him to be reflected in his eyes. A jumble of images circled in his mind: the fresh spring morning in Kashmir when he had received his acceptance letter from MIT; the plea of his widowed mother to stay in India; his broken promise that he would return when he received his doctorate; his terrible bewilderment, his suffocating sense of betrayal when he glimpsed an Archon and learned the true magnitude of the Totality Concept experiments; his one and only trip to New York City, attending the musical *Guys and Dolls* knowing full well that within a month the metropolis with its teeming millions, its culture, its venues of entertainment and smut would be consumed by a nuclear holocaust. Luck would never be a lady again.

"Something amuses you?" Salvo's voice held an iron edge.

Only then did Lakesh realize he had smiled slightly. He didn't bother with a reply. The figure of Baron Cobalt materialized in his mind—the baron, with his long limbs, graceful movements, golden eyes, high, hairless head and hybrid bloodline. The man whom he loathed, the man whom he had deceived for years, who represented the extinction of the human race, yet the only man who could save him from traveling an agonizing road to death.

Lakesh found he was sweating with fear, heart triphammering within his narrow chest, adrenaline coursing through his system like raging floodwaters. He could only speculate on the kind of readings his biotransponder was transmitting to the satellite uplink, then to the Cerberus redoubt.

He heard Pollard snicker. A jarring blow exploded a fireball of agony in his kidneys. Bile leaped up his throat. Through the wave of nausea, he was only dimly aware of half-falling over the bench, fingers scrabbling over the coarse wood, cheek scraping against a canvas strap.

Hands grabbed him under his armpits, heaved him up, turned him over. Lakesh resisted, but he was unable to prevent Pollard from forcing him back down on the bench and binding him securely with the restraining straps. As he struggled with Pollard, he half heard Salvo carefully instructing his subordinate to make sure his head had no support. Pollard obligingly arranged him so that his head hung over the edge of the bench. Pain spasmed in his neck.

"Now do you acknowledge your value?" Salvo's tone of voice was gentle, a mockery of sympathy.

Lakesh looked up into the man's dark eyes. They were deep pools of hatred, swirling with bright glints of madness.

"I'm afraid you'll have to do more to convince me," he replied hoarsely.

Salvo nodded. "That has always been my intention."

Both Pollard and Salvo left the tiny cell, shutting and locking the door securely behind them. Lakesh breathed deeply, not considering for a moment a cry for help. All he heard through the metal walls and door were pleas for mercy and aid and even a repeated request to be allowed to die.

In the years he had served in Cobaltville's Administrative Monolith, he had never visited C Level, the Magistrate Division, though it was just below B Level, the Historical Division, where he held the senior archivist post.

He knew C Level possessed classrooms, a weapons range, a vast armory, dormitories, office suites and a detention cell block, but he doubted that was where he was. At the bottom of E Level, the manufacturing facility, he had heard there was a sealed-off section where convicted felons were held pending execution.

Although ville laws were complex and often deliberately arbitrary, violators were never sentenced to a term of imprisonment in the cell blocks. Locking away a criminal either for rehabilitation or punishment was not part of the program.

Perpetrators of small crimes, those involved in petty thefts or low-level black marketeering in the Tartarus Pits were sentenced to permanent exile in the Outlands.

People convicted of crimes against the ville itself were served termination warrants and executed. If they were suspected of participating in activities that fit the baron's exceptionally loose definition of sedition, they were detained indefinitely, questioned incessantly, tortured inhumanely.

Lakesh had heard rumors of prisoners in the E Level section being flayed alive, their entrails unwrapped, their bones carefully broken into many, many pieces. The practices reserved for women were particularly vile. He had no idea if the rumors had any foundation, or if they were intentionally spread by the Magistrates themselves to further their already fearsome reputations.

He had never summoned up the courage to ask either Grant or Kane about what went on in the E Level cell blocks. The mere possibility that they would confirm the hushed whispers made him ill.

Thinking of them brought to mind Brigid Baptiste and Domi and their mission to Ireland. He had dispatched them there to test a theory, and he was less concerned about the results of the test than about their safe return.

He had no doubt the subcutaneous biochip transponder at the base of his wrinkled throat would continue to transmit his vital-signs data to the Cerberus monitoring station. The personnel there would be driven half-mad with fright by the readings, but they could do nothing to help him. They were all exiles from the network of villes. Although he had tried to break their farm-animal conditioning, they were still academics, rabbits shrinking in fear from the shadows cast by the baronial hierarchy.

As former Magistrates, only Kane and Grant possessed the natural aptitude for violence that could conceivably extricate him from the hands of Salvo. And they were gone, sent to a far corner of the nuke-scarred globe, on a mission he had believed to be of utmost priority.

Rage and loathing filled him. He knew what Salvo wanted to know, and it was so simple really, compared to what he could tell him. Salvo had bought into a piece of mole-data that Lakesh himself had sent burrowing through the ville network some twenty years before.

Salvo was utterly convinced of the existence of an underground resistance movement called the Preservationists. This was a group who allegedly followed a set of idealistic precepts to free humanity from the bondage of the barons by revealing the hidden history of Earth.

Lakesh's lips twitched at the irony. The Preservationists were a fiction, a straw adversary he had crafted for the barons to fear and chase after, while the real insurrectionist work proceeded elsewhere. He had learned the techniques of mis- and disinformation many, many years ago while working as a project overseer for the Totality Concept.

Salvo believed him to be a Preservationist, and that he had recruited Kane into their traitorous ranks. Baron Cobalt had charged Salvo with the responsibility of apprehending Kane by any means he deemed necessary, and Salvo was using the wide latitude he'd been given, a blanket endorsement that left him to act without consultation.

Obviously Baron Cobalt knew nothing of it, and Lakesh accepted some of the blame for putting his head in Salvo's noose. Posing as a slightly dotty pedant, he had assumed that his membership in the Trust, the baron's inner circle, would continue to ensure his untouchable status. But when Kane had thrown his entire ville-bred life away to save Brigid, an accused Preservationist, Lakesh should have known that Salvo's suspicions would eventually focus on him.

Not only had he been Brigid's direct supervisor, but he also had a tendency to disappear from the ville for days on end. No one dared to ask him to account for his time. He believed himself to be utterly safe, above direct reproach if not covert suspicion.

A few weeks before, when a seed of Intel had floated to him about an Archon operation in Idaho, the possibility that it might be planted had never occurred to him. Salvo, as director of the Grudge Task Force, had planted it, Lakesh had dug it up and foolishly passed it on without scrutiny. The crop that sprouted from the seed had very nearly resulted in Kane's apprehension and Brigid's postponed execution.

Though they managed to escape Salvo's trap, the man's suspicions were confirmed—an intelligence pipeline ran from Cobaltville and was fed, through a circuitous route, to Kane.

Lakesh tried to snort out a laugh, but only succeeded in blowing droplets of blood into the air. He doubted Salvo had access to sophisticated instruments of torture. He could and would cause extreme physical pain, but he would be unable to penetrate to the seat of his soul, where his true pain lived. He had borne the pain for a very long time, and nothing Salvo did could possibly approach it in duration and intensity.

The metal door rattled and scraped open. Pollard stepped in, carrying a heavy cast-iron electric generator with a handle attached to the armature spindle. Salvo followed, shutting the door behind him.

"Sorry about the delay," he said. "Had a bit of difficulty convincing one of my officers to give up this instrument. It was already in use."

Pollard placed the generator on the foot of the bench, removed two coils of wire from a pocket and affixed them to the terminals. The ends of the wires were connected to a pair of small alligator clips. Pollard thumbed them open and shut experimentally.

"Not very sophisticated," Lakesh murmured.

Salvo leaned over Lakesh, putting a hand on either side of his shoulders. He lowered his head to within a few inches of his face. Very softly he said, "Let there be no mistake, old man. I have the means and the inclination to hurt you very badly. It doesn't require sophisticated equipment. I shall hurt you and go on hurting you until I receive satisfactory answers to my questions."

"You haven't asked me any yet."

"Then I'll begin," said Salvo dryly. "Who are the Preservationists? Where are they headquartered? How many are there? Where can I find Kane?"

Lakesh had already worked out his answers. "I don't know."

Salvo pushed himself erect. "Not satisfactory. Not at all."

"I can't make anything more satisfactory than the truth."

Salvo smiled thinly and gave a go-ahead sign. "We'll see."

Pollard stepped forward, clips and wires in his right hand. With his left, he roughly unzipped the front of Lakesh's pale green bodysuit, then attached the clips to his nipples. The steel teeth bit cruelly into the tender flesh, but not a muscle quivered or an eyelid flicked in reaction to the pain.

"Give him a taste," Salvo ordered, staring down.

Lakesh watched as Pollard turned the handle, slowly and methodically at first. He felt a tingling in the area around the clips, but the sensation was not unpleasant. A smile creased Pollard's bulldog face, and he gave the handle a fierce, fast crank.

Without warning, the pins-and-needles prickling became a dazzling concussion of agony, fire flaming through his chest, searing its way through to his back. He felt clammy sweat spring out all over his body. Faintly he heard himself gasp.

Salvo nodded sharply to Pollard, who immediately stopped turning the handle. He leaned down over Lakesh. "There is much more, old man. Much worse. How much do you think you can take?"

Lakesh dragged in a shuddery breath but didn't answer.

"How long have you been a Preservationist?" demanded Salvo, his muddy brown eyes glinting. "Where are they? Where is Kane?"

"I don't know."

Lips compressed in a tight white line of fury, Salvo gripped Lakesh's bodysuit and ripped it open, the seams splitting to the crotch. He snatched the alligator clip from his right nipple, ripping the flesh in the process. He clamped it with a vicious flourish to his penis. Lakesh twitched, clenching his teeth against the biting pain.

"At your age," Salvo said in a gloating croon, "you should be happy to feel something down there."

Pollard spun the handle, the spindle noise rising to a high, screeching whine. Agony burst in sheets through Lakesh's loins, boring deep into his testicles. As if driven by thunderbolts, his pinioned body arched up off the bench, straining against the straps, then slammed down again. He writhed and convulsed, drenched in pain. Sweat ran from every pore. The pain suddenly ceased. He kept his eyes tightly closed and he heard nothing but the sobbing rasp of his own breathing.

Very close to his right ear, Salvo said thoughtfully, "I'm sure a man as educated as you doesn't view torture as an effective means of coercion. What you may not understand is how very difficult it is for a proud man—like you, for instance—to maintain his dignity when his entire universe becomes one of never ending pain.

"You come to realize that your self-image is all bravado, a persona, a sham, particularly when every function of your body is controlled by others. The humiliation is sometimes worse than the pain itself. Did you know that after a few more exposures to the voltage you'll lose control of your bladder and your bowels? You'll be wallowing in your own piss and shit, worse than any slagjacker in the lowest squat of the Pits. Even if you want to answer my questions, you'll find it easier to scream. In fact, that will be the only reason you'll find to keep breathing…just so you can scream.''

By degrees, Lakesh turned his head in the direction of Salvo's voice. He cracked open his eyelids. The man's smirking face filled his field of vision. His lips worked, he coughed up from deep in his lungs and spit a mixture of phlegm and saliva into where he thought Salvo's eyes would be. He had no idea if he hit his target.

Filling his chest with air, Lakesh began to sing, as loudly and as earnestly as he could. Even in his own ears, he knew he was hopelessly off-key. "'Luck be a lady, luck be a lady, lucky be a lady tooo-night!'"

The handle of the generator spun, and an endless wave of scorching pain swept his song into screaming fragments.

Chapter 2

Berlin, the Reich's Chancellery
April 30, 1945

Domi felt nothing, saw nothing, floating alone in a nothingness so vast and deep that it far exceeded her grasp of the concept of eternity.

She knew she wasn't dead, but she felt like a spirit or a ghost, wafting naked among the colorless gulfs of nonexistence. She experienced several emotions more or less simultaneously—fear, anger, then grief. Primarily she felt confusion.

Domi remembered stepping into the shimmering veil of light produced by the interphaser, but she couldn't recollect if that action had been a moment ago or a year. Or a century or even an aeon. If she were dead, surely she should remember her death and how it came about.

She screamed, but she couldn't hear it, not even an echoing murmur in the sea of silence. Then she sensed the currents, pulsing and running through the void, like filaments of a spiderweb, lacing the whole of infinity together.

One of the currents caught her, and she rode it. She slid with it, a mad plummet with no sense of direction, motion or destination. Then she floated down from the ceiling.

She took a slow look around the cubelike room, with its walls of mortared stone blocks feebly lit by a single naked lightbulb. The furnishings were few—worn chairs, a scarred wooden table scattered with papers and maps. Books were stacked against one wall. For all its clutter, the room had the look of temporary occupancy. No pictures hung on the walls, there were no windows and there was a total lack of personal items.

It did have a sofa, with a dead woman lying on it, though. Domi knew she was dead without looking at the small glass bottle lying on the floor next to her outstretched hand. Her face, peaceful in repose, was youthful and fairly attractive, despite her unflattering hairstyle.

Somehow Domi managed to move to the heavy closed door. Through it, she dimly heard the crumping detonations of heavy artillery and the steady *boom-boom* of exploding bombs. Gunfire crackled sporadically, distantly, but with a nerve-racking rhythm.

Domi reached out for the doorknob and realized with a numb shock that she couldn't see her hand. She knew she was standing there in front of it, but apparently hovering a couple feet above the floor.

The door suddenly opened, pulled from the outside. Framed within the doorway stood the small figure of a man in a starched, brownish tan uniform. He paused and stared directly at her. She shrank from his intense, penetrating eyes. They were all-seeing eyes, but they didn't see her. A lank lock of black hair curved down over his forehead, and a small square mustache smudged the area between his nose and upper lip.

Domi knew his name, although she had no idea how she knew it.

Adolf Hitler spoke over his shoulder in a language alien to her, but one she understood nevertheless.

"I am ready, Colonel."

He stepped into the room, steadfastly not looking at the corpse of the woman on the sofa. He was followed a heartbeat later by a tall, cadaverously thin shape in a black, overly decorated uniform. A Sam Browne belt crossed from his left shoulder to his right hip, buckled to a holster holding a square-butted handblaster.

Domi stared at him, not quite sure if she was looking at a man or something posing as one. His high-boned face was very pale, with sharp cheekbones and a jutting chin. A high-peaked cap sat at a jaunty angle on his hairless head. A silver skull-and-crossbones emblem glinted on the front of the cap. Shining against the lapels of the black collar were two silver pins, resembling twin lightning strokes.

His ears were very small and delicately shaped, nestled close to the skull. A pair of dark, curve-lensed sunglasses masked his eyes. His sensually shaped, chalk-colored lips barely moved as he said, "As you wish."

The man deftly unholstered the pistol, snapping back the slide with his left hand to chamber a round. At the *click-clack* of sound, Hitler spun around, mouth falling open in astonishment and fear. He stared at the hollow bore of the Walther P-38, and the momentary fear in his eyes was swamped by a wave of awesome arrogance, fueled by an equally awesome ego.

"How dare you?" he demanded, his voice rising to a shrill, strident cry. "I have kept our covenant, observed our pact! You are to see to my escape!"

The black-uniformed cadaver inclined his head in a short, taunting bow. "Too true, and so I shall. There is no more certain an escape than death."

Hitler's mouth worked, spittle flecking his lips. "I have served our cause faithfully—world power or ruin!"

"You certainly managed the latter," came the cold reply. "Unfortunately the agreement was to gain the former. The Thousand Year Reich is dust."

Hitler stabbed out with a shaking forefinger. "I always obeyed your bidding, I always followed the terms of the Directive!"

"That is a transparent untruth, Führer. If you had followed the terms, the Russians and the Americans would not be within shooting distance of this bunker."

Hitler tried to square his shoulders beneath his uniform jacket. "Your own failures to understand humanity and their concepts of personal freedom led to this. You have made the penalty for your failure my death."

The man in black tilted his head at a quizzical angle. "I am not meting out a penalty or a punishment. Your death will serve our cause. If a corpse is provided for identification, even if that identification is disputed, then the Allied search for you will not impede the progress of the program."

Hitler barked, "You speak of progress, of the program? The war is over!"

"*Your* war is over," replied the silky voice. "To us, it is merely yet another skirmish, the latest in a long series. We will regroup, refine and redefine the program. After all, we have much to offer the victors...certainly as much as we offered you."

Adolf Hitler opened his mouth wide, eyes wild and staring. A torrent of screamed words burst from his throat, so charged with hysterical fury they were almost incomprehensible. He screeched that he had been betrayed, that the man in black was a half-breed, a hybrid hellspawn, worse than the Gypsies, worse than the Jews—

The cadaver squeezed the trigger. The Walther made a flat, hand-clapping sound. The bullet entered Hitler's open mouth, drove through the back of his throat and exited at the rear of his head. His skull was framed by a mist of blood, white bone chips and gray brain matter. He swallowed hard, as if he were trying to dislodge a piece of gristle caught in his throat.

A flat ribbon of crimson spilled from his slack lips, and he sank to his hands and knees. He shook his head like a wounded, dazed animal. His arms folded beneath him, and he fell face-first to the concrete floor. Blood spread around his head in a widening pool.

Domi watched, her emotions detached from the swift brutality of the execution. One level of her mind understood nothing of what transpired. On another, far deeper, visceral level, she knew exactly why the crazed little man had to die.

The man in black holstered the pistol, stepped out

of the door and returned a moment later carrying a large, square metal can. He unscrewed the cap and poured the liquid contents over the body on the floor, drenching the uniform with gasoline.

He emptied the can, dropped it and backed out of the room, calling to someone down the corridor. From a jacket pocket, he withdrew a box of wooden matches. He was in the process of opening it when he stiffened, his head swiveling to and fro, like a hound casting for a far-off scent.

In a crooning, almost singsong voice, the man in black said, "I can't see you, but I feel you watching me. Whoever you are, wherever or whenever you came from, I trust your curiosity has been satisfied."

A thrill of fright shook Domi. She was invisible, even to herself, yet the cadaverous man knew of her presence. She gazed into his pallid, smiling face and felt an icy malevolence far greater than that exuded by the man called Hitler. She wanted to run, to fly, to flee, out of sight of that hideously pretty smile forever.

As soon as the desire raced through her, she felt the tugging of a current and she let it carry her up, flit her away, back into the nothingness where she knew she could be safe.

Chapter 3

Roswell, New Mexico
July 12, 1947

It was night, yet the desert blazed with light. Stars and constellations burned whitely against the deep blue-black of the western sky, and Brigid Baptiste fell out of it.

She rode the currents, as swift and as insubstantial as a dream. Below her, the rough terrain, burned a golden brown by the merciless summer sun, stretched away in all directions. A small patch of light glowed in the shadows, bright spots of color against the dull desert floor. Traffic swirled around the lights, vehicles, people on foot, long trucks with canvas-covered beds.

Brigid slipped lower, soundless, weightless, letting the currents surf around her. Almost all of the people below were men, and almost all of them wore drab olive green uniforms. Helmeted men brandishing rifles stood shoulder to shoulder in a tight wall of flesh around a huge humped object covered by staked-down tarpaulins.

She recognized the uniforms and insignias as that of the United States Army, a military body that had not existed for nearly two hundred years. Judging by the cumbersome configurations of the weapons and vehicles, she guessed not only where in time she was, but how she had arrived.

The quantum energies unleashed by the interphaser had opened a pathway, not just across linear space, but through the chronon structure of the space-time continuum. A chronon flow had carried her into the past, well over two centuries earlier than the moment she stepped into the interphaser's field effect, and thousands of miles from her point of entry.

Brigid understood the theory behind her journey, but she couldn't understand why she existed as only a mote, a wisp of consciousness. She couldn't feel her body or sense her friends. She was intangible, a ghost of herself, drawn like an iron particle by a great hidden magnet to this time and place.

Swooping down among the soldiers, through the roaring vehicles, she felt the rumble of the electric generators providing power for the field spotlights. She tasted a man's fear as she passed by, an acrid cloying in her mind, felt fragments of his unvoiced terror.

She slipped through the tarpaulins. A great silver disk, half-buried on one side by sand, rested on the desert floor. One part of the topside hull was a sheared tangle of gleaming alloy, as if it had exploded from within, or been struck from below by a powerful projectile.

Instantly she recognized the basic shape and design. She had seen one like it before, smaller, whole, yet unpowered in a subterranean vault in the Black Gobi. That had been—would be—roughly two and a half centuries from now.

Floating away from the disk, she allowed the currents to carry her in the direction they wished. They picked her up and rushed her headlong toward a large tent. The flaps were closed, guarded by a pair of grim-faced soldiers. She eased between them and then through the rough canvas.

The interior was lit by electric lamps hanging from the crisscrossed ceiling support poles. The illumination they cast struck dull gleams from the four plastic-shrouded bodies laid out in a row at the far end of the tent. She didn't bother inspecting them—she knew who and what lay wrapped within the semitransparent cocoons.

At least half a dozen men were packed within the canvas walls, but none of them went near the corpses or even looked in their direction. All but one were in uniform. That man sat on a camp stool, one leg crossed over the other, right ankle on left knee. His smartly tailored business suit was jet black, as was the narrow necktie over a spotless white shirt. He wore his clothes and held his body with that peculiar arrogant assurance that comes from perfect confidence in every aspect of one's life. He was so lean he was almost cadaverous, an aspect not helped by his narrow, high-boned and sunken-cheeked face. His complexion looked strange, even in the lamplight.

Brigid realized it was an unnatural, flat tan, due to the application of a flesh-colored cosmetic. His cupid's-bow mouth looked startlingly red. His short, crisp hair was neatly cut and combed, so neatly it was obviously a wig. The dark, curved lenses of sunglasses concealed his eyes.

A broad-chested man wearing a navy blue uniform

studded with silver buttons and gold braid on the
shoulder epaulets towered over him. His heavy-
jowled face shone with perspiration, and his lower lip
protruded pugnaciously. Brigid felt his fear and his
fury. Both emotions were directed at the seated man
in black, who regarded him calmly.

In an oily, uninflected and unaccented voice, he
said, "Of course, I realize this mishap will be difficult
to explain away, Admiral Hillenkoetter. But that is
the province of your part of the agreement."

Admiral Hillenkoetter's lips writhed in a silent
snarl. "Don't lecture me, you smug son of a bitch.
Your people were to tell us when they scheduled a
flyover. The report of the crash has already gone out
over the news wire, we have civilian witnesses—"

The man in black fluttered a dismissive hand
through the air. "All easily remedied, Admiral. Manipulate the media and eliminate the witnesses. Deny
everything."

Admiral Hillenkoetter's jaw muscles bunched.
Through clenched teeth, he growled, "As a bird colonel, you should know we've got a little thing in this
country called the Constitution—"

"A very noble yet exceptionally troublesome set of
ideals. I suggest we circumvent them as soon as possible. Or better yet, do away with them altogether
before they interfere with the Directive."

The Admiral gaped at the man, shocked into
speechlessness. Disbelief and outrage shone in his
eyes.

The sensual mouth of the man in black twitched in
a cold caricature of a smile. "Don't look so morally
offended, Admiral. If we truly abided by the spirit of

the Constitution, our government would have never granted amnesty and asylum to the Nazi scientists of the Totality Concept. The government would have never agreed to be a cosignatory of the Directive at the end of the war. By the standards espoused by that beloved document, you are a traitor to your country and its people."

Hillenkoetter's body flinched, as if he had received a blow. Tears sprang into his eyes, but they did not fall. "You bastard. I'm a soldier. I obey orders."

"As do we all," the man in black retorted. "And the orders are to conceal all evidence of this incident, by any means necessary." He nodded toward the semiopaque sheets covering the corpses. "Remove the bodies of the unfortunate crew to the base in Nevada. We'll fly the craft out of here as soon as a cargo plane is available."

He paused, adjusted his glasses and stated, "In fifty years, perhaps less, no one will ever remember what happened here at Roswell."

The man in black started to say something else, then froze, mouth half-open. His masked eyes shifted rapidly back and forth across the confines of the tent.

Admiral Hillenkoetter noticed and demanded, "Now what?"

In a low tone, the man replied, "I sense a presence that should not be here. A spy, perhaps."

Hillenkoetter turned, looked at the officers, then glared down at the man in black. "Impossible. I know all these men."

As the lenses of the sunglasses fixed on her, Brigid cringed away, desperate not to be seen. Intangible fingers of force tugged at Brigid, lifting her, propelling her up through the ceiling of the tent and toward the sky. She didn't resist, didn't struggle, though she wanted to stay and learn more. Somehow she knew she had learned enough, as if she had glimpsed a key to the lock of a dark mystery. But the key was useless and the knowledge was futile. A disembodied spirit could do nothing with them.

She concentrated on building an image of her body, on remembering Kane, Domi, Grant and Cerberus. She plunged through the sky, then into the gulfs of nothingness, driven by the wild panic to exist again.

Chapter 4

Dealey Plaza, Dallas, Texas
November 22, 1963

Though it had rained that morning, the storm clouds were breaking up, allowing shafts of sunshine to dry the streets and the clothing of the onlookers. The temperature climbed as they waited on both sides of Elm Street, and they shed raincoats and jackets.

Kane squinted his eyes against the sunlight before he realized he didn't have any eyes or lids to squint, or even a head to hold them. He floated along and over the sidewalk flanking Elm Street, sliding between and through the scattered crowd gathered there to catch a glimpse of somebody named John Fitzgerald Kennedy. He overheard enough to understand that the man held the position of President of the United States.

He didn't know what he was doing there under the noonday sun. He recalled penetrating the shimmering veil of energy sprouting from the apex of the interphaser, then fluttering like thistledown on unseen winds, a misty nothing dancing through nothing.

Then he felt currents pulling him, compelling him, and suddenly he stood on the sunlit street, behind him a grassy knoll and, looming a hundred yards to his left, a shabby, six-storied building.

The emotions from the men, women and children lining both sides of the blacktopped thoroughfare battered at him—excitement, resentment, curiosity, admiration, anger. And like ambient radiation, he sensed a cold resolve, a single-minded dedication to achieve an objective.

Kane bobbed with the current like a cork in a gently running stream. His attention focused on a tall, very lean man standing at the curb. He wore a black suit, sharply creased and impeccably tailored. His high-planed face held no particular expression and was strangely ruddy of complexion, his hair a dead, jet black. A pair of sunglasses concealed his eyes, as did many of the assembled onlookers, but his had large, curved lenses, impenetrably dark. He gripped a furled umbrella in his right hand.

Kane looked at him intently, wondering vaguely why the currents seemed to drag him toward this man in black. When he floated closer, he saw his ruddy complexion was artificial, a cosmetic heavily applied to disguise the natural pallor of his skin. His hair was fake, too, a wig fitted tightly over a hairless skull. His ears were small, and a tiny transceiver plug was snugged in the right one.

A ragged cheer suddenly erupted down the street. The man didn't turn his head. Kane saw the presidential motorcade turn onto the street from an adjacent boulevard. A pair of long, open-topped vehicles—somehow Kane knew they were called limousines—bracketed by helmeted men astride motorcycles, rolled slowly between the facing throng of on-lookers.

Kane watched President Kennedy, seated in the rear of the lead vehicle, smile and wave. He brushed impatiently at his windblown hair, but his smile didn't falter. A slender dark-haired woman in the seat beside him leaned over to say something to the people riding in front.

The first shot was muted, mushy, like a firecracker going off under a tin can. The President's body jerked, hands flying to his throat. His wife turned toward him, confused, not frightened.

The second shot sounded much louder, and Kane saw the bullet dig a gouge in the sidewalk to the left of the limousine. The man in black smoothly, deftly opened his umbrella and pumped it twice in the air over his head.

Immediately came triple cracking reports, the shots coming so fast the echoes swallowed each other. President Kennedy's body lurched forward, his wife reaching for him. The motorcade slowed as people began to scream, grabbing each other, dropping to the ground, their heads swiveling and necks craning.

The man in black stayed where he was. He shook the umbrella a third time. The sound of the sixth shot was an ear-knocking snap, as if a giant twig had been broken.

The right side of President Kennedy's head erupted in a slurry of blood, skull shards and brain matter. For a split second, a liquid halo of crimson surrounded his skull.

His body flailed back and to the left, slamming violently into his wife, who voiced a primal scream of soul-deep horror, denial and anguish. The limousine leaped ahead, engine roaring. It lunged past Kane down the boulevard, where it was lost in the shadows of an overpass.

The man in black calmly collapsed the umbrella and furled it, paying no attention to the running, shouting, shrieking chaos in the plaza. People dashed back and forth, some weeping, some blank-faced with shock. Kane noticed a couple of middle-aged men facing each other across the boulevard sharing a thumb's-up gesture.

The man in black displayed no emotion whatsoever. Tucking the umbrella under an arm, he strolled calmly down the sidewalk, away from the crowds of people racing up the face of the grassy knoll.

A red-faced police officer, blue uniform shirt damp with sweat, blocked the man's path, shouting garbled questions. The man made a casual show of withdrawing a wallet from an inner coat pocket and flipping it open. Sunlight glinted briefly from a silver badge.

The policeman respectfully and apologetically touched the brim of his cap with a finger, then sprinted around him, toward the swarm of people milling about at the knoll.

The man in black walked only a few yards more, stopped, took a handkerchief from a pocket and carefully spread it open on the curb. He sat down and waited.

He didn't wait long. A heavyset man in a checked, short-sleeved shirt crossed Elm Street, striding toward him. His sandy hair was cropped short in a bristle cut. He sat down on the curb beside him, breathing heavily, but not from exertion. He was excited and thrilled.

In a voice barely above a whisper, he announced, "Lee's trapped in the depository building. The mechanics are on their way to the airfield. Ferrie is standing by." His tone carried notes of barely contained ebullience.

The man in black replied flatly, "All other systems green."

The heavyset man's blunt features twisted in a scowl. "You don't seem very happy about it. We finally got rid of that Commie, nigger-lovin' sumbitch."

"Don't be vulgar, Howard," the man admonished gently. "This was simply a necessary extraction of a troublesome factor. Emotions have no place in the program."

Grunting, Howard heaved himself to his feet. "Colonel, you're one cold-blooded bastard."

"So I've been told, Howard. So I've been told."

Howard shuffled away, hands in his pockets, resolutely not looking at the crowd or the panicky stampede of police officers. The man in black watched him go, then said in a clear, ringing voice, "I know you're there, my friend. This is the third time I've felt your presence in eighteen years. If you are an observer, I hope your curiosity has at last been satisfied. If you are a spy, then what you have learned here today is of no use to you. You are impotent and powerless."

It was less the superior, self-confident tone than its subtle, underlying vibrations that triggered Kane's sudden rage, then a hatred so intense he felt a frenzied desire to be clothed in flesh again—simply so he could strangle what passed for life out of the black-clad man.

Effortlessly he arose from the curb, fastidiously folding the handkerchief and putting it back in his pocket. He angled the umbrella over his shoulder and sauntered away down the sidewalk.

Kane wanted to follow him, but invisible chains restrained him, pulled him away. He felt frustrated fury at his disembodied state. The light of the sun began to fade, and he fell up into an abyss of blind, eternal darkness, where direction and dimension had no meaning.

Chapter 5

Embassy Row, Washington, D.C.
January 19, 2001

Grant plummeted through the darkness. Nothing lived, nothing moved, nothing had ever been. The universe was blank and void and forever without life.

Grant knew he wasn't dead, even if he met all the other criteria. He saw nothing, heard nothing, but his mind and his memory still worked. Even as he whirled in an invisible maelstrom, he knew he still lived. Memories of words, actions, faces all neatly strung together like beads on a string passed through him.

Then the string snapped, and like the abrupt rising of a curtain of nothingness, light shattered the eternal darkness and Grant was able to see again. He had no idea where he was or what he was looking at.

The yellow-hued light was dim, exuded by a double fluourescent strip running along the low ceiling. The lights showed nothing but a concrete block wall, perfectly square slabs fitted together with such precision that not even a seam or corner interrupted the smooth, featureless expanse.

Slapping footfalls echoed from behind him. He started to turn, then realized he didn't have a head or a neck. He simply stretched out his awareness in the direction of the sound.

Two men strode purposefully, shoulder to shoulder along the narrow corridor. One was squat-legged and stout-bodied, his bushy eyebrows joining at the bridge of his thick nose. His salt-and-pepper hair was lavishly pomaded. A swelling belly strained against the buttons of his blue serge suit coat. The downturned corners of his broad mouth twitched slightly in a nervous tic that indicated barely suppressed apprehension.

His companion towered over him by nearly half a foot, although he looked to weigh half as much. His narrow face reminded Grant of a mask, a resemblance not alleviated by the black-lensed sunglasses over his eyes. His black suit and hair contrasted sharply with the deep, waxy pallor of his skin.

The men walked right toward Grant. Automatically he tried to move out of their path, but the squat-bodied man walked right through him. He couldn't understand where they were going, since the passage dead-ended at the blank wall.

The man in black removed a small oval object from a pocket and, without breaking stride, pointed it at the wall. The sonic key activated a hidden unlocking mechanism. With a faint click of solenoids opening, a rectangular section of the wall slid soundlessly upward into a concealed slot.

Grant felt an irresistible tug, as if he were attached to the black-suited man by an invisible tether. He trailed along, like a balloon bobbing at the end of a string.

The chamber beyond the portal was little more than

a hollow cube within a larger cube. An overhead lightbulb illuminated the strongroom, casting a cold white glow over the four-foot-long metal cylinder resting on a steel framework. It dominated almost all of the floor space.

The stout man eyed the object fearfully and muttered, "If only the ambassador knew that thing was down here."

Grant recognized the language as Russian, a tongue he should not have understood yet did.

The tall man replied softly, in the same language, "Vorishin is a pompous fool, Felix. That is why we arranged for him to occupy this post—what other diplomat would permit himself to be barred from a section in his own consulate?"

The question was rhetorical, and Felix responded to it with a grunt. He seemed transfixed by the metal-encased cylinder. The man in black reached for it, lifting up a small hinged panel on its dully gleaming skin. Felix backed up hastily, but there wasn't much room and he couldn't back up far.

Voice oily with amusement, the man said, "It's quite safe, Felix. Until the warhead is armed, it is little more than an ugly conversation piece."

Beneath the panel glowed a glass-fronted LED. The man in black touched an inset row of small buttons, tapping in a sequence. An electronic beep sounded from the cylinder. Digits scrolled and flashed over the face of the LED. The flashing stopped, and the numerals 024.060 shimmered there. As Grant watched, the 060 changed to 059.

In an unsteady voice, Felix asked, "Now what happens?"

The black-clad man closed the panel. "In twenty-four hours, give or take ten seconds, a free neutron will collide with a uranium 235 atom. The collision will split the uranium atom into two smaller atoms, which in turn will collide with two more atoms. The high-explosive wedge in the warhead will detonate, compressing the uranium atoms into a supercritical mass that will undergo instantaneous fission."

Felix growled, "You mock me, Colonel."

"Not at all," replied the man in black soothingly. "I am educating you. Due to the fission, a one-megaton detonation will occur, and the surrounding air will be heated to ten-million degrees centigrade. The fireball generated by it, traveling at tremendous speed, will vaporize everything and everyone within a five-mile radius. The president-elect and all dignitaries—including Ambassador Vorishin—attending the inauguration ceremony will vanish so completely it will be as if they never lived at all.

"The fireball is immediately followed by a pressure wave, moving at four hundred yards per second. This wave will generate winds of up to six hundred miles per hour, which will flatten every structure within ten miles."

He straightened his shoulders and in a dreamy, droning tone continued to speak. "Two minutes later, the pair of secondary warheads will detonate. What is left of the District of Columbia, a fair portion of Maryland, Virginia and the entire Atlantic Seaboard will be swept from the face of the earth by the terrible fire. Three minutes after that, General Frederickson will launch a retaliatory strike at the Russian heartland.

"The world will take its first and very final step over the threshold to a new genesis. The seeds planted millennia ago will finally burst forth. The Directive will have achieved its primary goal and will become an active Directorate."

The pallid face turned. Though he could not see his eyes, Grant knew he was staring directly at him. In English he announced, "And there is nothing you can do to prevent it. All the scattered threads of time have been sewn together in a Gordian knot." His long fingers drew a square in the air. "Time squared, so to speak. You can observe this defining moment of human evolution, yet you can have absolutely no effect on it."

Felix gaped openmouthed at the man, first in confusion, then fear. "Who are you talking to?"

The man in black chuckled. "An old acquaintance. I knew he—or she—would be here."

Felix's eyes darted back and forth, up and down. "Have you gone mad, Colonel?"

The black-clad man did not answer.

Felix cleared his throat loudly and edged toward the door. "We must leave now, Colonel. Our transportation to the South Dakota facility is waiting for us at Dulles."

The man in black snapped the fingers of his right hand as if he suddenly remembered something that had eluded him for days. "Oh, I forgot to tell you, Felix—your invitation to sit out Judgment Day has been rescinded."

Felix's body froze in midshuffle, eyes bulging in disbelief and shock. He stammered, "I—I don't understand, Colonel. My family, my wife and children, are already at the Anthill. They expect me to arrive today.''

Sympathetically the pale man replied, ''I regret to inform you that your family are still in your apartment.''

''Why?'' demanded Felix. ''You promised me they would be as safe as your own family!''

''I confess to a bit of dissembling there, Felix. I have no family. Alas, neither do you as of four hours ago.''

There wasn't much room in the chamber for Felix to stagger, but he fell against the wall, clutching at his heart, wheezing, eyes wild and bulging. His mouth opened and closed twice before he husked hoarsely, ''They are dead?''

''I am afraid so. Quite thoroughly.''

''*How?*'' The word came out as anguished bleat.

''Like this.''

The man's right hand darted out like the head of a striking serpent, a tiny plastic ampoule held between thumb and forefinger. A splash of clear, colorless fluid shone on Felix's cheek.

''A nerve toxin, derived from the VX agent,'' said the man blandly. ''Absorbed instantly through the pores of the skin, attacking the respiratory, heart and central nervous system. The effect is immediate, and a five-milligram dose is almost immediately fatal. I just administered fifteen milligrams.''

Felix's tongue protruded from his mouth, writhing like a blunt tentacle. A tremor shook his body, and the back of his skull struck the wall. Then, as if all of his muscles, tendons and ligaments contracted simultaneously, Felix seemed to shrink, fingers contorting into claws, arms drawing up, his joints locking. He remained in a half-upright position, like he had been stuck to the wall by adhesive.

"One of the more interesting ancillary effects is a condition very similar to rigor mortis. He'll stay that way for at least eight hours."

Grant knew the black-clad man addressed him, and felt a hot anger build up.

"Ah, you're upset with me. You know, I used to wonder who you were," the man continued sardonically, "but now I don't give a damn. Even if you're one of Operation Chronos's failed experiments, splashing and paddling along the temporal stream, trying to find your way back, what you've witnessed means absolutely nothing."

He glanced over at the immobile corpse of Felix. "Or is it the death of one man that outrages you? It is that short-sightedness, that lack of focus, that has brought about the race's extinction."

The man in black smiled.

The smile shook Grant. It was a leer that was the antithesis of anything human, completely devoid of any emotion other than a hate-fed hunger.

The black-clad man stepped out of the strongroom and into the corridor. Grant followed. The sonic key sealed the portal, and he slipped it back into a pocket. He peeled back a shirt cuff and consulted a timepiece strapped to his narrow wrist.

"Look at the time. As Felix said, my transportation awaits."

Grant gazed at him, fearing him, hating him.

The man in black took off his sunglasses. His inhumanly large, curved eyes didn't reflect the light.

Grant saw no pupils, only obsidian irises with a bare hint of white at the corners. They were fathomless apertures leading to the ends of the universe. He felt a distant wonder at the man's identity.

"You want a name? I suppose I owe you that much, but I've had so many over the years. At the moment I travel under the name of Air Force Colonel C. W. Thrush. Something of a joke, you see. A bird colonel with the name of a bird. I selected it from a poem by T. S. Eliot."

The man gestured theatrically with the sunglasses and quoted:

"Footfalls echo in the memory
Down the passage we did not take
Towards the door we never opened
Into the rose-garden.
...shall we follow
The deception of the thrush? Into our first world."

Putting on the sunglasses, he said, "Quite meaningful and symbolic if you think about it. I suggest you do so. You have plenty of time."

C. W. Thrush turned smartly on his heel and strode down the corridor. Grant couldn't follow him. A current washed over him, buffeting him up into the empty universe. Nothingness closed its doors, and time stopped.

He floated in endless space.

Then light began to pulse in brilliant flashes around him, and he heard a quiet mechanical whine climbing in pitch. He saw shapes, he heard sounds, then he felt pain burning through him.

Chapter 6

The whine of machinery climbed up out of the audible range, straining to hit an ultrasonic note. The needles on the power gauges flicked back and forth like metronomes setting crazed rhythms.

The sensor boards and indicator lights flashed erratically. Switching stations clicked. A console squirted a shower of sparks that smelled like burned orange blossoms.

The sound of the mat-trans unit cycling through its jump program reached a painfully high squeal, then laboriously descended in scale. Bry, the technician, had never heard anything like it before. The entire central control complex of Cerberus vibrated with a fierce determination to shake itself apart. The very air was like a heavy surf, pounding relentlessly against his eardrums and bones. Loose papers fluttered, pens shivered and rolled over surfaces.

"Another one coming through!" shrilled DeFore from behind him.

Bry spun his chair around, away from the madly blinking lights of the master console, and rose. Swiftly he crossed the high-ceilinged, vault-walled center to the open door of the anteroom leading to the gateway chamber. He wiped at the film of sweat sliding from the roots of his curly, copper-colored hair. Reaching the doorway, he immediately stepped aside to allow Auerbach to push the wheeled gurney through.

Domi lay curled in a fetal position atop it, looking as stiff and as cold as a corpse. Because of her albinism, it was impossible to tell her degree of pallor, but her breath came in short, ragged bursts.

DeFore stared at the brown-tinted armaglass door of the mat-trans unit, nibbling her full underlip, one hand resting on another gurney. She squinted away from the flashes of light bursting on the other side of the heavy translucent portal. The sound of a fierce, rushing wind swelled in volume, climbing in pitch.

"One-minute intervals," Bry declared, speaking loudly to be heard over the hurricane howl. "They've been materializing at one-minute intervals. The cycling system is overloading."

With a studied calm, DeFore said, "This should be Kane coming through now. He's the only one of the team we haven't retrieved."

Bry opened his mouth to retort, then turned it into a wordless hiss of anxiety. The dark-eyed, bronze-skinned woman was a medic not a tech, and would not understand the danger of the situation. Quantum energies could not truly be controlled; they could only be channeled.

Still, he knew she was anxious and fearful. Her white bodysuit showed half moons of perspiration at the armpits, and the intricate braid she favored for her ash blond hair had come undone. She hadn't bothered trying to pat it back into place, although loose tendrils hung about her face. The posture of her stocky body telegraphed tension.

Bry half closed his eyes against the brilliance of

the coruscating flares trapped within the walls of the jump chamber. Fortunately the properties of the arma-glass kept the wild energies contained. He couldn't bring himself to contemplate what would happen if they breached the walls.

DeFore's main worry lay with the physical conditions of her patients. They had materialized, one by one, in the redoubt's gateway completely unconscious, with their vital signs erratic. She was familiar with the symptoms of jump sickness or mat-trans shock, but the three people exhibited none of these.

Bry's primary concern focused on the maddeningly intricate Quantum Interphase Mat-Trans Inducer operational systems. Although Lakesh had trained him in its theory and functions over the course of his eighteen months in Cerberus, he often worried that he knew just enough about the mat-trans unit to get himself—and everyone else in the redoubt—into serious trouble.

Upon gateway activation, a million autoscanning elements committed to memory every feature of the jumpers' physical and mental composition—even, Bry supposed, down to the very subconscious. The data filtered through the system's memory banks, correlating it with a variation-range field. Once the autoscanning sequence was complete, the translation program kicked in, what Lakesh referred to as the "quincunx effect." Lower-dimensional space was translated, phased into a higher-dimensional space along a quantum path. The jumpers traveled this path, existing for a nanosecond of time as digital duplicates of themselves, in a place between a relativistic *here* and a relativistic *there*.

That much of the theory and concept Bry understood, even though it seemed fiendishly complicated, like a physicist's nightmare. He knew the pathways always had to lead to an active-destination gateway, whether it was across the country or on the other side of the world. If a destination lock wasn't achieved, or a transit line not opened, then jumpers could conceivably materialize at completely random points in linear space—or worse, endlessly speed through Cerberus's global mat-trans network, going absolutely nowhere with no chance of reconstitution.

But what had been happening in the Cerberus redoubt for the past four minutes flew in the face of Lakesh's instructions, completely circumventing all of Bry's training. The gateway had simply activated itself, as if receiving a transit-line signal from another unit. However, the monitoring stations didn't register an origin point, and the interlinked database support systems had done nothing but chatter to each other in computer gibberish.

When the unit cycled through the first materialization process, Brigid Baptiste lay unconscious on the hexagonal floor plates of the chamber. Bry alerted DeFore and had just begun to pull her out when the system activated again, and then again, each time depositing another senseless member of the jump team on the platform. The only one left to appear was Kane.

The light behind the armaglass dimmed, as did the keening wail of the gale-force wind. He winced as he heard another circuit crackle and spit from a console in the control center.

DeFore rushed across the anteroom, around the polished table and heaved up on the handle of the jump-chamber door. It opened easily, silently, on counter-balanced hinges. The last of the spark-shot tendrils of white mist curled away, seeming to be absorbed by the emitter array on the ceiling and the seams between the hexagonal floor plates.

Kneeling beside the crumpled figure of Kane, she placed an index finger at the base of his throat. His skin felt cold and clammy, and his pulse beat fast and thready. One side of his lean-cheeked face was lacerated and covered with caked, scabrous blood. His lower lip showed swelling, and the flesh around his right eye was puffy and discolored. Bruises showed in red-purple blotches around his throat. His thick, dark brown hair was soaked through with sweat. As was the case with the others, his clothes reeked of gunpowder and cordite.

Unlike the other members of the team, Kane's blue gray eyes were wide open, unseeing, staring and haunted. DeFore had seen the look before—and the recognition of it chilled her. In predark days it had been called the "thousand-yard stare" and was directly related to post-traumatic stress syndrome. Too much stress, too much fear, too much pain in a short period of time and even the strongest of nerves could break. She was very familiar with it. Her lover had worn the same nonexpression after a tenure with the Magistrates. That was, of course, after he had named her as a seditionist.

She put one hand before Kane's blank eyes and snapped her fingers. No reaction. She passed the small rad counter over him and grunted at the mild, mid-range green readings. Over her shoulder she called to Bry, "Give me a hand."

Kane held his body in a stiff, unnatural position, and she and Bry had difficulty dragging him out of the gateway chamber and heaving him onto the gurney.

"His eyes are open," Bry stated. "Is he conscious?"

DeFore grimly shook her head, pushing the stretcher ahead of her out of the anteroom. "No. He shows all the symptoms of a neurocognitive disorder. I don't think his injuries account for it. I'll let you know."

Bry closed the door of the mat-trans chamber with a sigh of relief. He stayed behind in the central control complex as DeFore wheeled Kane to the dispensary.

The needle gauges no longer flicked, the lights had stopped blinking and flashing, though the odor of molten circuit boards still hung fresh and sharp, only slightly less acrid due to the efficiency of the air-recycling system.

Sitting down at the main workstation, Bry began switching the appropriate toggles and tapping the proper keys to initiate the system-wide self-diagnosis program. He wasn't overly worried about a database failure, since the control complex had five dedicated and eight shared subprocessors, which continued operations even in the event of a mainframe failure. The possibility of a dysfunction in the shared data link between the gateway's imaging autosequencers and the target coordinate lock concerned him the most. If that happened, no one would be going anywhere or arriving through the mat-trans unit—including Lakesh, who had recently jumped to Cobaltville.

As the self-diagnostic began, the consoles of dials, switches, buttons and flickering lights that ran the length of the walls hummed. Monitor screens displayed shifting columns of numbers. Bry looked at the big Mercator-relief map of the world spanning the facing wall. Pinpoints of light shone steadily in almost every country, connected by a thin glowing pattern of lines. They represented the Cerberus network, the locations of all functioning gateway units across the planet. Most of the units were buried in subterranean military complexes, known as redoubts, in the United States. Only a handful of people knew they even existed, and only half a handful knew all their locations. The exact purpose of the units and of the related projects belonging to the Totality Concept vanished when the ultimate nuclear megacull destroyed civilization all over the world.

Bry routed the security vid-net signals through the main monitor, a four-foot screen of ground glass. As his fingers tapped the keyboard, the system of closed-circuit vid cameras transmitted interior and exterior images of the redoubt to the station.

The view of the dispensary was fairly close to what he expected to see. Grant, Domi, Brigid and Kane lay prone on the examination beds with DeFore and her assistant, Auerbach, hovering over them. Cotta had been pressed into service as an aide, though judging by the sour expression on his long-nosed face, he didn't enjoy it very much.

Bry grinned bleakly. He didn't much blame him. Less than five days before, Kane had kicked Cotta in the balls because of a perceived overstepping of authority.

Grant, who had been the first to appear in the chamber, was the first to show signs of returning consciousness. He stirred fitfully on the bed, opening his eyes and raising his head. DeFore bent over him, wielding a small hypodermic.

Bry swiftly switched the view to the dining hall, repressing a shudder. He was phobic on the matter of injections. Farrell and Rouch were seated around the remains of a very late supper. Rouch was a fairly new arrival, only a month out of Sharpeville. The black-haired woman with exotic Eurasian features was very attractive, and Farrell had wasted no time in making a play for her.

She, Domi, Baptiste and DeFore were the only females in the Cerberus redoubt. Auerbach had an unrequited crush on Baptiste, Domi was viewed as Grant's woman, though allegedly he had never touched her, and DeFore's brisk, no-nonsense mannerisms were intimidating. For the unattached male exiles in the installation, the pickings were exceptionally slim.

Depressing another key, he peeked in at the subterranean maintenance section. Wegmann dozed on a stool, his balding head resting against the huge wire cage enclosing the three ovoid nuclear generators. The big vanadium-shelled machines had provided the redoubt's power for the past two centuries and probably would continue to do so for the next five.

He transferred the view to the main corridors. No one walked the twenty-foot-wide passageways made of softly gleaming vanadium alloy. Great curving arches of metal and massive girders supported the high rock roof. There was no point in checking the redoubt's well-equipped armory or two dozen self-contained apartments. The installation had been built as the seat of Project Cerberus, a subdivision of Over-project Whisper, which in turn had been a primary component of the Totality Concept. At its height, the redoubt had probably housed well over a hundred people. Now it was full of shadowed corridors, empty rooms and sepulchral silences.

He didn't bother glancing in at Balam's holding facility. The very concept of the little entity imprisoned there awakened a primal dread within him. He had nothing but admiration for Banks, the creature's warder. Only he and Lakesh could spend more than a minute in close proximity to Balam without suffering nightmares for a week.

Bry checked the area around the main sec door. As usual, it was closed, locked tight, since the gateway brought people in and out. Vanadium alloy gleamed dully beneath peeling paint. The multiton door opened like an accordion, folding to one side, operated by a punched-in code and a hidden lever control. Nothing short of an antitank shell could even dent it.

Rendered on the wall near the lever, in garish primary colors, was a large illustration of a froth-mouthed black hound. Three snarling heads grew out of a single, exaggeratedly muscled neck, their jaws spewing flame and blood between great fangs. Three pairs of crimson eyes blazed malevolently. Underneath the image, in an ornate Gothic script, was written the single word Cerberus.

Bry often wondered about the identity of the artist—if he or she had used indelible pigments intentionally, if the artist had been military and whether there had been a reprimand for defacing government property.

He transferred the vid network to the exterior cameras, making sure to patch in the infrared-filter relays. As he expected, it was very dark, appropriately enough since the redoubt was built into a Montana mountain range known colloquially as the Darks. Once, in the centuries before America became the Deathlands, they had been known as the Bitterroot Range. In the generations since the nukecaust, a sinister mythology had been ascribed to the mountains, with their mysteriously shadowed forests and hell-deep, dangerous ravines.

For most of the people who lived in Cerberus, seeing a genuine night sky was something of a rarity. Inside the installation, time was measured by the controlled dimming and brightening of lights to simulate sunrise and sunset. Very few of the ville-bred exiles dared ventured outside of the sec door.

Cerberus was built in the mid 1990s, and no expense had been spared to make the installation a masterpiece of impenetrability. The trilevel, thirty-acre facility had come through the nukecaust in good condition. Its radiation shielding was still intact, and an elaborate system of heat-sensing warning devices, night-vision vid cameras and motion-trigger alarms surrounded the plateau that concealed it.

The road leading down from Cerberus to the foothills was little more than a cracked and twisted asphalt ribbon, skirting yawning chasms and cliffs. Acres of the mountainsides had collapsed during the nuke-triggered earthquakes nearly two centuries ago. It was almost impossible for anyone to reach the plateau by foot or by vehicle; therefore, Lakesh had seen to it that the facility was listed as irretrievably unsalvageable on all ville records.

Everything seemed secure, inside and outside of the redoubt. Tension slowly drained out of Bry, leaving him weary. The computer system signaled that it had completed its self-diagnosis. He knew he should run the results. Instead, he swallowed a yawn, rested his head on his forearms and wished he could go to sleep.

Chapter 7

Kane dreamed of being so cold that his blood congealed in his veins and his tongue froze to the roof of his mouth.

In his dream, he was a boy again, being led through an ice-walled tunnel by his father. He held on to his father's thumb, and it felt like an ice sculpture that leached out his warmth, his life. He shivered uncontrollably as he walked.

His father spoke, but he felt the words rather than heard them. The man's lips were welded shut by a crusty rime of frost.

You'll know much pain, boy, because you'll see too much of it. You'll know sadness because you'll live during the winter of the human race, and you won't know if there will ever be a spring. You'll be cut off from everything you knew and believed.

Kane knew his father spoke the truth. He had joined the Magistrates and proudly wore the armor and murdered for the baron. Any questions regarding right and justice were beaten out of him, all but one.

But you'll still be connected to your Other, and the day will come when you will embrace him or cut the connection forever. Whatever you decide to do, you will lose a part of yourself but gain a part of him.

Kane did not understand, since he was only a child. He wanted to ask his father the meaning of his words, but the tunnel slowly melted around them. The ceiling and walls flowed down in rivulets, then in a rushing white froth. His father melted, too, collapsing into the cold stream of death. Kane felt the frigid drops splash over his face, the tears of a man who had been frozen in a cryogenic canister, his body preserved to provide genetic material to create a new race to inherit the nuke-blasted earth.

And then Kane floated alone, in a comfortable void, dimly aware he no longer felt the marrow-chilling cold. Then he no longer felt so alone, because the Other came to keep him company. Shapeless it was, as formless as the deepest fear of death. The Other had no face, but Kane recognized it.

He heard a voice, a human voice, a woman's voice, speaking from far away. "Vital signs are stable. Increased EEG and EKG activity. Take off the cold compress."

The voice pushed the Other away, back into the void. At the same time, Kane felt himself rising slowly from the nothingness. He wasn't sure if he was happy about it.

The woman's voice spoke again, very close, a warm, husky whisper. "What is your name? Give me an honest answer. If you don't know, say so. I have to assess your condition and decide on a course of treatment. What is your name?"

He said, or hoped he said, "Kane."

Other voices spoke, a man's deep, rumbling tones and another woman's, a childish piping. It took Kane a long time to visualize the people who belonged to the voices. At first he tried to sink back into the void, but it was lost to him, washed away by the pain throbbing within the walls of his skull. He let the voices drone on, keeping his eyes shut.

Grant…DeFore…Domi…the names echoed in the hollow halls of his memory. The woman who had asked him his name was DeFore, and the lionlike grumble belonged to Grant. Domi spoke in a high, childlike tone. There were other names he knew he should remember, faces he knew he had seen somewhere. Cobaltville, maybe.

No, that didn't seem right, although a fragment of memory came to him about a small, pyramid-shaped device made of metal. His eyelids lifted. The lighting was muted, diffused and the world looked strange. Shadowy figures moved, wavered back and forth. The walls were white, the ceiling lit by a fluorescent strip.

The dispensary.

In the Cerberus redoubt.

Grant and Domi.

And Baptiste.

Kane opened his eyes fully and tried to sit up. Pain hit the left side of his head like a club, and the bed spun. He grasped the high rails on the sides and squeezed his eyes shut again until the spasm of vertigo passed. Clearing a dry-as-dust throat, he asked, "We made it?"

One of the shadow-shapes shifted close and coalesced into Grant. He came to the bedside and gently pushed Kane back onto the mattress. His ebony-colored, mustached face creased in a grin, but his heavy, prominent jaw quivered ever so slightly. He tried to speak, then averted his gaze, rubbing his eyes with the thumb and forefinger of one hand.

"Did we make it?" Kane asked again, a little dismayed by the weak raspiness of his voice.

Dropping his hand, Grant said gruffly, "Of course we did. We always do."

Though it required a great deal of effort, Kane balled his right hand into a fist, extending his index finger. Grant curved his own forefinger around it, a simple gesture signifiying they had survived another gamble.

"Domi?"

"Fine," she piped up, stepping around Grant to smile down at him.

If Kane hadn't remembered she was an albino, he would have mistaken her for a ghost. Her big crimson eyes gleamed out of a hollow-cheeked white face like a pair of polished rubies. Her short, ragged hair was equally without color. A slender yet insolently curved girl barely five feet tall, she had dispensed with her usual revealing garb of high-cut skirt and low-cut blouse. She wore the standard-issue white bodysuit, which gave her already ethereal appearance a wraith-like touch.

"And Baptiste?"

Uneasiness appeared on Grant's face. Blandly he answered, "She's fine, too. How do you feel?"

"Head hurts. Pain comes and goes, and I feel fuzzy, kind of disconnected. But it's better."

DeFore came to the foot of the bed, saying tersely, "I should hope so. You've been unconscious for thirty-nine hours."

With shooing motions of her hands, DeFore drove Grant and Domi away from the bedside. She peeled back Kane's right eyelid, the narrow, bright beam of the small penlight in her hand causing him to wince and flinch.

"Good," she declared, turning off the light and releasing him. "Pupils dilate and contract normally."

Kane blinked. "Why shouldn't they?"

DeFore smiled down at him patronizingly. "You're suffering from a concussion, tough-guy."

"Concussion?" he echoed.

"Strongbow really laid into you, remember?" Grant reminded him.

Until Grant mentioned it, he hadn't remembered. A splinter of memory came back to him—Strongbow's smashing attack, his teeth bared in a snarl, steely fingers sinking into the muscles of his throat while his free hand battered him about the head and face. He even recalled how the sour, reptilian stench of the man's exertions clogged his nostrils.

Defensively Kane said, "I've been bashed around before without being out of it for two days. Remember the Tushe Gun?"

"The head injuries you received in Mongolia made you particularly susceptible to a concussion," replied DeFore. "Making a mat-trans jump exacerbated your condition...or whatever kind of jump you four made."

"What do you mean?"

DeFore laid cool fingers on his wrist, checking his pulse. "I mean it wasn't a normal transit. Bry is still trying to figure it out."

"I'm all right now?"

"Except for a touch of dehydration, yes. X rays showed no skull fractures or other complications. Just the same, I think you should stay in here the rest of the night so you can be monitored. Head injuries are tricky.''

She turned and strode away.

Domi said, "I'll bring you food," and left the dispensary with her.

Kane waited a moment, then asked quietly, "Where's Baptiste?"

Grant gestured in the general direction of the control complex. "She's fine, like I said. She's busy."

Kane tried to scowl, but his face hurt too much. He settled for making a spitting sound of derision. "I'm glad to see she has all her priorities in order."

At the note of sarcasm in his partner's voice, Grant sighed heavily. "She gets an hourly update on your condition."

"I don't know if I can handle such an outpouring of naked concern for my well-being. What the hell is she so busy with? Another one of Lakesh's jolt-brained schemes to get us all chilled?"

Grant shook his head dolefully. "You might end up hoping for that."

Kane squinted up at him, ignoring the stinging twinge around his right eye. "What?"

"Brigid's trying to find Lakesh. He left for Cobaltville a couple of days ago and hasn't returned yet."

"So? He's been gone longer than that before."

Grant took a deep breath. "His biolink transponder has never transmitted these kind of signals before, though."

Kane knit his brows, staring at the big black man in confusion. "What's a biolink transponder?"

Passing a nervous hand over his gray-sprinkled hair, Grant replied lowly, "It's another detail of life in Cerberus that Lakesh withheld from us. The latest in a long line of need-to-know policies.''

He cast a searching glance toward the open door of the dispensary, then reached down and lowered the high rail of the bed. "You feel strong enough to walk?''

"We'll see," Kane replied, kicking away the sheet covering him. He eyed with distaste the thin, baggy undershorts he wore. He swung his legs over the side of the bed.

Grant supported his back and left arm as he slowly rose to a sitting position. The left side of his face itched, and his fingers gingerly explored the film of liquid bandage adhering to the lacerations ripped by Strongbow's fingernails.

His temples pounded with the effort of edging off the bed, and his neck muscles ached where the snake-eyed bastard had throttled him. He placed his feet on the floor and stood up, swaying, unnerved by how rubber kneed and light-headed he felt. He glanced down at his right hand, at the bruised band of flesh around the wrist. Strongbow had stomped him there, but his fingers flexed fine.

Grant helped him put on a calf-length robe and stayed beside him as he shuffled forward. With every step, the pain in his head abated and his stride became stronger.

The two men walked into the small laboratory and examination room adjacent to the dispensary. Kane had peeked into it briefly shortly after his arrival at the redoubt. Since it was filled with machines and medical instruments he didn't understand, he never made a return visit.

"What are we doing here?" he asked.

"Putting you on the need-to-know list," Grant answered dourly. "Better late than never."

From a black-topped trestle table he picked up a long-handled, two-pronged device that resembled the sensor probe used by Magistrates to verify and validate ID chips of ville citizens. This gadget, however, held a small neon tube between the prongs.

Squinting at it, Kane demanded, "What is that thing?"

"An ultraviolet-light projector."

"How do you know?"

"Because that's what DeFore told me it was."

Grant thumbed a stud on the handle, and an ectoplasmic, pale purple glow shone from the tube. Stepping around Kane, he pushed the wall light switch and plunged the room into semidarkness.

"Roll up your right sleeve," he instructed. "All the way."

Mystified, Kane pushed up the loose-fitting sleeve to his shoulder. Grant placed the projector a few inches above Kane's right bicep, the waxy light washing all color out of his flesh. Tiny dark markings were outlined against the skin, a series of symbols Kane recognized. They resembled three downward-pointing elongated triangles, topped by circles.

Kane stared at them, feeling a cold sickness in the pit of his stomach. Grant passed the light over the back of his right hand. Despite his deep brown complexion, identical symbols were visible.

"Brigid has them, too." Grant spoke quietly, grimly.

"What are they for?" Kane pitched his voice low

to conceal the growing tremor of rage underlying it. "To brand us like goddamn cattle?"

"No," announced DeFore sharply from the doorway as she turned on the overhead lights. "They're identity markings. And monitors."

She regarded Grant and Kane reproachfully, but didn't chastise them.

"They're the symbols of Overproject Excalibur, the insignia of the Archon Directorate." Kane spit out the words.

DeFore shook her head, taking the projector from Grant's hand. "I didn't know that."

"What do you know?"

"I already explained it to Brigid and Grant."

"I guessed I missed it," retorted Kane dryly. "I sort of had an appointment with a coma at the time. How about bringing me up-to-date?"

DeFore didn't react to the tone of his voice. She stated, "Standard ville ID chips are little pieces of silicon injected under the skin. They react to low-frequency sound waves emitted by Mag scanners. You know from your own experiences how easy those chips are to forge."

Kane nodded reluctantly. Much of his and Grant's duties as Magistrates had revolved around apprehending counterfeiters of bogus ID chips.

"Lakesh devised a new form of identity recognition, restricted to ville exiles, just in case our numbers increase to the point where we have trouble differentiating our players from those on the other side."

"We know who the players are on the other side," Kane snapped. "Everyone not in this redoubt."

With an obviously forced note of patience, DeFore

inquired, "Did you think that Lakesh's overall plan was to simply fill Cerberus with exiles until it burst at the seams? No, once we have the numbers, we'll be given new identities and smuggled back into the villes and the surrounding Outlands. We'll act as agents provocateurs."

Kane arched his eyebrows suspiciously. "For the past five or so months, I've questioned Lakesh about a master strategy. He never told me even the little you just did. Why?"

DeFore took a breath. "I've been here the longest time. Nearly three years. You know we have sec protocols. Probationary periods for new arrivals are part of them."

"Probationary!" Kane roared in furious disbelief. "Since I've been here, I've been shot at, blown up, beaten up and damn near drowned. I think I've passed the fucking initiation!"

DeFore cast her eyes downward in shame. Kane could see she knew he spoke the truth.

He hissed in a calming breath between his teeth, wincing as his head began to throb again. Flatly he demanded, "What's this about a monitor and a biolink transponder? You sewed something up inside of me?"

"No. The transponder is a radioactive chemical that bound itself to the glucose in your blood and a middle layer of epidermis. It's based on organic nanotechnology and perfectly safe. It transmits heart rate, brain-wave patterns, respiration, blood count and so forth. The signal is relayed by a Comsat satellite to the redoubt."

"How long have I had it in me?"

"It was injected after your return from Dulce," DeFore answered matter-of-factly. "While you were being treated for your injuries."

Knotting his fists, Kane took a menacing step toward her. "So all those injections were more than just painkillers and antibiotics. Why didn't you ask my—*our*—permission?"

DeFore hadn't retreated, but now her full lips compressed. "It wasn't optional, Kane. Part of the price of sanctuary. We need to know where the exiles are, what their physical conditions are at any given moment."

"In case we're recaptured," Grant said. "Or so she said."

Kane eyed him keenly. "You didn't happen to ask her if there's a suicide switch implanted in us, by chance, did you?"

Grant's eyes flashed in sudden surprise. He glanced challengingly toward DeFore. "That's an excellent question. Is there?"

She frowned. "Of course not. Admittedly we considered something along those lines, but Lakesh felt it's a bit too early to implement such measures."

"Why do the transponders look like the Overproject Excalibur insignia?"

She shrugged. "That I don't know, never having seen it. Perhaps it's Lakesh's way of being ironic, like a private joke. You know what his sense of humor is like."

"Yeah, he's a gifted comedian," Kane muttered darkly. He made a dismissive gesture with both hands, turning toward the door. "That's it. I'm done."

Anxiously DeFore asked, "What do you mean?"

He glanced back over a shoulder. "I mean as soon as I feel strong enough, I'm out of here." His voice went acid with bitterness. "He concocts these triple-stupe missions for us, and what have we accomplished? Nothing."

"Kane—" Grant began.

Kane whirled, bellowing, "*Nothing!* Dulce, Russia, Mongolia, England, Ireland. We run around shooting up those places, trying not to get shot up ourselves, and what's the payoff? The Archons still pull the strings of the barons, and the barons pull the strings to make us all dance. I'm through with dancing."

Grant gazed steadily at his partner, his conflicting emotions not showing on his face. He had heard Kane vent similar feelings before, but in those instances he was simply being contrary, blowing off steam. Now he heard the unmistakable edge of conviction in his voice, saw it in his eyes.

"Kane," Grant said quietly, "look at it objectively. The transponder is a small enough thing, isn't it?"

Kane uttered a sneering laugh. "In size or implication? It's still a deception, and how many small deceptions have to pile up until they make a big one?"

He continued on toward the door, respiration labored. "I'm going back to bed."

"Damn you," cried DeFore shrilly. "Didn't Grant tell you Lakesh is in Cobaltville?"

The angry urgency in her voice stopped him, turned him. "He did. I told him that's not unusual."

"What we receive from his transponder is. Lakesh's has been transmitting high-stress signals for the past two and half days."

"And?" Kane's response was flat and disinterested.

"That means he may be undergoing torture," DeFore barked.

"And that means," added Grant grimly, "he may talk."

Kane felt the icy touch of fear creep along his spine. "And if he talks, we may expect an assault force from Cobaltville. All of us better be prepared to evacuate. Does Baptiste know?"

"Yes," DeFore answered. "She's monitoring his vital signs in the control center. She's been trying to get a precise fix on his present location."

"Go fetch her," Kane said to Grant. "Tell her we're leaving."

Grant shook his head. "You tell her. You damn well know she won't abandon Lakesh."

Kane massaged his temples and uttered a half sigh, half groan. "I'll talk to her, then. Did my blaster make it back with me?"

"Of course. It's in the armory." Grant narrowed his eyes. "Why?"

"Go get it for me, would you? I think I might need it."

"To talk to Baptiste?" Grant's tone was skeptical.

Kane dropped his hands and gazed steadily into Grant's eyes. In a hoarse whisper, he said, "Yeah. To talk to Baptiste."

Chapter 8

Bracketed by two console screens in the darkened control center, Brigid Baptiste manipulated a pair of keyboards with her left and right hands. Since it was long after sunset, the overhead fluorescent strips had been dimmed to accommodate the internal clocks of the personnel. The only source of light came from the banks of data terminals. The only sound was the clatter of her fingers over the keyboards and the hum of disk-drive mechanisms.

Cotta manned the workstation behind her, but he didn't speak to her, as per her request not to interrupt her concentration.

On the screen to Brigid's left, the downlinked telemetry transmitted from Lakesh's transponder scrolled and changed. Flashing icons indicated heart and respiration rates, as well as brain-wave activity. The computer systems recorded every byte of data sent to the Comsat and directed down to the redoubt's hidden antenna array. Sophisticated scanning filters combed through the telemetry using special human biological encoding.

The digital data stream was then routed to the console on her right, though the locational program, to precisely isolate Lakesh's present position in time and space. The program considered and discarded thousands of possibilities within milliseconds.

Brigid had been engrossed in the computer activities for the past hour and a half, and her neck muscles felt stiff and her eyes stung from the strain of staring at the constantly shifting jumble of letters, numbers and symbols.

Pushing her chair back, Brigid stood up, taking off her former badge of office, a pair of wire-framed, rectangular-lensed eyeglasses. They were the only memento of the many years she had spent as an archivist in Cobaltville's Historical Division.

She rolled her head, hearing and feeling neck tendons pop. She stretched, hands at her hips, arching her back. She caught a reflection of herself in a monitor screen. The zipper on the front of her bodysuit had opened, and a bare patch of her full breasts gleamed as they strained at the fabric.

Immediately Brigid returned to a normal standing posture, swiftly restoring decorum to her bodysuit. She glanced surreptitiously over her shoulder at Cotta. He quickly dropped his gaze to the console. He had noticed, and she felt slightly embarrassed for him, then faintly amused.

Brigid rarely thought about her looks, about her tall, athletic body, although more than one male colleague in the division had made it plain they thought about it far more than she did.

Her one disadvantage was that she stood out in a crowd, a true liability for living in one of the baronies. It had been worse when she was younger, because she hadn't yet proved her intellect and her drive. Now, in her late twenties and away from Cobaltville, she wasn't devalued because of her appearance or her sex.

She had never considered her body more than anything than a package, locomotion for her brain. That is, until she had met Kane. In a state of half drunkenness, he'd barged in on her while she had been in a state of total undress. That meeting had ignited the fuse of events that triggered the explosion that sent them all into permanent exile.

Brigid brushed her fingers through her mane of redgold hair, which tumbled in wavy mounds onto her shoulders. On impulse, she inspected her face in the reflective surface of a monitor screen. She had almost never worn cosmetics in Cobaltville, since they were viewed as symbols of human vanity by the baron.

They were available in Cerberus, albeit two centuries old, but the habits of a lifetime couldn't be easily broken. Domi had once suggested she allow her to give her what she called a "makeover," but Brigid had refused. Somewhere in the large eyes of deepest, clearest emerald, or in her smoothly contoured cheekbones and finely aquiline nose, or perhaps the rosy complexion lightly dusted with freckles, lay the reason why she despised the superficial.

Grimacing at herself, Brigid turned away from her reflection. Until she met Kane, her appearance had been an afterthought. But she had found him the most attractive yet disquieting man she had ever met. She thought back to that night in her small flat in the residential Enclaves. Kane's thick dark hair was just barely combed, his blue gray eyes were so penetrating, they saw through her body to the soul beneath. She remembered how when he smiled his eyes squinted and when he laughed they disappeared. At the time, despite the fear his Mag's persona had evoked, she thought he was the handsomest man she had seen—

The outline of a figure appeared in the open doorway of the center. She turned quickly, and for a bewildered moment didn't recognize the man standing there. When she realized it was Kane, she tried unsuccessfully to avert her gaze.

His hair was an unruly, greasy mass, his face sporting a few days' worth of beard stubble. His complexion was sallow, eyes bagged and underlined with dark rings. His face still bore the discolored blotches of fading bruises, his lower lip swollen and puffy.

He wore an open robe that showed the ridiculously loose fitting undershorts that fell almost to his knees. Even in the dim light, Brigid saw he had lost weight, and the crisscross pattern of scars she always suspected he had were easily visible.

Kane looked like hell warmed over and left to congeal, but she tried not to think about it. She could not afford to be distracted, and she needed his input— even though he didn't look capable of inputting a foot into a sock at the moment. Deliberately she restrained herself from rushing to him. Kane was a proud man, absurdly so sometimes. She gazed with increasing consternation at his slow, shuffling approach, which showed none of the wolflike grace she had always silently admired.

Kane stopped midway, wiped sweat from his forehead with one of the belled sleeves of his robe, looked directly at Brigid with eyes full of pain and exhaustion and said, "I think I may faint. Maybe if you're not too busy, you can keep me from bashing out what's left of my brains on the floor."

She hurried to him, letting Kane put an arm around her shoulders. As she led him to a chair, she noticed Cotta unobtrusively edging out of the control center.

She pulled the chair closer with her foot and helped him to lower his weight gently into it. He clamped his teeth tight, then grunted, "Good to see you, Baptiste."

He leaned back in the chair, his breath coming in labored rasps. She stood behind him, cradling his head. For a long moment, neither one of them spoke. Absently she stroked his damp, stringy hair. At length Kane's respiration became more regular.

Softly she said, "Sorry I wasn't there when you woke up."

"Just as well. I wasn't in the best of moods. Did you miss me?"

She ran a hand up the back of his neck and through the longish hair hanging there. She didn't answer. The question confused her, made her emotions feel like they were trapped in a sandbag.

Right before they had risked the interphaser transit in England, Kane had grabbed her, held her, as if he were taking advantage of quite possibly the final opportunity to tell—or show—her how he felt about her.

He hadn't embraced her, hadn't kissed her, hadn't said anything more revealing than "See you on the other side, *anam-chara.*" Then he had walked into the interphase field and vanished into a pocket of nonspace between here and there and when and where.

She wasn't sure if Kane was aware she had learned the meaning of *anam-chara.* She doubted he did. It was an old Gaelic term, meaning "soul-friend."

Turning his head, Kane looked up at her. A little

of the old high-voltage insouciance glinted in his eyes. "I asked you a question."

"Yes," she said crisply, removing her hands from his head and stepping away. "We've got a situation, and I need your expertise."

She returned to her seat between the consoles. "Have you talked to Grant?"

"Yeah. Lakesh has gone missing."

"That's not quite accurate. We know where he is."

"Cobaltville."

Brigid nodded to the right-hand console. "I configured and triangulated the transponder signal. Here he is."

Kane rolled his wheeled chair to the station. On the screen glowed a jumble of lines, curves and squares, glowing green against black. The view was centered on a series of interconnected box shapes. Inside one of them, a red dot pulsed. He instantly recognized the layout.

"The Admin Monolith. Level E. The convicted-felon blocks. The Mags have him."

Brigid nodded grimly. "At least one Mag in particular. Salvo."

Kane leaned back, staring vacantly at the Mercator map on the far wall. "No surprise that Lakesh had the floor plan and the specs for the Admin Monolith in the database."

Brigid cast him a bright jade stare. "What's that supposed to mean?"

As if he hadn't heard, Kane continued, "No surprise that he bugged us, implanted us with those transponders without asking our permission or even mentioning them to us."

"I don't you think you grasp—"

He raised a peremptory hand. His voice was flat, unemotional. "Let's be straight with each other for once. Both of us hate to be wrong, so we tend to snipe at each other instead of communicate."

She looked at him in surprise. Quietly she said, "Go on, then. Be straight."

"I'm not going to put my head into the lion's den for that two-faced, double-crossing bag of bones. I'm tired of us—even his pet Domi—being used as versatile yet expendable tools."

Brigid's voice was tight. "He's suffering torture. What if he talks about this place?"

"Let him talk. Let this place be overrun. We'll be long gone, either through the gateway or overland in the Sandcat."

His blue gray eyes chilled her, as did his next words. "Maybe he's been captured or maybe it's what he wants us to think. Either way, Lakesh is on his own."

Brigid stared at him unblinkingly. She breathed, "You don't mean that, Kane."

"Every goddamn syllable."

She kept staring at him. Kane met her gaze unwaveringly. Finally, through gritted teeth, she said, "You bastard. You can pack up and run, but I'm going after him."

He shook his head gravely. "That's where you're mistaken, Baptiste. You're not going after him."

She made a wordless scoffing sound. "Who'll stop me?"

"I will. I'll break one of your legs if I have to, but you're not going to Cobaltville."

Brigid jackknifed up out of the chair, limbs trembling with the effort to control her anger. Her breasts rose and fell. "You couldn't break a biscuit in your condition, Kane."

She didn't see him tense the tendons of his right wrist, but she heard the actuator click, the faint, brief drone of a tiny electric motor and the solid slap of the butt of the Sin Eater sliding into his palm. Kane raised the big-bored handblaster. She glimpsed the holster strapped to his forearm beneath the sleeve of his robe.

He said, "Then I'll *shoot* you in the leg. Lakesh has put you in harm's way for the last time, Baptiste. All for nothing. It ends now."

Brigid held herself very still, very quiet. Inwardly she cursed herself for not suspecting that Kane's head trauma could induce a form of dementia. Gently she said, "You don't need a blaster with me, Kane."

He smiled without humor. "Don't patronize me. I'm not a jolt-brain, I'm not fused out. I'm thinking very clearly. I've made the decision and I'm sticking by it."

"What does Grant think? And Domi? What if they don't abide by the decision you've made for us?"

"They'll have the same choice you have—leg-breaking or leg-shooting."

She pulled in a deep, steadying breath. "There's more to this than simply saving Lakesh, you know."

He chuckled harshly. "I know. There always is in this place."

She ignored the sarcastic observation. "I've got the memory disk from the interphaser."

He looked at her blankly. "So what?"

"I can't analyze it."

"Why not? Aren't you a genius on top of having a photographic memory?"

She bristled but said only, "It's in Lakesh's own personal mathematical language. Multiple-option logarithmic philosophy. It's beyond me, beyond the encryption keys of the database."

A line of irritation appeared on Kane's forehead. "What's that got to do with anything?"

She fixed her green eyes on his pale, drawn face. In a voice pitched low, she asked, "What do you remember of the time between stepping into the interphase field in Strongbow's place and the time you woke up?"

His reply was immediate. "Nothing."

Tersely she said, "You're lying, Kane. Think." Lamely she added, "Please."

The line of irritation on his forehead joined creases of concentration. His eyes narrowed, he opened his mouth to speak, then shook his head in frustration.

"What?" she demanded.

"I had a dream, about my father...."

"Anything else? Anything at all?"

"I remember...like a jump dream, only..." He let out a shuddery breath and blinked up at her. "It was like I was in the past, long before the nuke, in a city. I was invisible, but I saw a man, a very important man, get chilled."

"An important man?"

"More important than just because he was a leader or famous. He was important because his death meant the next step of a plan could go forward."

Brigid said nothing, standing and waiting.

"I saw another man," continued Kane in a rush, "but he looked—I don't know how to describe him—but he looked *fake*…like somebody who really wasn't a man but only playing at being one."

He glanced up at her. "Does that make any sense?"

"Yes," she whispered. "Go on."

"This man—or whatever—was connected to the assassination, to the plan. He knew I was there. He told me I couldn't do anything to stop him."

Kane's jaw muscles bunched. "I hated him, like I hate the baron."

"The man you saw murdered," Brigid urged quietly, "do you remember his name?"

Pursing his lips, Kane ran his left hand through his hair. "Something with a hard *C* or a *K*. Keneely? Connaly?"

"Kennedy?"

Kane snapped his head up. "Yeah, Kennedy. Now I remember. One of the predark presidents."

"President John F. Kennedy," Brigid declared. "Thirty-fifth President of the United States. You were present at his assassination on November 22, 1963, in Dallas, Texas."

He eyed her in surprise, then with skepticism. "Could have been a jump dream."

"One that happens to coincide with an actual historical event, one that happened over two hundred years ago and one that few people outside of the Historical Division are even aware of anymore? You're not that obtuse, are you?"

He responded to her question with one of his own. "What made you ask if I remembered anything?"

"Because Grant, Domi and myself all experienced some kind of temporal shift during the interphase transit. We were noncorporeal, like you, visiting the past in a pan-physical state so we couldn't effect a causality violation even if we wanted to. Each of those past time periods seem to be pivotal points in history that apparently led to the present-day circumstances."

She paused, then declared, "The unifying factor in those events was the faux human you described."

"The what human?"

"From the French—it means 'fake.' When you saw him, was he dressed in black, wearing dark glasses?"

Almost reluctantly he nodded.

Brigid smiled coldly. "As he was in all of our experiences. A man in black, known in the vernacular of the twentieth century as an MIB."

With a weary impatience, Kane said, "Baptiste, I'm not interested in a faux MIB. He's not the topic."

Hotly Brigid retorted, "The hell he isn't."

She reached down to the left-hand console and plucked up a small CD-ROM disk. She held it between thumb and forefinger like it was a coin.

"Locked on this disk, in a language only Lakesh can translate, is the path to changing the road of the present. Remember what he told us about Operation Chronos?"

She wasn't certain if Kane could remember in his current fogged mental condition, so without waiting for his reply, she said briskly, "Chronos was a major component of the Totality Concept, spun off from the Project Cerberus successes."

Resentfully Kane said, "Yeah, the Totality Concept, a secret military undertaking that researched all sorts of crazy stuff—including time travel. But according to Lakesh, Operation Chronos only had one success.''

Brigid nodded, recalling what Lakesh had told her about the many failures of Chronos, of translating a test animal's head into the past while the rest of the wretched creature remained in the present. It wasn't until Lakesh's Project Cerberus phased a living subject along a quantum pathway and wholly reintegrated it did Operation Chronos work the bugs out of temporal dilation.

''Lakesh also said that Chronos disrupted the structure of time,'' Kane went on as if by rote, ''and triggered a probability wave dysfunction that then led to the nukecaust and then led to—''

He broke off, suddenly realizing the weight of his recitation and its implications. Brigid knew the thoughts chasing each other through his mind.

She said, ''Led to this lousy present time. Lakesh always claimed the holocaust was preventable, that Operation Chronos had created an alternate event horizon. He wasn't just theorizing, Kane. What all of us witnessed as an accidental byproduct of the interphaser proves that time travel is possible.''

Kane sighed, winced and asked, ''Even if we can go back in time, what good could we do, floating around like ghosts?''

''I believe that was a phenomenon related to the interphase field. Lakesh built it to interface with natural quantum vortex points like the megaliths in England and Ireland. The interphaser wasn't designed to operate as either a portable gateway unit or a time machine. Somehow, some way, it accidentally did both.''

She brandished the disk again. ''The reasons why and how it can be intentionally duplicated are embedded on this. It could be our only chance of setting right what the Archon Directorate put wrong all those centuries ago. Whatever you may think, I'm not determined to risk my life to rescue Lakesh for purely sentimental reasons.''

Kane exhaled a slow, contemplative breath.

Brigid gazed at him speculatively, then asked quietly, ''Kane, do you remember what you said to me back in Strongbow's place? You said you'd pay me back.''

His head came up in swift anger. ''You told me I owed you nothing.''

''I'm taking it back. I'm asking you to help me retrieve Lakesh before he dies or before he talks. Not even for his particular life, but for all the millions— the billions—of lives needlessly snuffed out in the nukecaust and the skydark.''

He didn't respond. His eyes were fixed and vacant on some faraway point.

''Kane,'' she pressed, hearing and despising the quaver of desperation in her voice, ''will you help me?''

Squeezing his eyes shut, Kane said bitterly, hoarsely, *''Anam-chara.''*

He pushed himself stiffly to his feet, as if he were ninety years old. He pushed the Sin Eater back into its forearm holster. ''Give me about an hour to clean up, dress and get something to eat. Then we'll discuss tactics.''

He walked toward the door of the control complex. Brigid called after him. He kept walking but said over his shoulder, "Now what?"

"Would you have really shot me?"

He stopped in midstride, turning toward her. A thin, slight smile played over his lips. "Of course not."

He lifted his right arm and patted the blaster under the sleeve of the robe. "Grant took out the bullets before he gave it to me. I guess he figured I wouldn't know the difference. Or you wouldn't."

"You tried to run a bluff," she said angrily.

He started walking again. "That makes two of us, Baptiste."

She almost hurled a stream of profanity at his retreating back, but swallowed it down. He was right.

Chapter 9

For a long time, longer than he could recall, the damp stone walls, the dim lightbulb burning overhead and the hard, hard bench had been Lakesh's universe. The broad straps locked over his midsection and his legs, as well as the leather cuffs buckled around his wrists, severely limited his horizons.

Pain, of course, was an integral part of his universe. It was the only means he had of marking the passage of time. When Salvo and Pollard—always together, never separately—made their visits, the pain and questions would begin. Sometimes there were no questions at all, just the infliction of pain. Lakesh found himself looking forward to the routine and grew a little anxious when it varied.

He retained enough clarity of reason to know that was the true horror of torture—the intimate, almost sexual relationship that sometimes developed between victim and victimizer. At first the psychological distance between the two was immense. But if the routine continued long enough, if the periods of isolation between them were extended, that divide narrowed until the victim actually welcomed the torturer, eager for any kind of exchange.

Although Lakesh had spent the first part of his adult life as a physicist, he had read more than scientific journals. At university he minored, for one semester at least, in psychology. He remembered a reference in one of the textbooks to the depraved Marquis de Sade and his justification for causing pain: "Heaven has decreed that it is your part to endure these sufferings, just as it is my part to inflict them."

Salvo had probably never heard of de Sade, but he was determined to be the perverted Frenchman's spiritual successor.

During the first few sessions, Lakesh had managed to construct a bunker in his mind where the pain couldn't reach. For a while, the mental walls had held fast against the assaults of electricity, of sleep deprivation, the withholding of even minimal amounts of food and water.

He wasn't sure when it had happened, but the pain had breached the walls and become all that there was. He couldn't remember a time without it or visualize a future where it did not reign. An infinitesimally tiny section of his mind recognized the onset of despair and despondency. That part, which still held cogent thoughts, set up a wailing, warning racket. Lakesh lay on the bench, closed his eyes and ignored it.

After what seemed like a chain of interlocking eternities, the door lock clicked. He heard footsteps, the murmur of voices, the door slamming shut. He didn't open his eyes until he felt a warm breath on his right cheek, smelled a stale odor.

Salvo's face hung a foot above his. The man's dark eyes were dull, no longer swirling with liquid madness. His breath came out of his nose and mouth in shallow puffs. He looked profoundly exhausted. His lips moved in a forced, stitched-on smile. "Have we had a moment of breakthrough, old man?"

Lakesh heard the soft, rustling whisper but couldn't summon up the energy or interest to respond to it.

Salvo waited, then said, "You haven't answered my question. That's very impolite."

Lakesh gazed unblinkingly into Salvo's eyes. He kept his gaze fixed and unremitting. Salvo blinked first, and Lakesh slowly closed his eyes.

Straightening up, Salvo ran a hand through his short dark hair. When his fingertips touched the wealed scar on his scalp, he jerked them away.

"The old prick is faking, sir," growled Pollard, putting his hand possessively on the electricity generator. "A few jolts of direct current will perk him up. Or we could start breaking some bones. Small ones at first."

Salvo shook his head slowly. "No, the shock would chill him. He's already prepared to die."

"Let him." Pollard's voice held a hard, eager edge. "The bastard is defying our authority. Death is the least of what he's earned."

Salvo studied the man strapped to the bench. The wrinkled skin looked like paper out of a predark book, the ash-colored hair was limp and the body was shriveled, the eyes sunk deep in their sockets. So much time, so much pain and so little to show for it.

Intellectually Salvo knew there was nothing remarkable or admirable about Lakesh's dogged resistance to torture. It was simply single-mindedness, a spiteful determination not to surrender anything through force. He had seen such stubbornness before, and it inevitably faltered, weakened and collapsed altogether. Sometimes it collapsed into gibbering insan-

ity, more often into a gradual wasting away, followed
by death.

He turned toward the door. "He's no good to us
dead. We need to restore him to some kind of health
so we can begin again. I'll arrange for a medic to
come down here and give him stimulants and vita-
mins. Until then, you're not to touch him, understand?"

Pollard grunted in angry disappointment, but he
muttered, "Understood, sir."

Salvo left the cell and strode through the cell
blocks, oblivious to the moans and screams filtering
from behind the metal braced doors. As he approached the termination room, he heard the explo-
sive rounds of four Sin Eaters firing simultaneously
and the unmistakable flat, wet slap of lead striking
flesh.

The door to the room was up, and he glanced into
the room as he walked past. The overhead fluorescent
lights blazed down on four Mags in full armor. Their
jet-black figures contrasted sharply with the blank,
featureless walls. Smoke twisted in pale planes in the
air.

A naked woman sagged in a set of wrist and leg
shackles against the far wall. It was pocked with old
and new bullet holes. The yellow bodysuit worn by
the condemned lay wadded on the floor in a corner.
They wore it only on the short, final walk from a cell
to the termination room.

Three rounds had drilled dark holes in her chest,
grouped neatly over her heart. The fourth had
punched through her forehead, and a thick mixture of
blood and brains oozed down the wall behind her.

Termination squads always consisted of four Mags, and one always aimed for the head. The Magistrate selected to fire the telling head shot was always known as the Chosen Man. It was part of some old, murky tradition Salvo had never quite understood or cared enough about to investigate.

Since the termination room was on E Level, the manufacturing facility, the corpse was left in a bin so it might be rendered down into its useful chemical components. Hair, bone, skin...none of it went to waste.

Months ago, the same fate was decreed for Brigid Baptiste's treasonous life, but one member of her termination squad had been Kane. He had penciled in a new ending.

The corridor ended at an elevator tube. Salvo tapped in his badge number on the keypad, the door panel slid aside and he stepped into the car. With a hissing squeal of hydraulics, the lift ascended from E Level to C Level. He stepped out into the Magistrate Division and went to his office.

It was small, far smaller than his ambitions, and shaped like an oval with one end sliced off. He eyed the stack of daily Intel reports transmitted along the ville network on his desk, but he didn't waste his time thumbing through them. He knew not one of them would contain even the vaguest clue to the whereabouts of Kane, Baptiste or Grant. Whatever hole they dug to hide themselves in, it was deep and dark, far from the eyes of the barons. Only Lakesh could point out the hole. At least Salvo hoped he could. No, *prayed* he could.

He stepped to the window behind his desk, staring

out at the fat-faced Colorado moon. He grudgingly admitted that Lakesh was a strong man, far stronger than he had ever imagined.

Human strength was not a quality to be admired any longer. The Program of Unification had been devoted to stamping it out, to crushing the spirit that fueled it. Humanity must be prevented from aspiring to any other future beyond simply surviving from day to day.

That spirit had very nearly been obliterated on January 20, 2001, when an atomic hellstorm effectively vaporized four-fifths of the planet's population. The twenty-five-year-long nuclear winter that followed the skydark accounted for millions more.

Salvo glanced down, below the latticework of residential Enclave towers connected to the Administrative Monolith, to the Tartarus Pits. A shroud of gray enveloped the westernmost blocks, completely obscuring them from view. Beneath the roiling canopy of fog and smoke, the Pits seethed with life. The people who lived in the rancid alleyways, shanties and crumbling squats fought and loved and died, frequently for very little.

The Pits were a microcosm of human history, he reflected ruefully.

He wondered about Lakesh's human spirit, why it was so tough and resilient. It was easy for a torturer to strip the victim of all symbols of identity and reduce him to a state of total dependency, whereby the provision of the bare necessities of life was dependent on cooperation.

Alternating pain with interrogation at irregular intervals and a lack of sleep was a standard method of completely disorienting a prisoner. But applying the process properly required the luxury of time, a commodity Salvo had in short supply. He cursed beneath his breath.

An old man who presumably had lived on the cushioned tyranny of the baron for most of his life should have broken within the first day. He should have sobbed like a child, begged to tell Salvo what he knew.

Now the third day drew to a close, and all that his and Pollard's efforts had elicited was an old song, performed off-key in a horribly cracked voice, about luck being a lady tonight.

After three days, Lakesh wasn't singing anymore.

Lakesh was dying, deliberately ending his life to spite him.

Salvo pivoted away from the window, absently fingering the scar seaming his forehead, cutting down to the corner of his left eye. He knew he couldn't detain Lakesh much longer, even though the man's unexplained absences from the ville were the subject of gossip and envy. On any given day, Baron Cobalt might summon him for a private audience, or even call an unscheduled meeting of the Trust.

Salvo had no idea why the baron seemed so attached to the ancient, stubborn historian. He had considered trumping up charges and manufacturing evidence against him like he had done with Abrams, but Baron Cobalt would be sure to detect a frame, not a coincidence.

Abrams had been summarily executed as a traitor only two sunrises ago. As the Magistrate Division administrator, Salvo was next in line to assume his position. However, he had yet to be informed, officially or otherwise, of a pending promotion.

Possibly the baron preferred him to remain in the field, as director of the Grudge Task Force until Kane had been apprehended. Since the Magistrate Division was, had been his life, as it had been his father's and grandfather's, he didn't find the prospect perturbing.

All Magistrates followed a patrilineal tradition, assuming the duties and positions of their fathers before them. They didn't have given names, each taking the surname of the father, as though the first Magistrate to bear the name was the same man as the last and shared the same destiny—to live, fight and die, usually violently, as they fulfilled their oaths to impose a new world order upon chaos.

Continuing the tradition of duty should have been a sufficient life purpose, and as Salvo was promoted through the ranks, he found each upgrade satisfying, but it was a numb kind of satisfaction. Always came the yearning, the craving for more.

He fed the cravings by actions that, if discovered, would have slated him for immediate execution. Through intimidated Pit denizens, particularly Boss Guana Teague, Salvo had covertly established a highly effective spy service, with conduits stretching into the Outlands. He always knew what was going on within a fifty-mile radius and who was doing it. Rarely did he use this inside knowledge for personal gain, except to shore up his growing, fearsome reputation as a merciless enforcer.

When, five years before, Abrams sponsored his induction into the Trust, Salvo felt that his talents and superior skills were being recognized at last. He belonged to the most elite body on Earth, the ultimate secret society, the continuation of many entrusted with the hidden history of humanity and its intertwined fate with the Archon Directorate.

In a short time, Salvo grew disenchanted again. He had more power, but not nearly enough. He still had to maintain the facade of a Mag commander, dealing with a hundred picayune details every day, forced to solve mundane problems that held no interest for him whatsoever. He desired an assignment that only he could perform, an assignment that would prove to Baron Cobalt and his fellow members of the Trust just how exceptionally valuable he was.

That assignment came to him some months ago, due in the main to fortuitous circumstances he had unknowingly help to set into motion.

Thinking about Teague, Milton Reeth and the processing center he had established in Mesa Verde canyon, always brought his thoughts back around to Kane.

He fingered the scar again, this time angrily, probing it with his fingers until he felt a pinch of pain. Kane had given him that scar nearly six months before, and less than two weeks ago had taunted him about it: "You've healed nicely. Not every asshole I've pistol-whipped can say that, you know."

He opened his mouth and spit his dental plate into his hand, glaring at it with loathing. Kane had given him the new set of teeth, too, by the simple expedience of booting out his real ones.

Memories of those weeks of pain during his recovery, of enduring the humiliation of defeat, drove away any lingering doubts about the reasons he had Lakesh in custody. The old man was the door leading to Kane, and he had to find a way to open it, either with a key or a battering ram.

Slipping his dentures back into his mouth, fitting them over his gums, he looked again at the position of the moon. In a few minutes, he would stroll down to the Mag sick bay and seek out Cahill. The middle-aged medic had a drinking problem, so he would be easy to entice into examining and treating Lakesh secretly.

As the trans-comm unit on his desk skirled with a high warble, Salvo stiffened, whirling around to face it. He waited for a second signal, hoping desperately it wouldn't come. When it did, he felt a pressure in his lungs and a loosening of his bowels. He stared at the small box of molded plastic and stamped metal as if it had terrifyingly transmogrified into a bat-winged scream-wing.

Baron Cobalt had summoned the Trust.

Chapter 10

As usual, the briefing took place in the dining hall. Although the third level held a formal briefing room, it was never used. Big and blue walled, with ten rows of theater-type seats facing a raised dais in front of a projection screen, the room was depressingly sterile and disturbingly cavernous.

The dining hall was more intimate, inasmuch as most of the briefings rarely involved more than six people. Seated around a table in a corner, Grant, Brigid, Kane, Domi and DeFore were sharing a pot of one of the few perks of living in Cerberus. Genuine coffee seemed to be one of the casualties of the nukecaust, almost completely disappearing from the face of the continental United States. A bitter synthetic gruel known as sub had replaced it. Whether the name derived from "substitute" or "substandard," no one knew. Fortunately the redoubt had tons of freeze-dried caches of the real stuff, stockpiled for the original residents of Cerberus.

DeFore thumbed through a stack of spreadsheet printouts. The jagged lines and squiggles meant very little to the others, but DeFore had red-circled sections of the graph.

She pointed to one circle. "Several days ago, the first signs of stress were transmitted. Increased brain-wave activity, heart rate and respiration became irregular. They stabilized for several hours, though still erratic. Then they spiked again, stayed that way for about three hours and flattened out. That's been the pattern for the past couple of days.''

Kane took a sip of coffee. ''In your medical opinion, Lakesh is undergoing torture?''

''That's the only answer for these consistently erratic readings.'' She eyed Kane surreptitiously, noting the slight unsteadiness in the hand lifting the cup to his lips. Though he had shaved, showered and attired himself in a white bodysuit, the standard uniform of Cerberus personnel, he still looked wan and weak.

Domi, craning her neck to look at the spreadsheet, said anxiously, ''He old man. Heart give out. He could die.''

DeFore's lips twitched in a slight smile. ''He's old, right enough, chronologically a shade under 250 years. Physically, though, he's around fifty. A very sound fifty, I might add.''

Brigid stared at her in surprise. ''How can that be? He was nearly fifty when he went into cryogenic stasis shortly after the nukecaust. He claimed he was revived about fifty years ago, so his physical age should be closer to a hundred.''

''He looks that old,'' Grant argued. ''Older.''

DeFore nodded, consulting another sheet of printout. ''True, but his major organs were replaced upon his resuscitation. He's got a new heart, a new set of lungs, knee joints made of polyethylene and he's on his second pair of eyes.''

''Eyes?'' Domi echoed incredulously.

''Eyes,'' confirmed DeFore. ''Haven't you ever

wondered why an East Indian has a pair of baby blues?''

Since none of them had ever met an East Indian other than Lakesh, they had no frame of reference, so none of them had ever wondered about his eye color.

''Therefore,'' DeFore went on, ''Lakesh is in very good physical condition. To have all that reconstructive and invasive surgery done, he obviously has a high tolerance for pain. Certain kinds, anyway.''

''You mean that doddering around he does is an *act?*'' Grant demanded.

''Essentially, yes. He found it kept him fairly free of suspicion.''

''Except for now,'' intoned Kane. ''The arrogant bastard has been playing the odds for years. He should have known they wouldn't always be in his favor. Salvo isn't a fool.''

Grimly Brigid said, ''No, but he's not quite sane, either.''

She did not elaborate on her meeting with the man when she awaited trial and execution for treason. Salvo had mentioned his deep hatred of Kane without delving into the reasons behind it. And during the disastrous op in Idaho a couple of weeks before, Salvo had indulged in a paroxysm of jealous, homicidal rage over the very concept that Kane had sacrificed and betrayed everything for her.

Grant interjected, ''Salvo may chill Lakesh if he's too stubborn to cooperate.''

''I think it's safe to assume he's been stubborn,'' Kane said. ''Otherwise, this place would be under a full Mag assault by now.''

''Speaking of Magistrates,'' said DeFore, ''do you

have an idea of what kind of techniques they may be using on him?''

Grant and Kane exchanged discomfited glances, both feeling a little on the spot. But as former Mags, they were the logical ones to provide that type of information.

''We were hard-contact Magistrates,'' Grant replied a bit defensively. ''Most interrogations were carried out by Intel officers.''

''Still, you'd have sat in on a session or two,'' stated Brigid.

Kane shrugged. ''Standard opening is to soften up the perp by physical abuse. A beating, just severe enough to cause pain but not permanent damage. If that didn't work, then electric shock was applied. Deprivation of sleep, food and water, except for the bare minimum to stay alive. No toilet privileges, so the perp lay in his own wastes. Depending on the nature of the crime, drugs were used.''

''Psychotropics?'' DeFore inquired. ''Truth drugs?''

Grant shook his head. ''Nerve toxins that would cause pain and convulsions. That was usually saved for near the end, after the perps had their arms and legs broken.''

Brigid winced, imagining the agony of muscles convulsing uncontrollably, of shattered limbs thrashing about in a seizure.

Crisply DeFore said, ''The victim would probably die of shock inside of a few minutes, especially if he were in a debilitated physical state. Judging by the transponder readings, they haven't resorted to that method yet.''

"Yet," Kane repeated coldly. "They will, probably sooner than later."

"Then it's of paramount importance we get Lakesh out of there, sooner rather than later." Try as she might, Brigid couldn't keep the note of fear out of her voice.

Kane drained the coffee from his cup, set it down on the table with a loud clatter. His drawn face held no definable expression, and his tone was colorless. "Our options of penetrating both Cobaltville and the Admin Monolith are very limited. We've got only two choices—overland in a Sandcat will require at least a week's travel time, but it's the least risky. The second choice is to use the gateway and jump directly from here. Lakesh said there's a secret mat-trans unit in the Monolith."

Grant scowled. "Yeah, on A Level. The baron's quarters."

"According to Lakesh," put in Brigid, "it's a unit known to very few outside of his personal staff. It's hidden away, more than likely unguarded."

In a troubled tone, DeFore said, "Bry ran a diagnostic on the system after all of you returned. If he'd found any problems, I guess he would have said so."

Doggedly Grant grated, "He's going to have to say for sure before I climb into that goddamn thing again."

Everyone at the table, in the entire installation, knew of Grant's violent antipathy toward the mat-trans chamber, so no one responded to his remark.

"What about gateway in Mesa Verde?" Domi asked. "One we used to get here? Mebbe we jump to there?"

Brigid answered before Kane. "It was a modular unit, set up in the Cliff Palace to transport outlanders to the genetics facility in New Mexico. After we used it to escape, it was dismantled."

"Besides," said Kane, "we'd still have to contend with the overland-travel problem. We'd be on foot and hiking for days through a hellzone. We'd be sick with rad poisoning long before we came within sight of Cobaltville."

He scanned the faces of the people sitting around the table, and his eyes settled on DeFore. "We'll need you on this op just in case Lakesh requires immediate medical attention."

The woman's liquid brown eyes widened in surprise, then fear. Kane knew he was asking a lot of her. As of one Lakesh's first exiles, spirited out of Ragnarville to the north, she was still so fearful of being apprehended again she rarely ventured beyond the redoubt's sec doors.

DeFore didn't voice her fears. She took a deep breath and nodded shortly. "Understood."

Kane turned toward Domi. "You know every slaghole in Tartarus, right?"

She grinned, bobbing her close-cropped white head in a decisive nod. "You betcha. Find my way around blindfolded."

"Let's hope it doesn't come to that," Kane responded dryly. "We'll need you in case we're cut off from the gateway when we have to make our escape."

Although born in the Outlands, Domi had entered Cobaltville with a bogus ID chip provided by the former pit boss of Tartarus, the late and largely unlamented Guana Teague. Every ville had its own planned ghetto, in Cobaltville it was a sublevel known as the Tartarus Pits. For outlanders like Domi, the Pits were the only aspect of ville society in which they could participate—if eking out a hellish existence in an environment one step removed from a septic tank could be considered participation.

Like many other young Outland women, Domi had been lured into the Pits by the promise of a better life, on the provision she supplied a term of sex service to Guana Teague. For months she was locked away, little better than a slave to the depraved lusts of the grotesque man-mountain of flab. The term of service came to an abrupt, nonnegotiable end when Domi cut Teague's throat.

Casting his eyes back toward DeFore, Kane asked, "Can we assume that Salvo knows nothing of Lakesh's biolink transponder?"

She nodded. "I served in Ragnarville's medical service for better than five years. If the villes had something like it, I would have heard about it."

Darkly Kane said, "I was a Mag for better than fifteen years, man and boy, and I never heard about the Archon Directorate until six months ago."

He brushed impatiently at a lock of hair falling over his forehead. For an instant, the vision of the man Kennedy performing a similar, absent gesture ghosted through his mind.

"Kane?" Brigid gazed him at closely.

Quickly he stated, "All right, we'll operate on the assumption this isn't a trap, orchestrated by either Lakesh or Salvo."

Offended by the comment, Brigid shot him a ice-eyed stare. She said, "We haven't much time."

Kane glanced at his wrist chron. "Grant, Domi, DeFore, we'll meet in the ready room at 1300 hours."

For a handful of seconds, Brigid wondered if Kane's omission of her name was an oversight. Only when he pushed back his chair did she ask, "What kind of equipment do you want me to bring?"

"None," he answered, rising to his feet.

She blinked at him. "Why not?"

"Because you're not going," he retorted sternly.

Her eyes widened, burning with the green flame of outrage. "Who gave you the authority to make that decision?"

"Consider it a field promotion, Baptiste. There's no reason for you to be a part of the team. An op like this requires a minimum number of personnel. Four is a nice round figure. More only adds a name to a possible casualty or prisoner list."

She glared at him, groping for a response.

In a lower, yet no less firm tone, he added, "What was it you called yourself a couple of weeks ago... 'Brigid Baptiste, girl hostage'?"

Brigid swept her furious gaze over Domi and Grant, looking for either support or sympathy. Domi averted her eyes, but Grant met her stare from beneath a furrowed brow. He said, "Kane's right. This is the riskiest op any of us have ever been on. DeFore's presence may be essential to bringing Lakesh back here alive. Yours isn't."

Kane stared at her coldly, calmly. She demanded, "Am I supposed to be grateful that you're looking out for my safety…or sparing me the embarrassment of being captured again?"

"No, not now. Later you might be."

"You said you'd help me retrieve him—"

"Which I'm doing," he broke in sharply. "There was absolutely nothing said about you going along. And don't delude yourself into thinking I'm trying to protect you. I didn't make this decision for chivalrous reasons."

"Why, then?"

"You said the interphaser's memory disk held the secret to time travel."

"I did, but I also said only Lakesh can analyze the data."

"And if Lakesh dies, or if none of us make it back, who is the next-most-qualified person in Cerberus to find the analysis key, no matter how long it might take?"

She did not reply. The lump swelling in her throat blocked any attempt to speak.

"Answer me." Kane spoke loudly, harshly.

Brigid coughed, managing to hoarsely husk out, "Me."

"Exactly. You. What was it you said? Something about saving billions of snuffed-out lives that weren't supposed to be snuffed out?"

"I have an eidetic memory," she snapped. "Perfect and total recall. I don't need you to remind me of anything."

"Good." He gestured to DeFore. "I'm going to need a painkiller that won't make me woozy and a stimulant to keep me alert."

"I can give you those."

To Grant, Kane said, "We'll go in fully armored. We can't silence the Sin Eaters, so we'll bring the Copperheads, too."

Grant nodded. "Affirm. We should take grens and a Syne."

The Syne, or Mnemosyne, was a digital decrypter, small enough to carry in one hand but capable of overriding the most complex of electronic locks.

Kane started walking toward the exit. Grant hurriedly swallowed the last mouthful of coffee in his cup and rose from his chair. Between clenched teeth, Brigid hissed, "That man is a vanadium-hearted son of a bitch."

Grant smiled, but it didn't reach his shadowed eyes. "Isn't he just. That's why Lakesh needs him."

Chapter 11

Salvo strode purposefully down the corridor, away from the office suites, past the recessed armory sec door. He turned right, down a narrow, windowless hallway. After twenty paces, it ended at a locked service access door. Salvo inserted a key into the lock and opened it.

Instead of a service access, there was an elevator shaft, barely large enough to accommodate two men. He stepped onto the lift disk and pulled the door shut behind him. Lock solenoids snapped into place automatically, and the disk shot upward.

It hissed to a stop, and Salvo opened the door, moving quickly across the down ramp and into a magnificently appointed foyer. Glittering light cast from many crystal chandeliers flooded every corner of the entrance hall.

A member of the elite Baronial Guard stood at stiff attention before the gold-and-ivory-inlaid double doors. Usually two of the red-and-white-uniformed men were on duty, but tonight only a burly blond man stood there. Since Salvo had never spoken to any of the guards, he didn't know this man's name. The Baronial Guard opened the right-hand door, and as he expected, he strode into a deep, almost primal dark.

Salvo kept walking, knowing where he was going. The baron's level was the only one in the monolith without windows, and he always kept his suite at a light level like a summer's evening dusk.

He wasn't surprised by the unexpected and unscheduled meeting of the Trust. This was Baron Cobalt's demonstration, held at a deliberately inconvenient hour without prior notice, to show that he was the unquestioned master of every detail in the lives of his servitors.

Salvo passed through a wide, low arch into another room and then another. As he approached the fifth and final room, his sure stride faltered.

Before him blazed an incandescent golden flare, glowing like a miniature sun in the gulfs of space. Salvo walked slowly toward it, an icy hand seeming to stroke his spine. Cold sweat beaded his skin. He came to a stop in the center of the enormous Persian carpet covering the floor and faced the archway.

It was awash with a pale yellow luminescence, like veils of smoke dusted with particles of gold. Beyond the veils, he saw a vague and familiar shape, swaying slightly.

No other members of the Trust stood in a formal semicircle on the carpet. The gong had not chimed thirteen times to announce Baron Cobalt's arrival. The entire ritual of assembling the Trust and the baron's theatrical appearance had been dispensed with.

Salvo was alone, completely and utterly alone with Baron Cobalt.

He heard a faint rasping sound. Distantly he realized the short hairs on the nape of his neck had lifted, scraping against the high collar of his uniform.

All the moisture dried in his mouth, and he fought

against the mad impulse to turn and race back the way he had come, like a panicked deer.

He accepted the fact he was afraid—no, terrified. His instincts had kicked in before his brain, the trapped animal buried within the human psyche cringing away before his reasoning centers grasped the uniquely awful import of the moment.

A vanishingly tiny percentage of people had private audiences with the baron, and those few were members of his personal staff. As far as Salvo knew, the general membership of the Trust did not even know his true appearance. Certainly Salvo had never seen Baron Cobalt without his theatrical trappings.

He knew the baron utilized a psychological ploy to intimidate and solidify the master-servant relationship between him and the Trust, but that knowledge didn't make it easier to endure. Salvo was still shaken with a primordial fear.

The hierarchy of barons claimed to be hybrids of human and Archons, the Directorate's plenipotentiaries on Earth. Salvo wasn't certain about those claims, since he had never seen an Archon, just as he had never seen one of the baronial hierarchy in the flesh. As far as he really knew, the barons could be new strains of mutie, genetically scrambled mutations spawned by the nukecaust. In the century comprising and following skydark, the Deathlands had swarmed with the monstrosities. One of the original reasons for drafting the Unification Program had been fear of a mutie uprising. Less than a hundred years before, a deluded mutie calling himself Lord Kaa had formed a sizable army of stickies and launched a war of conquest against villes in the Shens and the Carolinas.

But it wasn't the question of Baron Cobalt's half-human ancestry that sent fear exploding through him. It was the certainty that the baron could end his life on a whim and with a single word. Or worse, extend that life in sanity-shattering agony until, wearying of keeping him alive, the baron would speak another word—and Salvo would cease to exist, so suddenly and thoroughly it would be as if he had never lived at all.

The figure behind the gold-speckled curtain paced incessantly. In all these years, Salvo had never received any other impression of the baron's appearance that was different than his first: a gaunt man-shape under six feet tall, with unusually long arms and unusually short legs. His face was always in shadow, but occasionally Salvo caught glimpses of a long, narrow face and a high-domed, hairless skull. The color and shape of the baron's eyes were still a mystery to Salvo.

Baron Cobalt spoke as he shifted his lean body back and forth between the walls of the arch. His voice, as melodic and musical as a contralto flute, caressed Salvo's ears.

"You must be rather surprised to find yourself alone before me and not in the company of your fraternity."

Salvo lowered his head, not daring to speak for fear that the tremor in his voice would betray him.

"Abrams, as you know, was executed three days ago," the baron continued. "Perhaps you may have wondered why I have not formally named you his successor."

Baron Cobalt paused expectantly.

Salvo forced himself to whisper, "My lord baron has many matters of state to occupy him."

Baron Cobalt laughed, a high, birdlike trill. "You grovel nicely, Salvo, but it is not required at this time. As for my occupations, I confess my thoughts turn more and more toward the rancorous events of the last half year."

Salvo didn't have to ask Baron Cobalt to clarify, even had he the nerve to do so. The events of the past five and a half months were, in all likelihood, the most scandalous in the eighty-seven-year history of the unified villes.

Kane had learned too much during the op to chill Milton Reeth and shut down his processing center. Rather than have a decorated Magistrate chilled, Salvo had inducted him into the Trust. His reasons were many and so complex even he didn't understand them all. Primarily the prospect of holding Kane's fate in his hand had been too attractive to ignore.

The idea of forcing an independent man like Kane to become vulnerable to his slightest wish had been almost sexual in its intensity. He remembered how Abrams had accused him of hatching an ill-conceived and perverse plan. Even Lakesh commented that he possessed a talent for cruel irony.

Replaying the old historian's words, Salvo suddenly doubted himself. Setting up Abrams as a traitor had been a way to divert the baron from Salvo's real plans for Lakesh. Now he wondered if his loathing of Kane hadn't blinded him to reality.

Both Abrams and Lakesh had lodged objections to the induction of Kane. On Lakesh's part, his rebuke could have been a pose, but—

Baron Cobalt's voice yanked his attention outward. "Over the years, in the other villes, a few Magistrates turned renegade, but they didn't possess the knowledge of our true work like Kane. Most of them were tracked and put to...other uses. Kane's own father is the most recent example of that practice."

"Yes, Lord Baron," Salvo said deferentially.

As if he hadn't heard, the baron went on, "Your own father's relationship with the elder Kane was a bit on the curious side, wasn't it?"

Salvo's heart fluttered inside his chest like a captured bird.

Baron Cobalt's nervous pacing stopped. Though Salvo couldn't see his eyes, he felt the heat of his stare through the pastel curtain. "I also find it a bit on the curious side why you chose the name 'Grudge' for the task force I allowed you to form...a task force dedicated to the sole aim of running down a single traitor. A traitor you brought into my fold."

Sweat slid down Salvo's body beneath his uniform, making him feel like a two-legged bog. "My Lord—"

Baron Cobalt raised an imperious hand. "I admit I allowed my fury at Kane to cloud my reasoning. I am not accustomed to experiencing such strong, visceral emotions as anger and hatred, and therefore I did not perceive the pattern. At least not immediately. But when I did, I checked our genetic database."

Salvo could not disguise his mounting horror. "My Lord, I don't understand."

"Perhaps you truly do not." The baron sighed, as if in remorse. "Even after I explain it, you may still not understand. You have heard of Overproject Excalibur?''

Salvo nodded, thoughts racing wildly. Overproject Excalibur had been a division of the Totality Concept dealing with the bioengineering of life-forms. The three subdivisions of Excalibur were Calypso, Invictus and Joshua.

"Joshua's role in the Overproject was the mapping of human genomes to specific chromosomal functions and locations," Baron Cobalt stated. "Do you know why it had that aim?"

Salvo mutely he shook his head.

The baron began pacing again. "It was so the Directorate would have genetic samples of the best of the best after the nukecaust. In the vernacular of the time, it was known as 'purity control.'

"After the Program of Unification had been instituted, the egg cells were developed to embryos. Through ectogenesis techniques, fetal development outside of the body eliminated the role of the mother until after birth. The genes in the egg cells were manipulated to reduce the hereditary relevance of both parents, to break the connection between mother, father and child. That break was crucial in order for the Unification Program to succeed. The existence of the family as a unit of procreation and therefore as a social unit had to be eliminated."

Baron Cobalt returned to the center of the veiled archway and gestured toward him. "You and everyone else who enjoys full ville citizenship are the descendants of that undertaking. Sometimes a particularly desirable trait was grafted to an unrelated egg or an undesirable trait removed. As you may imagine, there were many failures over the past three generations. However, when there was a success, it was replicated over and over, occasionally with modifications. But the basic genetic foundation remained unchanged.''

The baron's voice dropped in pitch, acquiring a self-satisfied purr. ''The best example is myself and my brother barons. Contained within us are superior traits collected from an equal number of humans and Archons. Some of that genetic material was supplied by the Kane line.''

Salvo's startled intake of breath sounded like a rasp drawn over resined violin strings.

Baron Cobalt chuckled. ''Yes, that makes Kane and myself related after a fashion. I told him this myself, in Dulce, though I overstated it a bit for effect.'' He paused for a musing moment. ''Do you begin to understand what I am leading up to?''

Salvo's tongue stuck to the roof of his mouth. He could not speak.

''Do you know the difference between identical and fraternal twins? No? Identical twins result when a single fertilized egg splits and develops into two separate but duplicate organisms, a form of natural, accidental cloning.

''Fraternal twins, by contrast, occur when two different sperm fertilize two different eggs. Need I continue?''

The carpet seemed to split beneath Salvo's feet. He rocked, as if he tottered on the edge of an abyss—or on the crumbling lip of hell.

Baron Cobalt fell silent, swaying slightly, like a reed in a gentle breeze. Salvo glared at him through a cloud of tears. The baron said no more. He preferred to unleash all of Salvo's hidden demons and watch with amusement as they shredded and gutted everything that he was.

Say it, you inhuman bastard. Say it! And in saying it, damn my father as a liar, as a deceiver! He told me Kane's father had stolen the woman selected for him, pulled rank, laughed about his victory! Say it!

That my father lied when he claimed Kane's father set out to humiliate him, make him an object of scorn in the division! Tell me how the Kane line possessed qualities superior to the Salvos, and that's why the arrangement was changed!

Go ahead, my Lord Baron, tell me that I sprang from the Kane stock! Tell me that I've wasted all these years hating a man who is my own genetic brother. Tell me something I didn't already fucking know!

Baron Cobalt's voice swam with notes of melodic notes of cruelty. "I can see you've managed to grasp the subtleties. And finally we reach the apex of this intimate heart-to-heart.

"Salvo, you orchestrated the entire sequence of events, from the moment you chose Kane to be a member of the penetration squad into Mesa Verde. You sponsored him into the Trust, you performed an admirable job of arranging his escape and concealing your own complicity in it."

The baron's swaying motions increased, as if the breeze had become a stiff wind. "You petitioned me to form the Grudge Task Force so you could take a more active hand in Kane's seditious activities. When

Abrams became suspicious, you framed him with manufactured evidence.

"Now my good friend Lakesh has vanished. My guard reported you were last seen with him. I submit Lakesh grew suspicious, just like Abrams, but rather than setting him up—since not even you are so arrogant to believe I would accept the exposure of two traitors in such a short time—you absconded with him."

Salvo's stomach turned a series of flip-flops. He shivered, biting down on his tongue to keep his teeth from chattering. He croaked, "My Lord, you are mistaken."

Baron Cobalt shook his head slowly. "Although I fall prey to errors of judgment, I never make mistakes."

Salvo sensed shadows shifting behind him, and started to turn. Searing pain lanced from the back of his neck to the base of his spine. Faintly he heard a hissing crackle and the thud of his head hitting the nap of the carpet. He didn't feel it.

He lay stunned, blinking at the two figures looming. One wore the uniform of a Baronial Guardsman. He wielded a black, three-foot-long baton that Salvo dazedly identified as a Mag-issue Shockstick.

The second figure took him longer to recognize. He was a tall man, holding what at first glance seemed to be another Shockstick. On second glance, Salvo saw it was a cane, a walking stick. The man holding it had hair and a beard the color of iron. A smile of triumph creased his weather-beaten face.

Salvo's lips writhed, his senses reeling. He was barely able to say, in a whisper, "Abrams."

Baron Cobalt's voice cracked like a whip. "Get up."

When Salvo didn't immediately move, the guardsman thrust down threateningly with the tip of the Shockstick. He got to his knees and stayed there, shaking his head from side to side in horrified denial.

Baron Cobalt thrust aside the iridescent curtain and approached him, walking in a mannered, graceful stride. Salvo gazed at him, seeing clearly for the first time his master, his deity.

The baron's slender, gracile figure was encased in a golden bodysuit, which matched the almost translucent golden hue of his complexion. The smooth, almost poreless skin was stretched tight over protuberant facial bones, all sharp angles of cheeks, brow and chin. The elongated skull tapered from a high, round, completely bald skull down to a pointed chin.

There were no lines on the face, not even on the high forehead. Below them, large, slanting golden brown eyes stared out from deep sockets. The thin slash of the mouth showed only authority and amused contempt.

Salvo tried to keep his gaze steady, faintly recalling something he had read that those who look on the face of their god would be struck dead.

"Lord Baron," he whispered. "I am yours. Ever and always. I have served you faithfully."

The tiny nostrils in the fine, thin nose flared. "Humans serve only themselves, their own venal ambitions for power, for material goods. They need a cause to cloak their greed. That trait cannot seem to be bred out of the race. It must be burned out."

Baron Cobalt's eyes looked down upon him con-

templatively. He smiled a sad, almost fond smile. In
a measured tone, he said, ''We will begin that cleans-
ing with you.''

Chapter 12

At 1230 hours, Grant and Domi entered the armory. He pressed the flat toggle switch on the door frame, and the overhead fluorescent fixtures blazed with a white, sterile light.

The big square room was stacked nearly to the ceiling with wooden crates and boxes. Many of the crates were stenciled with the legend Property U.S. Army. Glass-fronted cases lined the four walls. Automatic assault rifles were neatly racked in a case, and a nearby open crate was filled with hundreds of rounds of 5.56 mm ammunition. There were many makes and models of subguns, as well as dozens of semiautomatic blasters, complete with holsters and belts. Heavy-assault weaponry occupied the north wall, bazookas, tripod-mounted M-249 machine guns, mortars and rocket launchers.

All the ordnance, from the smallest-caliber blaster to the Sandcat and Hussar Hotspur Land Rover in an adjacent chamber, was of predark manufacture. Caches of matériel had been laid down in hermetically sealed Continuity of Government installations before the nukecaust. Protected from the ravages of the outraged environment, most of the munitions and hardware were as pristine as the day when they rolled off the assembly line.

Grant strode to the suit of Magistrate body armor

mounted on a metal framework in a corner. The framework holding Kane's armor gleamed nakedly in the light. He had suited up at least an hour previously, but Grant preferred to spend as little time as possible inside the polycarbonate exoskeleton.

For one thing, this particular suit of armor hadn't been fitted to his physique like Kane's armor had. It had belonged to a Mag named Anson who had briefly joined Lakesh's exiles some years before. Anson ended the association by blowing out his brains with his own regulation Sin Eater. Learning the truth behind the nukecaust and the future of Earth had been too much for him to bear.

He had left behind his armor, and though a big man, he wasn't as big as Grant. Pieces of it pinched and chafed him in places where a man wasn't meant to be pinched and chafed.

Grant removed the pieces from the framework, inspecting each one quickly, habitually. Though relatively lightweight, the polycarbonate was sufficiently dense to deflect every caliber of projectile, up to and including a .45-caliber bullet. It absorbed and redistributed a bullet's kinetic impact, minimizing the chance of incurring hydrostatic shock.

Before leaving his quarters, he had donned the Kevlar undersheathing, a black, high-collared bodysuit with Velcro tabs at the wrists and ankles. He stepped into the calf-length, thick-treaded boots with their metal-reinforced toes, buckling and strapping them tight. He touched the fourteen-inch combat knife in the boot scabbard, making sure it was properly sheathed.

Domi helped him into the armor. Her slender, petite

form was all but swallowed by a dark green, baggy coverall, the uniform of an Enclave custodian. A green wool stocking cap concealed most of her white hair. Holstered beneath the coverall, snugged in shoulder leather, was a Detonics .45 Combat Master handblaster. She had carried it with her on the op to Britain and Ireland, and despite doubts it might be too much gun for such a small girl, she had wielded it with deadly efficiency.

A tool bag hung by a strap from her right shoulder, but it held none of the accoutrements of a custodian's trade. It contained two spare ammo clips and three spherical frag grens of the MU-50 series, developed by the military two centuries ago.

Domi held up the molded breastplate, connected to the back plate by tiny hinges. Grant stepped into it, and she closed it like a clamshell around his massive torso. She fiddled with the side locks and said sternly, "Suck in gut."

Grant obediently sucked it in, feeling a twinge from his right rib cage, where, four days before, several 9 mm rounds had pounded. Fortunately his Kevlar-weave coat had prevented penetration. He had been worried about broken or cracked ribs, but DeFore had diagnosed only minor rupturing of the intercostal cartilage.

Domi snapped shut all the torso seams while he tugged on the leggings, then the long gauntlets. After he had secured the arm and shin guards, he looked like a statue carved from obsidian. The red disk-shaped badge affixed to the molded left pectoral provided the only spot of color anywhere on the polycarbonate carapace. It depicted a stylized, balanced scales of justice against a nine-spoked wheel, symbolizing the wheel of law in the nine baronies.

Grant buckled the holstered Sin Eater to his right forearm and tested the spring-release mechanism. The handblaster leaped into his waiting hand, the butt unfolding and slapping into his palm. He made sure his index finger was extended, since the Sin Eater had no trigger guard or safety. It fired immediately upon touching the crooked forefinger.

Satisfied, he pushed the weapon back into the holster and removed the helmet from the framework. He didn't put it on. Unlike the rest of the armor, it was a shade too large. Tucking it under his left arm, he went to a gun case, sliding back the glass door. From it, he selected his close-assault weapon.

A chopped-down autoblaster, the Copperhead was barely two feet in length. The magazine held fifteen rounds of 4.85 mm steel-jacketed rounds, which could be fired at a rate of 700 rounds per minute. Even with its optical image intensifier and laser autotarget scope, the Copperhead weighed less than eight pounds.

From a notched wooden rack at the rear of the case, Grant took a black, six-inch-long cylinder and screwed it carefully into the blaster's bore. The two-stage sound and muzzle-flash arrestor suppressed even full-auto reports to no more than rustling whispers.

He attached the Copperhead to a magnetic clip on his belt and announced, "I'm primed. What about you?"

Domi shrugged. "As can be."

She gazed up at him uncertainly, as if she wanted to say something else, but unsure of the words to use.

Gruffly he asked, "What? We're coming up on the jump point."

In a swift burst, Domi said, "That doctor lady not warrior like rest of us. Don't want baby-sit her fat ass."

Grant heaved a sigh redolent with an I-should-have-known undercurrent. Domi claimed to be in love with him, viewing him as a gallant black knight who had rescued her from the shackles of Guana Teague's slavery. In reality, quite the reverse was true. Teague had been crushing the life out of Grant beneath his three-hundred-plus pounds of flab when Domi expertly slit his throat.

Regardless of the facts, Domi had attached herself to him and, though her attempts at outright seduction were less frequent, she still made it fiercely clear that Grant was hers and hers alone.

Not too long before, she had expressed jealousy of DeFore, suspecting the woman of having designs on Grant. He had no idea if the medic had such an intent. She was a mature woman, certainly attractive and closer to his own age than Domi, though there was nothing between them but a guarded friendship.

Of course, he reflected, he had fought hard to make sure there was nothing but friendship between him and Domi, too, but he feared it was a fight he would eventually lose. He had no idea of Domi's true age, and neither did she. She could be as young as sixteen or as old as twenty-six, but either way, he was pushing forty and felt twice as old. He couldn't deny he was attracted to her youthfulness, her high spirits and her uninhibited sexuality.

Arranging his face into a fearsome scowl, he rumbled dangerously, "DeFore's not your concern. You will do what Kane and me tell you to do without argument or you'll be left behind. There's no place on an op for any kind of bullshit. You got me, girl?"

Crimson anger glinted in her eyes for a moment, then she ducked her head, nodding in grudging assent.

They went out into the corridor, Domi hurrying to match his long-legged stride. They entered the central control complex, passed down the aisle between banks of instruments and into the ready room. As Grant figured, Kane, DeFore and Brigid were already there. So was Bry, drumming his fingers nervously on the table, speaking gravely to Kane.

"I've run two diagnostics. Though I found some circuit damage to a couple of the secondary support systems, the unit itself checks out fine. I just wish I knew the modulation of the matter stream which brought you here. If I could analyze the frequency, I'd have no doubts whatsoever."

"Doubts?" Grant repeated challengingly. "What kind of doubts?"

Brigid smiled wanly. "Nothing serious. Bry is still confused about the quantum path we traveled to arrive here from England. I've already told him that he can't analyze the event frequency until Lakesh decrypts the interphaser memory disk."

"You found the access-activation code for the Cobaltville unit?" Kane asked.

Bry nodded. "It was in the database. I've already programmed it into the target-lock coordinate scanner."

Grant asked, "What about the way Lakesh rigged the target autosequence initiator? Is that still intact?"

Bry smiled confidently. "Don't worry about it. The Cerberus jump lines are still out of phase with the other units in the network. Your origin point will be untraceable."

Kane commented distractedly, "That's a small edge, but it'll have to do."

His black armor was identical to Grant's, except the red badge was missing from the pectoral. Only a couple of weeks ago, during the sour Idaho op, Salvo had personally pried it off. Kane hadn't wanted it retrieved.

Now a decision made on bitter impulse might hold lethal repercussions. Mag badges were keyed to photoelectric field sensors that gave the officers unimpeded access to all divisions, all levels of the monolith.

More than likely, the frequencies of their badges had long ago been deactivated, but knowing from experience the cumbersome pace of ville bureaucracy, a slight chance existed the codes were still active.

In addition to that worry, the tiny image-enhancing sensor mounted on the forepart of Kane's helmet did not function. Connected to the red-tinted visor, it intensified ambient light to permit limited night vision. The microchannel feeding the signal to the visor had been damaged in Idaho, and there had been no time to repair it before their mission to Britain and Ireland.

Though the likelihood of finding themselves in complete darkness was slim, Kane had stowed a Nighthawk microlight and a pair of Mag-issue dark-vision glasses in the compartments of his belt. Affixed to his left wrist by an expandable band was a miniaturized motion detector. It was made of molded plastic and stamped metal, and the top face consisted of a liquid-crystal digital display window.

Kane had appropriated it from an officer of the Grudge Task Force. The small device wasn't standard Magistrate issue. He assumed it was of predark origin, found in COG Stockpiles, then hidden away by the barons during the Program of Unification. Lakesh had stated that only a fraction of twentieth-century tech was available, even to the ville elite.

Grant watched DeFore run a final check on the contents of the medical kit lying open on the table. She wore the powder blue bodysuit of ville medical services. The left breast bore an embroidered likeness of the ancient caduceus symbol, two snakes intertwined and facing each other around a leafy staff.

Grant gazed at the symbol, feeling slightly queasy. After his encounter with Lord Strongbow and his Dragoons, he had hoped to never again see any scaled creature that slithered and hissed.

When he heard the faint, angry hiss from his left, he very nearly jumped straight up. Startled, he swung his head around and down to see Domi glaring at him and then at DeFore. She had followed his gaze and assumed he was transfixed not by the serpent insignia but the woman's bosom.

He opened his mouth to voice a profane rebuke, but Kane announced, "There's not much point in discussing tactics. Though the Administrative Monolith specs were in the database, they didn't include A Level. I've only been there once and didn't have much of a chance to look around. I don't know the location of the gateway unit, but if we can find our way from there to the baron's reception area, I'll be able to take us to a hidden lift that we can use to reach E Level.

"I doubt there's much business at this hour, so the only opposition is the Baronial Guard. They're show soldiers, and as far as I know, they're not even armed. If we're lucky, Grant's badge will get us through the checkpoints."

DeFore eyed him uneasily. "And if we're not lucky and we're cut off from the gateway?"

"There's a secret way down to Tartarus, but we'll have to reach the Enclaves, the fourth-level living quarters, to get to it."

Kane scanned the faces of the people in the room. "Any questions?"

DeFore closed and shouldered the medical kit. "Millions."

"I'll answer one."

She anxiously wet her lips. "If Lakesh is still alive, but too injured to move, too far gone for medical treatment to do any good, if in short, it's a negative prognosis, what should I do?"

A heavy silence draped the room. Eyes shifted back and forth. Finally Brigid spoke in a calm, uninflected tone. "Euthanasia."

Kane nodded. "It's the only logical recourse. If we can't bring him back, we'll have to silence him."

Curtly Brigid said, "That's not why I made the suggestion."

"I know," Kane replied diffidently. He slipped on his helmet, snapping shut the under-jaw lock guards. His eyes were masked by the slightly concave red visor, and only a portion of his mouth and chin was visible. He made sure the Copperhead at his belt was within easy reach.

Grant put on his helmet. As he did so, he stated, "You're running the show, Kane. But I want a couple of promises from you."

Kane glanced at him, saying nothing.

"I want your promise you won't go after either Baron Cobalt or Salvo," Grant continued. "If we bump into them, that's a different matter. Our mission is to get in and get out, a penetration. Not a vendetta."

Kane regarded him dispassionately for a moment, then said flatly, "No promises, except that I'll keep our mission priorities in mind."

As he turned toward the door leading to the mattrans chamber, Brigid plucked at Grant's arm, whispering urgently, "You'll have to watch him."

Grant grunted in acknowledgment of her words, but he was grimly aware that he could do very little to rein in Kane when the man's warrior heart beat hot and fast. He owed Salvo and the baron a debt, and only blood could wash it away.

Brigid stared after him, eyes bright with worry. Grant felt a pang of sympathy for her. She didn't know Kane, not really. Certainly she had witnessed his melancholies, his humors, his angers. But she had never seen him as juggernaut of vengeance, so crazed by berserker fury he was willing to die in order to deal death to his enemies.

Grant had seen that mad rage only a couple of times in the dozen years he had partnered with him. Once, when a cornered jolt-walker had stabbed him, and again, only a few months before, when he flung himself into combat against the loathsome hybrid horde in Dulce. Although Brigid had been there, she had been too busy fighting for her own life to notice the battle-madness driving Kane.

If the proximity of Salvo or Baron Cobalt triggered that fury, Grant knew he could do little to contain it. Kane was as likely to chill him as the objects of his hatred if he tried to stop him.

Domi patted Brigid's arm soothingly. "You not worry. I look out for him. He come back to you."

Brigid eyed her in surprise, then in irritation. "That's not what I'm worried about."

Domi went toward the jump chamber, grinning over her shoulder. "Whatever you say."

They went through the anteroom and entered the gateway unit. Right above the keypad encoding panel, imprinted in faded maroon letters, were the words Entry Absolutely Forbidden To All But B-12 Cleared Personnel. Mat-Trans. Even Lakesh didn't know who the B-12-cleared personnel had been and what had become of them, though he had opined they had probably jumped from the installation after the nuke, desperately searching for a place better than Cerberus and doubtlessly not finding it.

Grant closed the heavy armaglass door behind them, the lock mechanism triggering the automatic jump initiator. Under his breath, he murmured his pre-jump mantra, "I hate these fucking things, I hate these fucking things."

He glanced toward DeFore, who took deep, calming breaths. Though her face was composed, her eyes darted back and forth, up and down. She had only

made one mat-trans jump before, when she had fled
Ragnarville three years ago.

Domi, who possessed only a bit more jump experience than DeFore, appeared as if she were about to
nod off from boredom.

Kane stood stiff and grim, facing the door, not
looking at his companions.

The familiar humming vibration arose, climbing to
a high-pitched drone. The hexagonal metal disks
above and below exuded a shimmering glow that
slowly intensified. The fine mist gathered and climbed
from the floor and wafted down from the ceiling. Tiny
crackling static discharges flared in the vapor. The
insubstantial tendrils thickened, curling around to en-
gulf them.

None of them felt any pain, only a mild shock and
then a dissolution as deep and as dark as death.

Chapter 13

During his years as a hard-contact field Magistrate, Salvo often wondered about death, since it could come unannounced at any moment. He knew predark religions were cluttered with contradictory lore regarding the immortality of the soul, rewards, punishments, heavens, hells, purgatories.

Although none of it made any sense to him or had the slightest impact on his day-to-day duties, he still found himself in dark, private hours contemplating the means and manner of his own death.

A bullet to the brain was preferable, he figured, to being maimed in say, a Deathbird crash. With a bullet, one second he would be alive and in the next second, he would not. That manner of death was elegant in its simplicity, and he approved of it and gave it no more thought. As for the manner, he presumed that would take care of itself.

Now he found himself devoting more emotional and mental energy to the subject than he had ever dreamed he would.

As he knelt on the carpet before Baron Cobalt, still tingling from the Shockstick's voltage, he heard a wheezy sneeze of sound from behind him. A sharp pain stabbed through the side of his neck. He didn't need to pluck out the tiny hypodermic to realize a guardsman had shot him with a dart gun. Nor did he need to wonder why his entire body went limp within three seconds.

The drug coursing through his bloodstream and scrambling his nervous system was a synthesis of chlordiazepoxide and carbachol. It was the same stuff he had used on Brigid Baptiste and Kane a couple of weeks before in Idaho. He also had administered it to Lakesh just three days ago.

The compound had been developed by the Intel section of the Magistrate Division for crowd control in the instance of another Pit uprising. Salvo had appropriated it for the Grudge Task Force. He might have smiled at the irony, but his facial muscles no longer worked.

Although he breathed normally and was entirely conscious, he had no control over so much as a single toe joint. It was not an uncomfortable sensation—his body was numb and barely responded to tactile sensation. He doubted he would react even to a continuous Shockstick assault.

Another pair of guardsmen appeared, and they dragged him effortlessly away from Baron Cobalt and the smirking Abrams. His heels dug shallow grooves in the nap of the carpet. They pulled him through archway after archway, then to the left, down a tight, narrow passage that was more tunnel than corridor.

Salvo knew very little about the layout of A Level. As the baron's aerie, it was a place of mystery. He had heard it was a labyrinth of connecting chambers, hidden passageways and secret rooms, deliberately designed as a fortress within a fortress. In the exceptionally unlikely instance of assassins reaching the top level of the monolith, they would never be able to find the baron before they themselves were found.

The passage opened into a small, dome-shaped chamber. The guardsmen laid Salvo down on the smooth floor and arranged him in position—flat on his back with his arms close to his sides, feet together. He noted that barely six inches separated the crown of his head and the soles of his boots from the curving walls.

The two guardsmen backed out of the chamber, into the narrow mouth of the passageway. Dully gleaming steel clamps came up out of disguised floor slots and seized Salvo's wrists and legs. Two more rose from the either side of his hips and joined over his waist.

Then the floor on which he lay began to turn over. The clamps held his body firmly in place, though his head drooped at the end of a lax-muscled neck. The floor completed its rollover, and he stared into total darkness.

Faintly he heard servo motors pumping hydraulic pressure to a hidden complex of gears and cables. The floor descended slowly, smoothly, straight down inside the walls of a circular shaft.

Salvo knew he should be terrified, imagining what awaited him at the bottom. He doubted it would be as merciful as a single bullet to the brain. More than likely, he would be slowly crushed, pulverized like a slab of meat on a butcher's block. Perhaps he would be lowered onto a forest of razor-pointed spikes, impaled by fractions over a period of hours.

Although he easily conjured up the images of such deaths, he was unable to respond to them in any meaningful, emotional degree. One thought dominated: his death was not supposed to be like this, but he felt more disappointed than frightened.

Finally he realized the compound that had turned his body into a sack of flour had also tranquilized him. Indifferently his eyes recorded a portal irising open beneath him. The dim light emanated as an eerie, blue green glow.

The descent halted smoothly, with a scrape of metal brackets sliding into flanges. Three pairs of white-gloved and -sleeved arms entered his narrow range of vision. The hands pressed up against him as the clamps clicked open. He felt himself lowered facedown on a wheeled stretcher. Strong hands deftly positioned his head so he could breathe unimpeded.

Salvo was borne swiftly down a short stretch of narrow corridor. The three figures didn't speak to him or one another, but he heard, or thought he heard, one of them humming to itself. He didn't recognize the tune, if tune it was.

A pair of metal-sheathed double doors swung wide, and Salvo rolled into a small room shaped like a hollow triangle. The four walls slanting up, presumably to meet in the center of the ceiling. Even though he could still roll his eyes, he couldn't see very much.

Chrome-collared sockets of different diameters studded the walls. They looked strange and threatening, but he couldn't bring himself to wonder or worry about their purpose.

He heard metallic clickings and he glimpsed the white-sleeved arms hovering around and over his prone body. They cut away his uniform, stripping it from his arms and legs. His underclothes were methodically snipped apart, his boots pulled off.

Salvo lay on his belly, naked, staring straight ahead. He saw only a small vid monitor module mounted on a wheeled tripod, cables snaking down from it to the floor. Seeing the vid screen made him think briefly about the Mesa Verde operation. Baron Cobalt had given him the task of providing clean genetic material to the Dulce installation. Salvo had assigned the gathering of the material to Milton Reeth, but when the slagger encountered problems supplying healthy bodies, he began substituting Dregs, diseased outcasts of the hellzones.

Salvo had led a Mag squad to Reeth's Mesa Verde slaghole, chilling him and everyone who had taken part in the smuggling operation. After that, Salvo had taken direct charge of supplying the bodies to Dulce, but he hadn't been able to accomplish very much due to Kane's treachery.

Aloofly he wondered if Baron Cobalt intended to practice the let-the-punishment-fit-the-crime philosophy by dissecting him and transporting his blood, soft organs and bone marrow to the installation in New Mexico.

Of course, he reminded himself, such action presupposed the destruction Kane, Grant and the Baptiste whore inflicted on the facility had been repaired. From what he had been told, the incubation chamber had been all but obliterated and the cryogenic storage area severely damaged.

Above him, from the center of the ceiling by the sound of it, came a hissing squeak. A sling-and-strap contrivance descended into his restricted field of vision. Hands fitted themselves under his arms and hips, rolling him over, heaving him up into a sitting posture. He saw the figures with the white gloves, but he might as well not have for all he could glean of their identities.

Three slender shapes he hoped were men stood around him. Since their features were completely concealed by white linen skullcaps, surgical masks and round-lensed goggles, he based his assessment of their sex due to the flat fall of the gowns covering their bodies. His mind classified them as attendants, and he felt a distant relief they weren't women.

Many years ago, shortly after receiving his duty badge at age sixteen, his first assignment had been to the Intel section. His superior officer, an affected, pompous martinet named Landenberg, personally supervised the questioning of attractive female suspects.

It was easy for Salvo to ingratiate himself with Landenberg, whose primary personality trait was an overweening, even monstrous vanity. Landenberg arranged circumstances so his flattery-prone protégé could lose his virginity in the line of duty.

Salvo recalled every detail of that two minutes, although it was nearly twenty years in the past. He remembered the woman, spread-eagled naked and manacled across the blood-stained bench, and how she had thanked him when he removed the electrode from between her legs. Then she spit at him when he unzipped the fly of his uniform.

When Landenberg received a mandatory administrative transfer, Salvo took over his duties. He found a certain luxury in them, until a night one of the prisoners managed to free herself long enough to sink her teeth into his penis, which, tragically, was exposed at the moment.

After his recovery from what passed as reconstructive surgery, he asked for and received a transfer from the Intel section. The vivid recollection of that instant of shock, agony and blood had prevented him from indulging in a similar luxury with Brigid Baptiste while she was in custody.

The white-gowned attendants lifted Salvo's 210 pounds seemingly without strain and placed him in the sling, strapping him securely, fastening clamps to his wrists and ankles. His buttocks and the underpart of his body sagged through the straps toward the floor.

One of the masked figures held up a small hypodermic syringe. Salvo watched disinterestedly as the point of the needle plunged into his right arm, piercing the collateral radial artery inside the elbow joint. When the needle was withdrawn, a tiny pinpoint of blood oozed out. A gloved hand swabbed it away with a tuft of cotton pinched between thumb and forefinger.

The three attendants stepped to the sockets on the walls, then posed motionless, their glassy, goggled eyes fixed on Salvo as if they were waiting for a signal.

A moment later, the trio moved simultaneously, adjusting the ring collars of the sockets and drawing out segmented conduits made of flexible, silvery metal. They reminded Salvo of tentacles. The attendants attached a pair of the conduits to the clamps around his wrists, and another pair was affixed to his ankles.

An attendant pulled a fifth tentacle toward Salvo's

face. He eyed its blunt tip incuriously. The masked figure twisted a metal cuff at its end, and an aperture opened. A cluster of small, jointed, spidery legs sprang out, like the petals of a particularly ugly flower. The legs spread to encompass the width of his face. Tiny extruder hooks dug into the flesh of his cheeks and temples, catching and holding tightly.

With a peculiar hiss, the conduits attached to his wrists and ankles began to retract into their sockets. Salvo felt the strain in his muscles and he wondered what purpose disjointing him could possibly serve. He couldn't feel pain, anyway.

The movement stopped, and he hung awkwardly in the sling, limbs spread-eagled. He peered out between the chromed spider legs. Nothing happened for what seemed like a long time. Then he became aware of pain.

The induced lethargy and paralysis slowly seeped away from his body and mind. Whatever he had been injected with, it counteracted the effects of the tranquilizing compound.

Although he had been unable to emotionally react to it at the time, his brain had recorded every minutia of his experiences. Now it all crested to the surface of his mind and dragged a cry of terror from his lips. Salvo struggled against the tentacles, twisting his head frantically to dislodge the cluster of legs hooked into his face. He accomplished nothing but a fireburst of pain.

From the center of the conduit's aperture extended a straight, tiny filament, like a thread made of steel. He tried to watch its approach, but his eyes crossed and his vision blurred. When he felt the light touch at the bridge of his nose, he cried out violently.

Baron Cobalt's voice wafted to him, electronically filtered so well that it sounded as if he were standing right beside him. His musical voice said, "Salvo, you have no conception of the depth of my sorrow that you are here. The grief is almost more than I can bear."

Desperately Salvo blurted, "Lord Baron, you must allow me the opportunity to speak."

"Certainly I will. That is why you are here. You must speak and you must speak the truth. However, I hope you sympathize with my difficulty in separating the truth from untruths. I propose to end that confusion quite decisively. Do you know where you are?"

The sudden question took Salvo by surprise. He couldn't shake his head or trust himself to speak, so he closed his eyes.

"Despite what you may think," Baron Cobalt said, "this is not a torture chamber like the crude little dungeons you maintain on E Level. No, this is my own private surgery. Would it surprise you to learn that even the barons fall prey to illnesses, to injuries, to weaknesses of mortal flesh?"

Salvo kept his eyes closed, wishing he could shut out the baron's voice, as well.

"Yes, though I am representative of the new human, improved and modified, I am frail, I am vulnerable. Obviously it would not do for the commonweal to know the barons are as mortal as they are. If the apelings who grub in the Pits or slouch through the Outlands should learn the barons can sicken and die just like them, keeping humanity in heavy harness would be very difficult. Do you not agree?''

Salvo did not respond.

''Thusly,'' continued the baron, ''we have private and very secret medical facilities at our disposal. To date, I have never had to make use of them except when Kane—''

Baron Cobalt's words broke off. Salvo heard a ragged intake of breath. After a long minute of dreadful silence, the voice spoke again, silky soft. ''I really don't know all the capabilities of this facility, though I admit to a certain fascination with them. Let us both collaborate to divine their mysteries.''

Salvo's eyes snapped open. He felt a cold metal pressure probing between his protruding buttocks. He tried to thrash, then shouted, ''Stop! I'll tell you anything!''

The baron's laughter fluted through the chamber, the memory of his beauty making his laughter more than cruel. ''I know that, Salvo. But do not expect me to ask you questions. Whatever I want to know, you will volunteer. Perhaps not gladly, but at least there will be little confusion in separating the falsehoods from the facts.''

The tiny filament poised at the bridge of his nose suddenly plunged through the lump of flesh between his eyes. He felt it spinning, drilling, boring through the epidermal layers then into the ethmoid bone. He jerked spasmodically, his face contorting in a silent scream.

''Of course, the process of clearing away confusion is accomplished slowly,'' Baron Cobalt said. ''It takes time. Therefore, I will leave you in the gifted hands of my surgeons. When the process is completed, they will alert me. You will be a cooperative patient, won't you?''

Salvo did his best to scream, but nothing came out except a sob of despair and horror.

Chapter 14

Kane blinked and the world swam mistily back into reality. He swayed on unsteady legs, a bit surprised to see he had ended the mat-trans jump in the same standing posture in which he had begun it.

Usually, no matter how jumpers arranged themselves before a transit, they arrived at their destinations flat on their backs. This time Kane remained upright, but he faced away from the door, staring at the pewter-colored armaglass back wall. He felt remarkably clear-headed, for which he breathed a sigh of relief. Sometimes even the cleanest of jumps had debilitating effects.

Grant, DeFore and Domi stirred on the hexagonal floor plates, their prone bodies surrounded by fading wisps of vapor. Kane had once overhead a discussion between Lakesh and Bry about the source and substance of the mat-trans mist. Lakesh had gone into an abstruse dissertation about plasma wave forms that only resembled vapor.

With a startled intake of breath, DeFore pushed herself up into a sitting position, staring around fearfully. She patted her arms and legs and murmured, "Thank God."

Domi uncoiled from the floor with an effortless, fluid grace, ruby eyes sharp and clear. She nodded curtly to Kane, an acknowledgment she felt fine.

Grant lifted his head, glanced around, then climbed to his feet. "Not bad," he commented. "How do you feel, DeFore?"

She smiled wanly, taking his outstretched hand. "A slight headache, a touch of vertigo. Nothing like genuine jump sickness, I imagine."

"That's for damn sure," he declared vehemently.

Kane repressed a smile. Grant always held up their jump to Russia as the standard for bad transits. The Cerberus gateway link had been unable to establish a link with the Russian unit's autosequence initiators. The matter-stream carrier-wave modulations couldn't be synchronized, which resulted in a severe bout of jump sickness—vomiting, excruciating head pain, weakness and hallucinations.

"What about you, Kane?" asked DeFore. "Stimulants and pain relievers still holding up?"

Kane only nodded, turning toward the door. He levered the door open, shouldered it aside a few inches and took a swift, appraising look around. The anteroom was small, just large enough for a round marble table and two chairs. A green-tinted light strip ran the length of the ceiling to the door. He saw no vid spy-eyes on the ceiling.

Hand on the Copperhead, he stepped out, feeling the pointman's tension build in him like subtle electricity. Bent in a half crouch, he walked cautiously, heel-to-toe, to the doorway. Grant followed him. DeFore and Domi remained behind in the chamber.

Listening, not thinking, Kane thumbed the solenoid stud on the door frame, unlocking the panel. He pushed it once, a short jab that noiselessly slid the door open just enough to see what lay beyond it. As he expected, he saw a small control room, less than half the size of the one at Cerberus. Consoles and light panels chattered and flickered. On the far side of them was another door.

Kane opened the portal all the way and moved among the banks of electronic equipment. He repeated the careful process with the second door, seeing only a span of empty corridor curving away to the left. Turning, he gestured to Grant, who gestured to Domi and DeFore still waiting watchfully in the jump chamber.

They came out and all of them joined Kane.

Grant whispered, "Where are we?"

"I haven't the faintest idea," replied Kane. "The corridor dead-ends here, so we've only got one direction to choose. If the place is spy-wired, we'll just have to act like we know where we're going. Standard deployment."

Grant said, "Big neg on that. I'll take point."

Kane started to object, then shrugged. In a hard-contact penetration, he always assumed the point position. His senses were uncannily acute when something nasty lurked around a corner, but in these circumstances, his lack of a badge could alert even the most dim-witted Baronial Guardsmen.

As it was, Mags in full armor were not exactly common sights in the Administrative Monolith, certainly not on A Level. The standard Magistrate duty uniform consisted of a gray bodysuit and a long, black, Kevlar-weave overcoat.

However, an armored Magistrate was a fearsome figure, exploiting the instinctive human terror of the unknown. The armor's psychological effect might buy them precious time.

Kane handed the motion detector to Grant, who slipped it over his left wrist, where it wouldn't interfere with the operation of the Sin Eater's spring-powered holster.

Domi and DeFore fell in behind Grant. Kane brought up the rear. Grant opened the door all the way and walked out into the corridor, sweeping the motion detector to the left and right.

"Clean," he announced.

The four of them quietly negotiated the corridor, following the curving wall. The floor was of a shiny green material, cut in square tiles. They searched for but saw no spy-eye lenses anywhere.

They reached an open archway, and after consulting the motion detector, Grant led them beneath it. The four people traversed a long series of arches. Nowhere did they see any windows or doors. Each arch merely opened up into another stretch of silent hallway.

"Why don't we come to a room?" grumbled Grant.

Kane didn't answer. His sole visit to A Level was nearly a half year in the past. During the trip, he had been forced to wear opaque goggles. After his induction into the Trust, he was so emotionally numbed and physically enervated, he had paid scant attention to the return route. He retained vague recollections of archways and feebly lit chambers on the way to the hidden elevator but very little beyond that.

The motion detector suddenly emitted a discordant beep, so sudden and startling, they all stumbled to a halt. Swiftly Grant raised it to eye level, noting the two red dots pulsing at the far edge of the LCD.

"Two contacts," he announced. "Ten yards, approaching our position." He ground his teeth, muttering angrily, "No place for us to hide."

"We'll brazen it out," replied Kane.

Grant snorted. "That's your solution for everything."

They began walking again, a stiffness born of fear apparent in DeFore's back and shoulders. Within seconds, the measured tread of marching boots reached them. In the passage between two archways appeared a pair of men in white uniform jackets, red trousers and polished black knee boots. Kane's lips twisted in a smirk.

Magistrates held Baronial Guardsmen in contempt, and they certainly had no patience with their studied arrogance. Guardsmen's duties consisted of strutting around A Level, opening doors and sneering at the infrequent visitor seeking an audience with Baron Cobalt. No one knew the number of guardsmen or how one was selected. Certainly they didn't come from the ranks of the Magistrate Division.

The two guardsmen were identically trim and blue-eyed, though one had blond hair and the other black. They made up for the color difference by styling their hair the same way. Both of their faces were clear of complexion, subtly sculpted to be the epitome of male beauty.

When they caught sight of Grant, their blue eyes widened and then slitted. The distance between them and the Cerberus party narrowed. Kane hoped they could pass each other without question.

The blond guardsman raised an imperious hand, palm outward. "Halt. What business do you Magistrates have here at such an hour?"

Not slowing his pace, Grant responded in the same haughty tone, "It is Magistrate business, none of yours."

The dark-haired guardsman stretched his right arm straight out, the fingers on a direct line with Grant's duty badge. "If your business is in regard to your commanding officer, then you will share his fate once the baron hears of this intrusion."

It took an instant for the meaning of the remark to penetrate. Grant came to a sudden halt, so suddenly that Domi nearly trod on his heels. The guardsman kept his arm extended, his middle finger only two inches from Grant's polycarbonate-sheathed chest.

"Commanding officer," repeated Grant. "Salvo?"

The blond guardsman's lips twisted in a sneer. "Who else? Do you entertain the absurd notion of intervening on his behalf with the lord baron?"

Kane could not contain himself. "Salvo is here? Explain."

The dark-haired man's eyes flicked away from Grant, toward Kane. They passed over Domi and DeFore. He demanded, "Why are Magistrates escorting a medic and custodian? *You* explain."

"Very well," Grant said mildly, taking a relaxed half step forward.

His right fist hammered upward, catching the black-haired guardsman under the jaw, twisting his head back brutally on his neck. Grant spun toward the second man, positive the first guardsman would hit the floor unconscious, perhaps even dead. Grant wasn't as fast as Kane, but he was a good deal stronger, and when he struck, he usually struck only once.

His left leg arced toward the blond guardsman's crotch. He caught only the briefest of glimpse of the dark-haired man stumbling back a pace, not falling or even appearing to be surprised.

The sight shocked Grant, skewed his timing and balance. His boot missed the guardsman's testicles, impacting on the pelvic bone instead. Then a fist seemed to come from nowhere. The right side of his lantern jaw took a punch so fast and so hard, amoebae-shaped floaters swam across his eyes and the not-quite-snug helmet wobbled on his head.

Kane could scarcely believe it when Grant staggered sideways, smashed to the floor by the guardsman's lightning-quick left cross. He snarled wordlessly, shoving DeFore aside with one hand, snatching the Copperhead from his belt with the other. He squeezed the trigger, firing a 3-round burst a finger's width over the top of Domi's head. The silenced shots sounded like an old emphysemic man spitting out mucus.

The guardsmen moved swiftly, bounding away from one another. Two of the three rounds missed. One caught the black-haired man on the right side of his head. Hanks of hair, a flap of scalp and piece of ear exploded outward in a clot of blood.

The guardsman stumbled, arms windmilling, his boot soles squeaking on the floor, seeking purchase. When the man regained his balance, he rushed toward Kane.

He had little time to think and even less to act.

Kane hurled himself to one side, away from Domi and DeFore, noting that the blond man was launching a kick at the fallen Grant.

Kane squeezed off another triburst at the wounded guardsman. He weaved and dodged without breaking stride. A bullet ripped a chunk of flesh from the web of the man's left hand, between thumb and forefinger. The other two gouged furrows in the wall.

The Baronial Guardsman cannonaded into Kane with the full force of his weight, sweeping him up and off his feet, all but knocking the wind out of him. If not for the kinetic-energy-absorption properties of the armor, Kane realized his ribs and clavicle would have shattered.

The Copperhead clattered from his hand when he hit the floor, but he reached for and snatched a fistful of uniform-jacket sleeve. He tried to drag the man down with him.

He instantly realized he had made a mistake. The guardsman obligingly allowed himself to be dragged, crashing his body weight against Kane, its full force concentrated in the knee pounding at the center of his abdomen. With a quiver of shock, Kane felt the poly-carbonate bend inward at the moment and point of impact.

His thoughts wheeled like a flock of panicked birds. The guardsman weighed far more than he guessed, probably tipping the scales at close to three hundred pounds of solid muscle. He was incredibly strong, preternaturally swift and agile. With a quiver of loathing, Kane realized the Baronial Guardsman were not selected—they were *made*.

Kane's left hand groped upward, clawing at the

loose flap of flesh hanging from the blood-spattered side of the man's head. He ripped it and the mangled ear away. Blood flowed, but sluggishly, thin and pale. The guardsman did not show pain. Very white and even teeth flashed in a cold, mocking grin. He jammed his thumbs beneath the under-jaw locking guard of Kane's helmet and heaved. Strained metal creaked.

As the blond guardsman's boot snapped toward his face, Grant's hands came together, catching the ankle and twisting savagely. The guardsman spun in the direction of the twist, leaping from the floor in a graceful pirouette. As he revolved in midair, his free foot slashed sideways across Grant's visor. It blunted the impact, but the helmet slid askew.

Grant released the ankle, one hand realigning the helmet, the other whipping up his Copperhead. He fired immediately before establishing solid target acquisition. A trio of dark holes appeared in the white uniform jacket, sewing red-rimmed coins from navel to sternum.

The blond man staggered and Grant shot him again, through the throat. Gobbets of muscle and tissue tore away. A few globs of blood spewed from his lips, but he didn't fall. With a liquid snarl of rage, the man hurled himself at Grant, fists knotted.

The corridor suddenly shivered with a thunderclap. The guardsman's left cheek erupted in scarlet, gelatinous spray, his perfectly shaped nose vanishing in a bloody smear.

The Baronial Guardsman's blue eyes registered outraged astonishment. He fell backward, vomiting blood, fingers snatching futilely at the air, as if to grab handfuls of life.

Domi pivoted, framing the back of the black-haired guardsman's head in the Combat Master's sights. He was too busy trying to tear off Kane's helmet or head to react to the sound of the shot.

As Domi's finger tightened on the trigger, Kane's Sin Eater slapped into his hand, the blaster discharging at the same instant. The 248-grain bullet punched a ragged path through the cleft in the man's chin, shattering his excellent teeth. A torrent of blood and bone splinters cascaded through his mouth and nostrils.

The Combat Master bucked in Domi's double-fisted grip. The .45-caliber round crashed into the occipital area of the guardsman's head, ripping an untidy groove in his carefully groomed hair. The impact of the slug drove him forward, and the broad cranial bone at his hairline split open. He hit the floor tiles on his face. For a couple of seconds, his feet twitched like landed fish.

Kane and Grant scrambled erect at the same time, both breathing hard, staring at each other in shock. Rubbing his jaw, Grant panted, "Brazen it out, my ass."

Domi swung her blaster to cover first one corpse, then the other, her face as expressionless as a porcelain mask. She whispered, "Bad men. Very bad men."

Kane saw no reason to respond. Automatically he checked his wrist chron. Less than thirty seconds had elapsed since they first exchanged words with the guardsmen. The time compression of combat was always disconcerting.

DeFore rose on trembling knees, facing Kane. "You called them 'show soldiers'?"

He sighed. "Well, they *did* put on a show, didn't they?"

"The bastards nearly chilled us," growled Grant. "That's not my idea of entertainment."

Turning to Domi, he said, "I should ream you out for pulling and shooting an unsilenced blaster without an express order."

Her chalk white lips quirked in a smile. "Didn't figure you'd mind."

"You figured right. Thanks."

As Kane bent to pick up his Copperhead, he saw a small shard of scarlet-tinted skull near the guardsman's head. He picked it up, shook off a gummy strand of brain matter, inspected it and tossed it to DeFore. "What's that look like to you?"

She examined the thick, gray white chunk of material, turning it over in her hands. Her eyes narrowed. Stooping cautiously over the blond-haired corpse, she opened his uniform jacket, peered at the penetration wounds made by Grant's subgun, then gingerly probed his chest and rib cage.

In a tone that sounded enthralled and revolted at the same time, DeFore said, "So much for natural selection."

"What?" asked Grant in irritation.

"The bones of your show soldiers are bonded with some kind of ceramic, doubling their density and strength. The muscle attachments are correspondingly thick and strong. The epidermis and body wall is very tough, especially where the inner organs have to be protected. See, there's no transient cavitation around the bullet perforations."

She straightened up. "They're like the *Übermensch,* the superman the Nazis dreamed of creating over two centuries ago."

Kane holstered the Sin Eater. "Supermen serving as bodyguards." He snorted derisively. "Didn't set their sights very high, did they?"

DeFore shrugged. "I doubt they had much of a choice. Their IQ's are probably somewhere below their shoe sizes. They were bred to be human gorillas, not physicists."

Grant checked the motion detector, sweeping it in the direction the Baronial Guardsmen had come from. "No contacts. Think anybody heard the shots?"

Kane shook his head. "Let's be optimistic and say no." He nudged the black-haired corpse with the toe of a boot. "Do you have a read on what they said about Salvo?"

With a grim satisfaction, Grant replied, "I hope it means the son of a bitch is drowning in the baron's shit."

"But why? He told me Baron Cobalt put him in charge of the Grudge Task Force. That shows he has confidence in him."

"Maybe the baron isn't happy with his performance. You and Brigid got away from him, remember."

"That was weeks ago," Kane argued. "If that's the reason, he would have double-dipped Salvo long before now. Something is definitely going on."

DeFore broke in impatiently. "Whatever is going on, it has nothing to do with our mission."

"You seem very sure of that," retorted Kane darkly. "I wish I could be."

Chapter 15

Nothing could be done to hide the corpses of the guardsmen, so they let them lie where they died. They walked in the direction from which the two men had come, Grant resuming pointman position.

Out of habit, Kane kept checking their backtrack. He wouldn't have been overly surprised to see one or both of the Baronial Guardsmen stirring, rising to their feet. Their very existence shook his confidence in himself, and he wondered why such superior specimens of humanity were created solely to safeguard the baron. If only fifty of them were introduced into the ranks of the Magistrate Division, the need for high-powered blasters and armor would dwindle.

But as DeFore had said, their intellects were wanting. If the Baronial Guardsmen possessed intelligences to match their physiques, they could pose a very real threat to the security of the villes. Superior abilities always bred superior ambitions.

Bleakly he thought of the hybrids at Dulce and Strongbow's mutagenically altered Dragoons in Britain. Even without Archon involvement, the race to resculpt the image in which evolution had shaped man would still be under way. He recalled Baptiste's wry reference to a faux human. The guardsmen, the hybrids and the Dragoons weren't fake, but they certainly weren't human as Kane understand humanity.

Lakesh once commented that the first genetic engineers, back in the twentieth century, had met powerful and outspoken opposition, but the opposition didn't prevail. The temptation to play God was too seductive. As Lakesh had explained, if the Directorate's plans for humankind succeeded, in a hundred years, there would be many humankinds.

Kane knew there were no grounds for doubting it.

The arched hallway ended in a small modular chamber. At the center of it, a spiral staircase curled down into a round opening. Grant made a motion-detector sweep, gestured all was clear and mounted the staircase.

"Careful now," Kane whispered unnecessarily.

The four people crept down the stairs one by one, six feet apart, walking stealthily on the balls of their feet. Though the steps didn't creak beneath their weight, everyone's breathing sounded frighteningly loud to Kane. Every second, he expected to see the blaze of a blaster from the gloom below them.

To his surprised relief, the stairway's spiral ended in a low-ceilinged corridor. The four of them gathered at the bottom step. Grant looked up. The ceiling was only three feet above his head. Glancing toward Kane, he asked, "You remember coming down or going up stairs?"

He shook his head.

Grunting softly in irritation, Grant pointed the motion detector down the corridor, moving it back and forth. It emitted an electronic beep. On the LCD, a cluster of three dots pulsed at the upper edge of the display window.

"Three contacts," he said. "They're not moving fast or far."

Kane turned on the Copperhead's laser auto-targeter. To Domi, he said, "Leather that cannon. Let us handle this."

Disdainfully she retorted, "Like you did bad men?" But she holstered the Combat Master.

The four people crept down the corridor. As with the upper level, the walls were painted a pale metallic green. The light strips exuded a blue glow. No vid spy-eyes hung from the ceiling, but they passed beneath a round portal slightly recessed in a metal frame. It looked to be seven feet in diameter. Kane had no idea whatsoever of its purpose, but he felt distinctly uneasy walking underneath it.

The passageway doglegged to the right and ended at a set of swinging doors. Grant pointed to the motion detector, then to the doors. Kane nodded, understanding the three contacts were in the room beyond. Sidling up beside Grant, he took a position at the right-hand door. They swiftly hand signed to one another, agreeing to enter quietly, stealthily.

Then they heard the aspirated scream.

The sound raised the hairs on the backs of their necks, made their skins tingle with gooseflesh, sent a jolt of adrenaline speeding through their systems. The scream contained wailing notes of an animal in agony, of a soul stricken with such terror that a retreat into insanity was the only sane option. For an instant, the echoes of a woman's scream in Dealey Plaza bounded through Kane's memory.

He felt the blood pound in his temples. He slammed into the door with his shoulder, crashing it open on its hinges, lunging into a pyramid-shaped chamber. In a flash, his eyes registered fragmented images of three masked and gowned figures, of a cold white light reflecting from polished metal fixtures, of a naked, spread-eagled man writhing in a sling. A chrome-plated serpent arched in front of him, the metal spider legs sprouting from its head hugging his face. Another gleaming serpent lay coiled on the floor beneath the man's buttocks, part of it stretched up and out. Its head was not visible, and Kane didn't want to speculate on where it might be.

The three gowned and goggled figures reacted quickly to the sudden, noisy appearance of the black-armored intruder. They rushed to all points of the room, as if following a prearranged contingency plan.

Kane put the targeting pipper on the nearest masked figure, the red kill dot blooming on the white gown like a tiny pinhead of blood. A triburst stitched holes in the figure's upper chest, knocking it backward and down.

He shifted the barrel, retargeted and fired again, the pipper flicking across a white-clothed back. The burst twisted the figure's legs beneath the body in mid-stride, sending it flying against the wall.

The third masked figure reached for a red button set high on the far wall. The pipper from Grant's autotargeter touched the skull cap. He stroked the Copperhead's trigger, and the trio of 4.85 mm steel-jacketed rounds shattered the goggles, slapped the figure sideways. The gowned man-shape struck the wall, bounced off and fell heavily to the floor.

Kane stepped farther into the room, swinging the

silenced bore of his subgun from left to right. He saw
no other targets, so he focused his attention on the
man hanging helpless in the sling. His dark eyes
rolled wildly toward Kane, blinking back tears. In-
coherent sounds bubbled from his ashen lips. Kane
leaned forward and saw the tiny filament embedded
in the fleshy mound at the bridge of his nose.

Grasping the metal tentacle at the point where the
cluster of legs sprouted, he gave it an experimental
tug. Crimson points appeared in the sallow flesh
pierced by the small hooks.

"Be careful, for God's sake!" Salvo gasped.

Kane laughed, a dark, cold sound without humor.
"What for? You think I give a shit what happens to
you? I only wish I had time to stay and watch your
brains get cored out."

He glanced down at the tentacle attached to Salvo's
pale, flabby buttocks. "And your bowels, too."

"The baron!" The words rushed from Salvo's
mouth. "He could be watching!"

Both Kane and Grant swiveled their heads, looking
all over the room. A miniature spy-eye lens protruded
from the ceiling. Grant aimed and fired immediately,
the bullets wrecking the delicate lens and tiny mike.

As pieces of surveillance equipment clattered down
to the floor, Kane asked Salvo, "Baron Cobalt rigged
you like this?"

"Yes," Salvo panted.

"Why?"

"Get me loose and I'll tell you."

"You shit-faced son of a stickie whore," Kane
snarled, rapping on the chrome tentacle with the barrel of his Copperhead. The hose quivered with the

impact, and the tiny hooks tore scarlet-edged furrows in Salvo's face. He yelped in pain.

Grant heard the bloodthirsty hum vibrating in Kane's voice, but he wasn't about to intervene. Quietly he said, "We've no time for this. Remember the mission priorities."

Kane acted like he hadn't heard. He shook the tentacle. "Do you know where Lakesh is?"

A sound very much like a relieved, satisfied sigh came from Salvo's mouth. "So you *do* know him. I was right."

"I won't ask you again."

"Let me loose," Salvo asked, his voice cracked. "I'll take you to him."

"Fuck you," snapped Kane. "We'll find him ourselves. We know he's on E Level."

"No, no. It's worse than you think. He's hurt, he may die."

The sharp click of a round chambering into a blaster echoed in the room. Domi stepped aggressively toward Salvo, the Combat Master's bore centered on his naked chest. DeFore followed her.

"You tortured him," Domi grated. "We know. You chill my people in Cuprum. Lakesh dies, I bigtime, long-time chill you."

Salvo could not cringe away, but a new wave of fear rippled through the mud-colored pools of his eyes. They flicked frantically to Grant.

"You've always been a reasonable man," he blurted. "Steady and smart. If the baron doesn't know you're here yet, he will soon. If you turn me loose, I swear I'll help you get out of here and save Lakesh."

"Kane tells me there's a secret lift tube on A

Level," Grant said stonily. "Do you know where it is?"

Salvo tried to nod, then grimaced as the hooks ripped more skin. "I can't tell you, I'll have to show you. Get me loose. Please."

Kane beckoned to DeFore and pointed to the pair of metal tentacles affixed to Salvo's face and buttocks. "Do you know what this stuff is?"

She eyed the lower conduit and shook her head in puzzlement. "Unless Baron Cobalt is curious about the condition of Salvo's colon, I see no medical reason for it. My guess is that it's simply for humiliation purposes, maybe to cause pain."

Smiling thinly, Kane asked Salvo, "Does that sound reasonable? Are you humiliated yet?"

Salvo only moaned faintly.

DeFore examined the flexible metal tentacle attached to Salvo's face. "I think I know what this is. An advanced psychosurgery instrument designed to deliver a tiny electronic device into the brain."

"An implant?" questioned Kane. "Like the kind the Tushe Gun used to control his followers?"

She shook her head. "I don't think so, since the microneedle is aligned with the so-called silent area of the brain."

Busy with opening the clamp around Salvo's right wrist, Grant asked him, "Did the baron tell you what he was doing to you?"

"All he said was that he could learn all he needed to know from me without asking any questions."

Domi suddenly exclaimed, "Look!"

She pointed at the blurry images flickering over a small vid screen mounted on a wheeled tripod. Shifting bands of color shimmered across it. A distorted image formed and dissolved so quickly Kane caught only the briefest, almost subliminal glimpses of it. But he was sure he had seen himself, wearing his gray uniform beneath his long Mag coat, sitting cross-legged in a chair.

The patterns of light and color wavered again, then resolved into a ghostly vision of Baptiste, hair in disarray, looking up in fear, blood streaming from her nose. An instant later, the screen filled with Lakesh's face, contorted in a silent scream.

DeFore said excitedly, "That thing in Salvo's head is an organo-metallic synapse, making a link between the brain and a computer database. It's recording his memories!"

Salvo groaned.

Grant demanded, "How is that possible?"

Speaking quickly, DeFore answered, "Linking the human brain to a computer was a theoretical study in artificial intelligence back in the twentieth century...biotechnology melded with cybernetics. In principle, there's no reason why information stored in the brain can't be transmitted to a computer."

Grant freed Salvo's right hand from the clamp, and the man flailed at the metal claws covering his face. "Get it off!"

"Stop!" DeFore half shouted. "Though the brain feels no pain, violent removal of the link might cause permanent shock. You could die."

"In that case," said Kane, "let him do it."

Grant closed his big hand around Salvo's wrist and pried his fingers loose from the spidery legs. "Somebody better think of something fast—like Salvo said, the baron could find out we're here any second.''

Kane quickly studied the tentacle-and-claw device, then gripped the metal cuff around the aperture and gave it a clockwise twist. The hook-tipped spider legs spread open, and the filament withdrew from the bridge of Salvo's nose. A tiny pearl of blood oozed from the puncture. Salvo hissed in pain and then in relief. Scarlet strings crawled from the six lacerations on his face.

The aperture swallowed the spider legs, and the tentacle retracted into a wall socket. At the same moment, the conduit positioned at Salvo's rear withdrew. He squirmed in discomfort and demanded, ''Get my other hand loose.''

Grant smacked the side of his head with the back of his gauntlet. ''Say please.''

Salvo spoke in a contrite whisper. ''I'm sorry. Please, get me loose.''

Grant released his left hand from the clamp and helped him out of the sling. Salvo massaged his wrists, obviously embarrassed by his nudity and fighting hard to regain control of his emotions.

In a fair imitation of his old authoritarian manner, he said crisply. ''Someone will have to find me some clothes, stat. Mine are ruined.''

Kane struck him with an open hand across the face. Salvo spun almost completely around. If not for grasping the straps of the sling, he would have fallen.

Grabbing him in a painful grip at the back of his short neck, Kane forced his head in the direction of the nearest masked and gowned corpse. ''There you are,'' he growled. ''Just your size, too. Be quick about it.''

He pushed Salvo to his knees beside the stiff form. His fingers fumbled at the snap-buttons of the surgical gown, popping them open. As he tugged at it, he recoiled and cried out.

Kane stepped quickly over, on the verge of hitting Salvo again. Instead, he saw what had evoked the outburst. Instead of bullet-flayed and bloody flesh beneath the gown, chromed steel gleamed in the overhead lights. He muttered, ''What the hell—that's not a man, it's some kind of machine.''

DeFore came to his side, stared for a speechless second, then stooped to pluck away the mask, cap and goggles. The head was like a human skull molded of burnished chrome, with small red photoreceptors set in deep sockets. The mouth hung half-open, showing silvery teeth in a macabre grin. The tubular neck was articulated, like the segmented, tentaclelike conduits in the room. The chest looked disproportionately broad, and it sported three bullet punctures. By peering through them, Kane discerned a glitter of broken circuitry.

''A robot,'' DeFore declared. ''Known in cybernetic circles as a droid. Lakesh told me the military fooled around with robotic security forces to install in the Totality Concept redoubts. They ended experimentation in the late 1990s because they didn't have the ability to generalize.''

''That's bad for a droid?'' inquired Kane.

''Bad for people, more like it. The sec droids tended to chill any personnel who even slightly matched their programmed enemy profile. Lakesh said he saw a test where a droid blew away a Congressional aide because he wore a mustache similar to a known terrorist's.''

She tapped the chest, and it rang dully. ''Good thing you shot it here. That's where its comp controls are located. The head is probably superfluous, mainly for symmetry.''

Grant blew out a heavy, disgusted breath. ''Nice place, A Level. I wonder what else the baron has tucked away up here—a stickie masseuse?''

Domi's sudden shriek of pain galvanized them, spun them around in adrenaline-fueled whirls. She sprawled awkwardly forward, arms out-flung. She bumped into the tripodal vid monitor and sent it careening across the room. As she fell, all of them saw the four rents slashed in the back of her coverall.

Behind her stood a droid, its head canted at an unnatural angle, flopping limply on a bullet-smashed neck joint. Light glittered from the four razor-sharp blades projecting from the fingers of its right glove.

It moved swiftly toward Domi, humming oddly like an electric clockwork mechanism. The bladed hand swept up in a vicious arc.

Chapter 16

Kane and Grant triggered their Copperheads in unison, firing from the hip.

Six bullets punched and gouged holes through the droid's chest, into the real brain of the thing. The delicate complex of microprocessors, printed circuits and data chips exploded from within.

The droid froze, completely immobile, its arm raised to slash. The electric hum wound down into silence. A thread-thin spark jumped from a bullet hole.

DeFore quickly knelt beside Domi, pulling her to a sitting position. The girl winced, biting her lip, as the medic examined the oozing lacerations on her back. Crimson lines shone startlingly bright against the bone whiteness of her skin.

"Superficial," announced DeFore, opening her medical kit. "Only the top epidermal layer was penetrated. She'll heal without any perceptible scarring."

While Salvo completed stripping the droid attendant of its gown, DeFore sterilized Domi's cuts with antiseptic and sprayed them with a film of liquid bandage. She climbed stiffly to her feet, eyed the motionless droid with loathing and fetched it a kick. It toppled over, clattering loudly to the floor.

Kane turned to Salvo. "Show us the way out."

The man hesitated, averted his gaze and leaned

over to pick up his boots. "You never said how you got here. I guess there's a gateway unit I don't know about, right?"

Kane planted the sole of his boot on Salvo's up-thrust rear and shoved, pushing him to his hands and knees. "Show us the way out or you'll die with your boots off."

Salvo swung his head up, fear and anger shining in his eyes. He glanced toward Grant. "If you let him touch me again, you'll never reach Lakesh."

Grant presented the image of seriously pondering Salvo's ultimatum, then raised his Copperhead, centering the laser killdot in the middle of his broad forehead. Flatly he said, "Fine. I'll see to it he won't touch you again."

Salvo's mouth dropped open. Kane reached down and hauled him roughly to his feet by a fistful of gown. "The way out."

Nodding in resignation, Salvo stuffed his feet into his boots and shuffled toward the double doors. He led them down the corridor in the direction they had come. Kane was about to order him to halt when Salvo stopped beneath the disk-shaped portal on the ceiling. He pointed toward it.

"That's a lift tube. It brought me down here from the baron's reception area."

Grant eyed it skeptically. "There's got to be another way up."

"Probably is," Salvo agreed, gesturing vaguely down the corridor, "but we don't have the time to look for it. Just because you blasted the vid eye, doesn't mean the baron isn't aware of what we're doing and where we are."

The sickly blue light strip did unflattering things to Salvo's sallow complexion and dark eyes. He kept twisting his head to look in both directions, and a trembling seized him. He clenched his teeth to keep them from chattering.

The note of almost superstitious terror in his voice when he mentioned the baron indicated he was on the brink of hysteria. Kane gripped his right shoulder, digging his fingers painfully into a clump of ganglia. Salvo tensed under the touch, but Kane held him fast.

"Find the spine, Salvo," he grated. "Be more afraid of me than of Baron Cobalt."

Releasing him, Kane tilted his head back to study the ring collar around the portal. Moving a few inches to the center of it, he lifted his left hand and waved it back and forth. The iris opened with a pneumatic hiss.

"Figured there had to be a photoelectric sensor," he said, pleased his guess was correct.

Recessed slightly inside the mouth of the opening, they saw a flat disk with an arrangement of metal clamps protruding from it. To an unasked question, Salvo quickly explained how he had been paralyzed and secured to the elevator disk.

"The thing will turn over once it reaches another floor," he said. "At least two above us. That's the baron's audience area and the location of the lift."

After a hurried discussion, it was decided Grant would make the initial recce, staying in contact with Kane via the helmet comm-link. Forming a stirrup with his hands, Kane heaved Grant up high enough to grip the largest clamp. Almost immediately the disk rose upward, pulling Grant into a tube of darkness.

Kane stood beneath the open portal, watching, feeling the chill finger of tension stroke at the buttons of his spine. When a crescent of dim light appeared and expanded, he asked, "What's going on?"

Grant's voice whispered in his ear. "Like Salvo said, it's turning over."

Metallic clicks echoed down the shaft. For a moment, a circle of light bisected by a dark line glowed, then vanished. A moment later, Grant said, "Zone is clear. No motion contacts. There's a button on the floor here. It probably sends the lift back down."

The metal-on-metal noises sounded again, and again dim light showed in a circle at the top of the tube.

"It works," declared Grant. "All of you come up at the same time."

Although apprehension showed in DeFore's eyes, she allowed Kane to hoist her up to grab hold of the wrist shackles. Domi, the smallest of the group, lithely bounded up to grip the ankle clamps. Kane helped Salvo reached the flattened U of steel that had crossed his middle, then used his extended hand to pull himself up beside Salvo.

A jittery smile played over Salvo's lips. "Kind of like the old days, isn't it?"

"Not the old days I remember," Kane retorted coldly.

Salvo looked away.

The disk ascended into the shaft. The time it took to traverse the shaft was very brief. Kane's arms and hands weren't even feeling the strain of supporting his weight when the platform began its rollover. Grant helped DeFore into the small domed chamber. Domi sprang to her feet with a flourish, as if she was showing off for Grant's benefit.

The five people moved into the tunnel-like passage, Grant keeping one eye on the motion detector. When they emerged into a feebly lit, arched room, Kane restrained a shudder of repellent recognition. To Salvo, he said, "Take us to the elevator."

Salvo looked around indecisively, saying nothing.

Grant turned on him. Through gritted teeth, he said, "The only reason you're alive is because you said you knew the way. Show us now and live, or don't and die. There's no middle ground."

Salvo shuffled forward, Grant walking beside him. Like the gateway-unit floor, they passed under numerous archways, though these were broader, taller, more ornate in construction and design. The lighting was barely above a gray gloom.

As they moved along, Kane's flesh crawled under his armor. He understood Salvo's awed dread of Baron Cobalt even if he had little patience for it. A lifetime of conditioning made all the ville bred vulnerable to the baron's theatrical trappings. They stimulated and exploited all the primitive, archetypal fears locked within the human psyche. Even the memory of his hand locked in a stranglehold around Baron Cobalt's throat did little to pump up Kane's own courage.

Salvo suddenly came to a halt, venting a heavy sigh of relief. Across a broad hall, through an archway, loomed huge gold-and-ivory-chased double doors.

Kane recognized them and echoed Salvo's sigh with one of his own.

"Aren't there always a pair of guardsmen posted on the other side?" he asked Salvo.

"When I came here a while ago, only one was on duty."

Grant consulted the motion sensor. "If he's there, he's not moving."

They crossed the hall and gathered at the doors. Kane listened intently, shook his head to indicate he heard nothing, then exchanged quick hand signals with Grant.

Gesturing to the others to back away and spread out, Grant faced the right-hand door. Kane half crouched behind him, Copperhead at his shoulder.

Grant knocked sharply on the door. A moment later, a latch clicked, the handle turned and the door opened. Brilliant light spilled from the chandelier-illuminated foyer beyond, silhouetting the burly Baronial Guardsman as he peered into the gloom. The expression on his face was one of almost comical wonder. His expression didn't alter even when the red laser light flashed onto his forehead. Kane's Copperhead spit once, and the dot on the man's forehead widened and changed color.

Grant grabbed him by his jacket, yanking him forward. He noted fleetingly that the back of his skull bulged unnaturally. The subgun's round had penetrated the thick cranial bone, but had lost its velocity in the process, pushing the man's brains ahead of it in a thick wad. Still, he was no less dead. After dragging him to the far side of the doors, Grant deposited him in a patch of shadow.

In an urgent whisper, Salvo said, "The lift is out the doors to our left and up a ramp. I'm not sure if it'll take us directly to E Level, but there's no reason why it shouldn't. Trouble is, it can only hold two of us at a time."

"Who's with Lakesh right now?" demanded Kane.

"Pollard."

"Figures."

"He's waiting for me in Lakesh's cell."

"Which cell is that?"

"Third from the last on the left. Pollard expects me to bring a medic."

"That's good," DeFore said.

"We'll have to stop on Level C so I can get another uniform," continued Salvo. "I can't go into the cell blocks dressed like this."

"You're damn right you can't," Kane said, "and you won't. Grant, DeFore, you two will go. We'll wait for you here."

Salvo's eyes went wild with fear. "No! You're not keeping me here. The baron—"

"You're staying with us. If the Mags get wind of us, you'll make a nice hostage."

"But Pollard is expecting—"

"A medic," Kane interrupted again. "Escorted by a Mag, not necessarily by you."

"He'll recognize Grant," objected Salvo desperately.

Running a finger over his mustache, Grant said, "Not right away. For his sake, you'd better hope his memory is as bad as his breath."

He turned to Kane. "How long will you wait for us to come back?"

Before he could answer, Domi declared sharply, "Until you come back. Long as it takes."

"Look," said Salvo reasonably, "why don't we three use the gateway and go back to wherever it is you came from. We'll wait for them there."

Almost negligently, as if he were working the stiffness out of a shoulder muscle, Kane raised his right arm, then drove the elbow into the side of Salvo's jaw. He staggered backward, but Kane paid him no attention.

"Like Domi said, as long as it takes. If the baron finds us, I'll do my damnedest to finish what I started in Dulce."

Grant nodded brusquely and handed his Copperhead to Domi. "This is an assault weapon, so there'd be no reason for a Mag to carry it in the monolith."

He tapped the side of his helmet. "To be on the safe side, let's observe comm-link silence. Too much of a chance our frequencies could be monitored. When we're on our way back, I'll give you our one-word signal."

He turned, checked the motion detector, then pushed open the doors just wide enough to admit him and DeFore. As he slipped through, he faced Kane and extended the index finger of his right hand and brought it smartly to his nose. Smiling, Kane returned the one-percent salute, a gesture reserved for those missions with grave risks and a small chance of success.

Domi closed the doors after them, plunging their surroundings back into semidarkness. They moved back to the archway across the hall. Salvo walked slowly, reluctantly. Kane knew why. Without Grant to act as something of a moderating influence, he feared to be alone with him and the fierce, ruby-eyed ghost girl.

They took up position inside the arch. Kane slid up his helmet's visor and put on the dark-vision glasses. The treated lenses weren't as effective as a functioning light enhancer, but they were better than relying solely on his eyes to penetrate the gloom. Fortunately Domi's natural night vision was so acute as to be uncanny.

Kane stepped in close to Salvo. "Now, you and I are going to pass the time with a talk. And like Baron Cobalt, I want only the truth. Unlike him, though, I won't implant a microneedle in your brain to get it—I'll implant a bullet."

Salvo tried to step back, but Domi prodded his kidneys with the muzzle of the Copperhead. "What do you want to know?"

"We'll start with why and how you fell out of the baron's favor. Talk."

Salvo wetted his lips, glanced at the red-eyed wraith glaring at him over the barrel of the subgun and talked.

Chapter 17

Grant hadn't been to E Level in well over twenty years. He had served on a termination squad, and the memories of that day were still vivid. He did not relish them.

A minor uprising had erupted in the Pits due to a water shortage. Thirty people were picked at random, classified as ringleaders, convicted and executed. As the Chosen Man, Grant had fired the killing head shots to all thirty of them over the course of an afternoon.

The so-called ringleaders had been an eclectic mixture of ages, colors, genders, weights and sizes. By the time the last one had been shackled to the termination wall, Grant's emotions were numbed, shocked into a coma by the near constant thunder of blasterfire and the stench of cordite and blood.

It wasn't until the next day when he remembered his thirtieth and last bullet had been fired into the head of a malnourished fourteen-year-old boy.

Through some stroke of good fortune or a glitch in orders or misfiled paperwork, he never served in a termination squad again.

He recalled that as the small elevator descended swiftly. It was so cramped he and DeFore were jammed against each other face-to-face. Though she didn't speak, he fancied he could feel her heart pounding even through his armor. He tried to think of something reassuring to say, but no words came to mind. To even suggest to her that a risk-fraught undertaking like this would turn out fine would be an outright lie.

Grant bit back a sigh. Being back in Cobaltville, in the Administrative Monolith, evoked such a maelstrom of conflicting emotions he couldn't express a single one. Fear, anger, humiliation, homesickness—all of them warred within him.

The disk eased to a hissing halt. As it did, he heard the heavy throb of machinery and smelled the astringent odor of superheated metal. The door panel swung outward, the mechanical cacophony doubling in volume, heat pressing into them like a physical assault, the smells cloying and throat-closing.

The small elevator shaft opened into the main manufacturing facility of Cobaltville. As Grant cautiously stepped out, he saw the door panel was concealed by a false wall hidden by spools of heavy-gauge cable and other stacked odds and ends. He looked around, found a small bucket and used it to prop the door partially open.

Quickly he and DeFore skirted the edge of a vista of great machines, toward the wide entranceway. Mechs and techs, wearing protective goggles and headgear, operated conveyor belts, drill presses, forges, smelters, crucibles. Every piece of machinery seemed to rattle, clank and roar, as well as spitting sparks and jets of steam.

Although they were well away from the main mechanical array, they felt their bones shivering in rhythm with the crashing machinery. The close air was overlaid with the thick odors of grease and metal turning molten.

Following the wall, Grant and DeFore made it through the square entrance and into a wide corridor. Both of them felt better as the noise and heat fell away behind them.

Grant side-mouthed to her, "If you're questioned by a Mag, say Salvo sent you."

DeFore nodded, dabbing at the film of perspiration on her upper lip, composing her face into a detached mask of professionalism.

They turned at an L junction and strode on. A gray-uniformed Magistrate approached them, frowning over a sheaf of papers attached to a clipboard. Grant sensed DeFore tensing up.

"Steady," he whispered. "Eyes front."

She did as he said, and the Magistrate glanced at them disinterestedly and passed by without a word.

As they walked past the termination room, Grant noticed patches of fresh blood shining dully on the bullet-pocked wall, but he didn't point them out to DeFore.

The corridor angled to the right and narrowed, lined on both sides by narrow metal doors. Moans, hideously shrill squealings and hysterical gibbering filtered through them. The stern tones of Mags, demanding answers to questions, undercut the din of human suffering. The effluvia of unwashed bodies, of excrement, urine and blood, was so noxious DeFore couldn't help gagging.

"Oh, my God, Grant," she whispered. "I can't do this—"

"Steady," he said sharply. "We're almost there."

The cells were unnumbered, so Grant counted them as they walked. When they reached the door described by Salvo, he listened for a moment, heard nothing on the other side, then pounded on the metal paneling.

Pollard's suspicious voice demanded, "Who?"

Grant nudged DeFore. She announced, "Medical services, dispatched by Salvo."

The knob rattled, and Pollard pulled the door open. He grumbled, "I expected Cahill."

DeFore stepped in quickly. Grant followed, ducking his head beneath the low frame. He had to give DeFore credit. She looked at the wasted body on the bench that bore only a vague resemblance to Lakesh, but didn't react emotionally.

Moving to his side, she opened the medical kit. Grant shifted his gaze to the electricity generator at the foot of the bench. As he figured, they'd been dosing Lakesh with "Old Sparky," as the portable generators were called. He tried to keep his face averted from Pollard without being too obvious about it. Pollard's blunt features compressed in a scowl, due either to exasperation or suspicion.

"Took your fucking time about getting down here," he said in the booming, aggressive voice Grant knew so well and despised. "Where's Salvo?"

"Business with the baron," DeFore answered distractedly.

Pollard's low brow acquired new creases. He looked toward Grant, and his eyes narrowed. "Seems like I ought to know you. Do I?"

Grant shrugged. "Do you?"

Despite his nonchalant tone, he carefully watched

NO RISK, NO OBLIGATION TO BUY...NOW OR EVER!

GUARANTEED

PLAY "ROLL A DOUBLE" AND YOU GET FREE GIFTS! HERE'S HOW TO PLAY:

1. Peel off label from front cover. Place it in space provided at right. With a coin, carefully scratch off the silver dice. Then check the claim chart to see what we have for you – FOUR FREE BOOKS and a mystery gift – ALL YOURS! ALL FREE!

2. Send back this card and you'll receive hot-off-the-press Gold Eagle books, never before published. These books have a total cover price of $18.50, but they are yours to keep absolutely free.

3. There's no catch. You're under no obligation to buy anything. We charge nothing – ZERO – for your first shipment. And you don't have to make any minimum number of purchases – not even one!

4. The fact is thousands of readers enjoy receiving books by mail from the Gold Eagle Reader Service™. They like the convenience of home delivery; they like getting the best new novels BEFORE they're available in stores...and they think our discount prices are dynamite!

5. We hope that after receiving your free books you'll want to remain a subscriber. But the choice is yours – to continue or cancel, any time at all! So why not take us up on our invitation, with no risk of any kind? You'll be glad you did!

the play of thoughts and emotions on Pollard's face as the man tried to place his bearing, voice and jaw-line.

Grant saw the microsecond when Pollard found the match. His burly body stiffened, his small eyes widened, his nostrils flared.

Grant brought up his right leg, fast and straight, the boot slamming into Pollard's groin. The man grunted, folding in the direction of the sudden, sickening pain. Grant rammed his head forward, hearing teeth and cartilage break against the forepart of his helmet.

Before Pollard began to fall, Grant dropped his right fist, weighted by the holstered Sin Eater, like a pile driver on the back of his exposed neck. Pollard went down, striking the corner of the bench with his head, lacerating his eyebrow.

"This is for Mesa Verde," Grant grated between clenched teeth, then slammed the metal-reinforced toe of his boot into Pollard's side. He heard the crunching of ribs.

Pollard's beefy hand fluttered on the floor like a butterfly too fat to take flight. Grant stomped on the back of it, crushing the delicate metacarpal bones. "This is for Lakesh."

He slammed the heel of his left boot into the side of Pollard's head. The man gave a deep, groaning sigh as if he were drifting off to sleep. The sigh turned into a gurgling rattle. "And this is because I feel like it."

DeFore asked, "Did you chill him?"

Grant turned toward her. "Does it matter?"

"Not to me."

Once Grant got a good look at Lakesh, he understood the woman's callous tone. He was ashen and gaunt, his bodysuit ripped and soiled with his own wastes. Red abrasions showed bright on his skin. His eyes, puffed and bloodshot, held no recognition of the woman leaning over him. From his open mouth came a wordless gargle, either a plea or an inquiry.

Grant choked back the curse forcing its way past his lips. He drew the combat knife from his boot sheath and slashed through the restraining straps.

DeFore removed a stethoscope from her kit and listened to Lakesh's heart, took his pulse and examined his eyes, moving from one task to the other with a grim, brisk efficiency.

"Can he be moved?" asked Grant.

"He has a touch of acidosis due to dehydration, agnosia, maybe even a pneumococcal infection. There's fluid on his lungs."

Grant listened to her diagnosis, which meant nothing to him. "Can he be moved?" he demanded.

She took a small hypodermic syringe from the medical kit, holding it up to the feeble light for a moment. "He shouldn't be."

"That's not what I asked."

Rolling up Lakesh's right sleeve, she injected the amber-colored contents of the syringe into his arm. "I can't find any broken bones, so yes, he can be moved, though as a medic I'd be remiss if I recommended it. I'm giving him a shot of antibiotics, then I'll administer a stimulant compound and an analgesic for pain. There's not much I can do to rehydrate him except to give him an alkalinizing solution for the acidosis."

Doubtfully Grant said, "The way you're juicing him up, he may just float out of here."

"Let me do my job," she replied hotly.

Grant let her. He occupied himself by frisking Pollard, making sure he wasn't carrying a comm unit. The pockets of his uniform were empty, except for a pair of nylon wrist cuffs. As he patted him down, a faint moan bubbled past his lips. The man still lived. Grant knew a dozen ways to chill him without using his knife or blaster, but while he was considering methods, he heard Lakesh speak.

Grant stood up and leaned over him. Lakesh's rheumy blue eyes contained a dim spark, but they were still glazed and unfocused. His lips writhed, and reedy sounds Grant couldn't identify whispered out. All he understood were references to luck and a lady.

"What's he saying?" Grant asked DeFore.

She smiled wanly. "He's singing."

DeFore slapped Lakesh across the face, once, twice, three times. They weren't gentle, attention-getting taps. The cell echoed with the loud smack of flesh striking flesh. Lakesh's head rolled and wobbled on his neck. He coughed rackingly, from deep in his lungs. His eyes widened. DeFore paused, hand upraised.

In his thin, reedy voice, Lakesh said, "Such extreme criticisms of my song stylings are appreciated but unnecessary."

DeFore leaned forward, putting both hands on either side of his face. "Who are you?"

Weakly he replied, "My name is Mohandas Lakesh Singh. I was born in—"

"Who am I?" she interrupted.

Unhesitatingly he answered, "Your name is De-Fore. You were born thirty-five years ago in Ragnarville, of the genotype—"

"Do you know where you are, what has happened to you?"

Lakesh squeezed his eyes shut, dragged in a raspy inhalation. "Very clearly. But I do not know how long I have been here."

"Three days. I'm going to sit you up. Grant, give me hand."

Lakesh's eyes opened, registering the big black figure in armor looming over him. "Friend Grant is here, too. Imagine that. How was the Emerald Isle, friend Grant?"

"Green," he replied gruffly, helping DeFore raise the man to a sitting position. He was dismayed by how light he felt.

"Darlingest Domi? Dearest Brigid? Friend Kane?"

"Kane and Domi are here, waiting for us on A Level. Brigid is back at Cerberus."

Lakesh nodded, his head wobbling loosely on his pipe stem of a neck. "You traced me through the transponder?"

"Yeah." Grant briefly contemplated voicing a derogatory opinion about Lakesh's secretiveness, but decided E Level wasn't the place. He said, "We're taking you out of here, but it may be dangerous."

Vaguely Lakesh muttered, "Out of here? Of course, the gateway on A Level. How do we get there? Oh, that's right. The lift."

His eyes squinted in the direction of Pollard's gray, supine shape. "Without my glasses, I can't see very well. Please tell me that's Salvo."

"Sorry," replied Grant. "It's Pollard."

Lakesh made a move to edge off the bench. Fearfully he said, "Salvo could come back at any second!"

"Salvo's taken care of," DeFore told him. "In fact, without him, I'm not sure if we'd have been able to reach you."

Lakesh's seamed face contorted in befuddlement. "I don't understand."

"Never mind that now. Try to stand up."

With her help, Lakesh put his feet on the floor. He stood carefully, swaying back and forth, as if he stood on a rocking boat deck. Experimentally he took a few tottering steps. He breathed harshly, unsteadily.

"I'm very weak," he said bitterly.

"And you stink like a swampie's hind end, too," Grant said brusquely, "but neither can be helped. Put your hands behind your back."

Lakesh stared at him in sudden suspicion. "Why?"

Showing him the wrist cuffs, Grant explained, "You're my prisoner. That's how we'll get you out of here."

Falteringly Lakesh asked, "What if I'm recognized?"

"I don't think it's common knowledge Salvo had the senior archivist imprisoned down here. Besides, the way you look right now, Baron Cobalt wouldn't know you."

Reluctantly Lakesh put his hands at the small of his back, crossing his wrists. Grant slipped the cuffs around them, not tightening or locking them into place. If Lakesh needed to use his hands, he could wriggle free in a matter of seconds.

In a stronger voice, Lakesh said, "I'm feeling a little better. I don't hurt as much. My thinking seems clearer."

"Euphoric reaction to the drugs," DeFore warned. "All they do is mask your pain and overall debilitated condition. Take it easy."

Lakesh paced around the cell, trying to step sprightly. "Nonsense. I can whip my weight in wild—"

His knees buckled and Grant caught him. Ruefully Lakesh muttered, "Roses."

Grant pulled him upright. "Let's go. Don't stop for anything or anyone. If we're questioned, we'll do like Kane says and brazen it out."

Then they went out the door, into the narrow passageway, Grant gripping Lakesh by the collar of his bodysuit. To a casual observer, it appeared a Mag was manhandling a frail prisoner, but Grant was really keeping him erect.

They marched into the main corridor, past the termination wall and around the L junction. Grant realized he had been holding his breath, and he released it in a prolonged sigh. The mechanical din of the manufacturing complex sounded as soothing and as welcoming as a band striking up a homecoming fanfare.

"Hey! Magistrate! You!"

The voice came from behind them, and it struck chords of recognition within Grant. He tried to increase his stride, hustling Lakesh ahead of him.

"Hey, I'm talking to you!" Rapid footfalls slapped against the floor. Grant slowed to a halt, turning around, DeFore shifting so she was slightly behind him. He kept his grip on Lakesh, holding him in front.

An armored Magistrate approached him at a dog trot. Three other Mags in full armor clustered at the angle of the L, watching curiously. Grant knew they had to be a termination squad, and they obviously wondered if the old man in the strange Mag's custody was their scheduled target.

It took Grant a moment of ransacking his memory to identify the man coming toward them. When he recognized him, he groaned inwardly. It was Mac-Murphy, a man he had served with for many years and with whom he had shared the dangers of the Mesa Verde penetration. He tried to align Lakesh so the exposed lower portion of his face was hidden behind his head.

MacMurphy slowed to a walk. "Is that slagger written in for a termination?"

"No," Grant responded, trying but failing to pitch his voice higher to disguise his deep, rumbling timbre. "The baron wants to question him personally."

"Then why are you dragging him through manufacturing?"

Grant's thoughts raced wildly, but he couldn't improvise a plausible lie. The elevator hidden in the complex wasn't known to rank-and-file Magistrates. Mentioning it would only initiate an immediate investigation.

MacMurphy fixed his visored stare on Lakesh, on the small rainbow-striped insignia of the Historical Division on the soiled and ripped bodysuit. "He's an archivist. What's he done?"

Before Grant could invent a crime, MacMurphy thrust his head forward. "For fuck's sake! It's what's-his-name himself! What's going on?"

Quietly, regretfully Grant said, "It's very simple."

His Sin Eater roared, the blaster hidden by Lakesh until the instant he brought it around his body. The high-velocity round smashed into the center of MacMurphy's chest, not penetrating the armor but swatting him off his feet, driving the air from his lungs, the kinetic impact numbing his limbs.

Grant didn't wait for the reactions of the other three Mags. He whirled, literally hoisting Lakesh clear of the floor and rushed toward the square entranceway. DeFore ran in front of them, hoping Grant's armored back would deflect the brunt of the blasterfire.

Once inside the manufacturing facility, Grant shouted to DeFore that they should run at an angle toward the nearest machines. The route took them away from the hidden elevator tube, but provided them with cover.

The grinding, rattling racket was so intense Grant couldn't hear blasterfire, but he saw a spark jump from a dark gray iron framework a foot ahead of him. Faintly, through his helmet comm-link, he heard a babble of orders and counterorders. He couldn't understand the words, but he didn't need to. The tactics employed by Magistrates were rarely subtle or clever. The termination squad would fan out in the facility, try to outflank them and, though backup had no doubt been summoned, the squad wouldn't wait for their arrival before moving in.

Grant, DeFore and Lakesh moved quickly through the vast complex, feeling the deafening thunder of machinery in their bones. They breathed shallowly against the thick smell of molten metal.

Clouds of steam fogged Grant's visor, and he constantly had to palm it clean. Lakesh did his best to move swiftly, though when he recoiled from a spark shower, he lost his balance and nearly fell. Grant's fist at the collar of his bodysuit kept him on his feet.

On the other side of a clattering conveyor belt, three black shapes materialized out of a billow of steam. The Magistrates moved uncertainly, swiping at their occluded visors. While their vision was temporarily impaired, Grant opened fire, the booming reports of the Sin Eater completely swallowed by the crashing of machines.

Grant shot one man in the head, the bullet driving through his visor and punching him backward. He aimed for the stomach of the second man, who folded, falling out of sight. The third armored man returned the fire wildly with a triburst that whistled well past Grant and up into the catwalks.

Grant squeezed the trigger again. Part of the Magistrate's jaw tore away in a red gout. He clutched at his face, spinning on his toes in a 360-degree turn. He fell half across the conveyor belt, and it whisked him away, toward the open, glowing maw of a smelter.

Scanning the zone, Grant saw no sign of the fourth member of the squad. Possibly MacMurphy had been incapacitated and was still out in the corridor. He couldn't see the man he had belly-shot, either, but he didn't care to circle or climb over the belt to check his condition. He pulled Lakesh along like a straw-stuffed dummy and began running again.

The three of them backtracked a few yards and left the mechanical maze. The air felt a little cleaner, a bit cooler. The elevator-shaft door was still propped open. They scrambled in, the fit very tight and exceptionally uncomfortable. DeFore had to reach behind Lakesh to pull the door closed.

As she did, there came the clang of a bullet striking metal. The panel shivered and was torn from her grasp. Cursing, Grant half crushed the woman against the wall while he stretched out to grab it and yank it shut. The lock caught automatically. Immediately the disk beneath their feet rose upward. Over Grant's comm-link he heard shouts. Backup had arrived and had spotted the concealed elevator shaft.

What would come next was easy to predict. Since the Mags couldn't report to Salvo, they would have no option but to go up the chain of command and contact Abrams, the division administrator. According to Kane, he was a member of the Trust and would know exactly where the elevator would deposit them.

DeFore uttered a shaky laugh of exultation. "We made it!"

Grant opened the comm-link to Kane and softly, disgustedly, said, *"Merde."*

Chapter 18

When Kane heard that single soft word, spoken in a tone he knew well, he shushed Salvo into silence. His ear filled with comm-link chatter, curses, orders, instructions to countermand those orders, demands to find Salvo. When he heard a profanity-salted reference to the renegade Mag making his escape in a hitherto unknown elevator, he repeated Grant's voice signal, but in English, with a great deal more heat. *"Shit!"*

Salvo and Domi stared at him uncomprehendingly but with anxiety shining in their eyes.

Grimly Kane told them, "Grant's on his way back up. The Mags are on the alert. They're trying to find you, Salvo. Time to start earning your keep as a bargaining chip."

Swallowing hard, Salvo replied, "When they can't find me, they'll raise Abrams."

"Yeah, up one link in the chain of command. So?"

"So, Abrams won't look at me as hostage material." Salvo lifted his hands in a lame, resigned gesture. "I framed him, used him as a pawn in my plan to expose Lakesh. It didn't work. Baron Cobalt saw right through it."

Kane stared at him in baffled anger. "That makes more sense than being punished for your task force's fuckup in Idaho. Do you know where Abrams is now?''

Salvo nodded. "Here, on A Level."

He squared his shoulders, trying to focus on Kane in the gloom. His voice held an accusatory note. "It was your fault the frame didn't work, Kane. You damn near chilled Abrams in Dulce, so trying to convince the baron he was your clandestine partner-in-sedition put the skids on it. He believes *I'm* your partner."

Salvo uttered a bitter, incredulous laugh. "*Me*. Your partner. Anything you touch turns to shit, Kane."

Acknowledging the comment with a scornful chuckle, Kane said, "If you have no value as a hostage, you have no value to me."

He gestured toward Domi. "Give me the Copperhead."

Salvo bleated in fright, tried to turn, but Domi hammered him to his knees with the butt of the subgun. Fiercely she whispered, "I chill him, for what he did to my people."

Kane managed to control his hate-fueled fury long enough to consider the girl's words. Salvo had deceived him, manipulated him, tried to trick him into standing aside while Baptiste and Grant were terminated. The man was directly responsible for his exile, for the loss of his identity and life path.

But Salvo had overseen the murders and mutilations of Domi's people. The outlander girl did not have much of a past, but what there was of it, Salvo had ruthlessly expunged.

Kane nodded to her. "Do it."

Domi jammed the bore of the Copperhead against the back of Salvo's head, where it joined with his neck. In an extraordinarily calm voice, he said, "No guts for chilling your own brother. I should have known."

The remark was so odd it didn't penetrate Kane's rage-clouded consciousness for a moment. When it did, he waved Domi back and demanded, "What the fuck is that supposed to mean?"

"It's the main reason Baron Cobalt thought I was in collusion with you, Kane. Something you never knew, something I thought no one knew but me. We're related. Genetic twins. The baron found that out."

Kane stared down at him, fighting off a shudder. "You're a lying sack of shit."

Salvo shook his head. "I wish I were," he replied venomously. "I'd give anything for it to be a lie. I've known it for years, Kane. We're brothers."

Domi snarled, "He try talk his way out of taking last train West. Not listen to him, Kane."

Domi's admonition came too late. Kane had listened and heard the note of conviction in Salvo's voice. His heart beat faster when he recalled how he had privately acknowledged the strange link between Salvo and himself. He remembered that Salvo had told Baptiste their fathers were enemies, but that Salvo had made sure Kane was unaware of that fact.

He remembered Salvo's irrational outburst in Idaho, when he blamed Baptiste for Kane's treason and was outraged Kane had dared to choose her over him.

The memory of his dream and his father's words

ghosted through Kane's mind: *But you'll still be connected to your Other, and the day will come when you will embrace him or cut the connection forever. Whatever you decide to do, you will lose a part of yourself but gain a part of him.*

Kane knew the Program of Unification had practiced the divide-and-conquer philosophy mercilessly, indoctrinating humanity with the belief that they were all weak and venal, bereft of the capacity to govern themselves. As humankind as a whole had been divided in the name of unity, so had brothers, sisters, mothers, fathers and children.

"Chill him!" Domi's voice came as an urgent hiss.

"Shut up," snapped Kane. He stepped closer to Salvo. "Why should I believe a word you say?"

Salvo sighed heavily. "Logically, no reason at all. Emotionally is a different matter. Trust your instincts, your feelings."

Kane gazed down at him, studying his short, gray-threaded hair, a shade darker than his own, the same shade as his father's. He looked carefully at the set of the jaw, the placement of the eyes. He looked at the scar the barrel of his Sin Eater had stamped on his forehead and he felt nothing, not even when his stare locked with the mud-colored eyes.

With a great weariness, he said, "I feel about as brotherly toward you as I would a muck-sucker, and I put an equal value on your life."

Domi made a feral sound, half growl and half chuckle. She tensed like a snow leopardess preparing to leap on her prey.

"But I'll spare it," continued Kane, ignoring Domi's outraged glare and wordless cry of disappointment. "Where we're going, we have ways to test whether you're lying. Besides, there's...*someone* I want you to meet."

Salvo caught his emphasis on the word. "Who?"

Kane didn't answer. A sudden rectangle of light pierced the gloom, and he spun to see the double doors swinging open. Domi raised the Copperhead to her shoulder.

Grant, DeFore and a third figure slipped through, pulling the doors shut. In the short span of seconds when they were backlit by the foyer's chandeliers, Kane couldn't recognize the emaciated scarecrow held between them. Domi murmured in horror and rushed across the hall. She took Grant's position on Lakesh's right and helped him toward the archway. Salvo shifted uncomfortably, starting to rise.

Kane pressed the Sin Eater's bore into the side of his head. "Stay. Lakesh may prefer you at his feet."

Grant reached the arch first. "You heard my signal?"

"Yeah. Bad?"

"Bad enough. Mags will be on their way up."

Lakesh resolutely ignored the kneeling Salvo. His creaky voice whispered, "Friend Kane. I'm afraid they got me."

"How do you feel?"

"Bloody awful, but our medic in residence got me on my feet."

Lakesh did look awful and smelled worse, but Kane figured he knew it and saw no reason to mention it.

Domi demanded, "Take cuffs off him."

Grant reached around to free Lakesh's wrists, but

Kane interposed, "Leave them. Salvo isn't worth shit as a hostage. One of the reasons Baron Cobalt hung him up for a high colonic was to question him about Lakesh's whereabouts."

Lakesh chuckled. "Really? I'm gratified. And I assumed Salvo would take the unfortunate Abrams's place."

"Abrams isn't unfortunate," Kane replied, "and he isn't dead. The baron turned Salvo's double-cross into a triple."

Lakesh chuckled again. "'O, what a tangled web we weave when first we—'" The remainder of the quote turned into a coughing fit.

Kane heard the liquid burble in the man's lungs and winced. DeFore said, "He's pre-pneumonic, due to lying on his back for three days and nights without proper nutrition."

Salvo, obviously discomfited by being spoken about as if he weren't there, said shortly, "We've got to get out."

With great effort, Lakesh got his coughing spasm under control. Hoarsely, sounding half-strangled, he said, "I can take you on a more direct route to the gateway than the one friend Grant described. I'm amazed you found your way to this area at all."

Kane nudged Salvo with a boot. "Get up."

Grant rumbled threateningly, "We're not taking him. If he's no use as a hostage to get us through the Mags, he'll just slow us up. Flash-blast his slagging ass and be done with it."

"Yes," Domi asserted.

As Salvo climbed to his feet, Kane said, "I've got

my reasons for keeping him alive—at least for a little while.''

"Which are?" Grant asked angrily.

Calmly Lakesh said, ''They are too complex and personal to delve into right now. Let's not argue.''

Both Kane and Salvo gave the man a searching glance. Though the old man could not see very far in the murk, he nodded toward them with a sad smile. He knows, Kane thought. The bastard knows.

Grant took point again. DeFore and Domi supported Lakesh, with Salvo following and Kane bringing up the rear. They passed under another curving arch and into a wing debouching to the right. Commlink chatter didn't begin again, but neither Kane nor Grant was comforted by its absence.

Quietly Grant said, ''No alarms have sounded yet.''

Lakesh replied, ''Silent alarms up here, friend Grant. Clanging bells and screaming sirens would disturb Baron Cobalt's delicate sensibilities.''

They entered a room ten feet across, its illumination supplied by flames in graceful, slim tapers set in sockets about the floor. The chamber was very quiet, as if upon entering it they had stepped into a vault of silence.

''A meditation nook,'' Lakesh explained. Though he spoke in a normal tone of voice, it sounded oddly hushed, as if his words wafted up from the bottom of a miles-deep pit. ''For the use of the baron's personal staff, so they may work out the knotty mysteries of existence.''

There seemed to be no door out of the room except the one by which they entered. The walls were completely smooth and featureless. Kane scanned all the corners, even the ceiling, and didn't see a spy-eye lens.

Domi pointed to a thread-thin vertical rectangle running from the floor to the ceiling. She grinned. "Secret door, I betcha."

Lakesh smiled. "Like all knots and mysteries, they are simple once you work out the combination. Friend Grant, you have the necessary musculature for this task. Please do as I say. It will speed matters considerably."

Following Lakesh's instructions, Grant stepped to the wall and pressed both hands against it, leaning his entire weight into it and pushing with all of his strength. His arms trembled a bit with the effort.

Kane expected the rectangle to rotate on pivots concealed in the floor and ceiling. Instead, the entire wall in front of them began to rise, except for a rectangular panel.

"Pressure actuators," said Lakesh. "Much like the ones ancient architects built into Egyptian and Toltec pyramids. This one is hydraulically operated, rather than relying on stone counterweights."

The rising wall revealed a railed gallery encircling and overlooking a six-foot-diameter, metal-walled shaft. A tiny dot of light far below marked the bottom. Cool air gusted steadily out of it, ruffling hair and stinging eyes.

"An air-circulation venting core," Lakesh explained. "Drops straight down some two hundred yards."

"Nice," said DeFore, edging away from the rail. "What good will that do us?"

"We need only climb down twenty feet. We'll find a duct facing the mat-trans chamber."

Kane peered down into the shaft. Glowing slits marked the levels. "I don't see a ladder, and you're not in any shape for rapeling, even if we had the equipment."

Lakesh inclined his head toward the opposite side of the opening. "Domi, darlingest one, be a good girl and go over there."

Obediently she did as he said, standing and staring at them over the railing. "Now what?"

"Look down. Near your right foot, you'll see a round button, inset in the floor, almost flush with it. Yes, that's the one. Step on it hard."

From above descended a flat metal disk, only a few inches smaller in diameter than the mouth of the shaft. A gleaming column of steel extended from the center of it, up into a network of cables and pulleys. Lakesh pointed his chin toward it. "A maintenance lift. Safe and simple."

Kane cast him an annoyed glance. "If you knew about all of this, why wasn't it in the database?"

Lakesh attempted a feeble imitation of his impish smile. "It is, friend Kane. But in a private file, personally encrypted by me. The secrets of A Level cannot be shared with all and sundry."

"Good attitude to have," Grant said dourly. "If they'd been shared with all and sundry, we could have gotten you out of here hours ago."

He touched the swelling at his jaw. "And with no delays along the way."

The disk stopped an inch above the lip of the shaft. DeFore found a catch-release lock and swung open a section of the railing. As she helped Lakesh onto the platform, he said, "A valid reprimand and one I accept without rancor. Friend Kane, I once accused you of being an overconfident, reckless fool. Truly an instance of the pot calling the kettle black."

Grant and Kane exchanged short, puzzled glances over the exact meaning of the proverb, but they understood the context.

Everyone clustered around the central column on the disk. Salvo had to be nudged at blasterpoint to join them. His position put him face-to-face with Lakesh.

Somberly he said, "I suppose you hate me."

Very earnestly Lakesh replied, "You have no idea."

"Would it make a difference if I told you I thought I was acting in the best interests of the baron, of the Trust, of the villes?"

"None at all," said Lakesh, turning his head away.

The platform dropped very slowly and smoothly, pausing automatically for thirty seconds at a covered hatchway on a lower level.

"A Level is the only one with more than one floor," Lakesh stated. "Three to be exact."

"Found that out ourselves," Domi chirped.

Kane moved closer to Lakesh. "Salvo told me he got nothing out of you except some bad singing."

Lakesh's glassy eyes squinted toward him. "That surprises you?"

Stolidly Kane retorted, "In fact, it does."

"I knew someone would come for me."

"It was touch-and-go on that point," replied Kane darkly. "If something hadn't happened that only you can figure out, you might still be singing your life away in the cell blocks.''

Lakesh's only response was a cough.

The platform sighed to another stop, and Grant reached out to wrestle with the hatchway's release lever. He slammed it to one side and pushed the hatch open. A tunnel-like passage, narrow and low ceilinged, stretched away along iron grillwork. Not too far ahead, a wedge of dim light marked an opening.

After making a motion-sensor sweep, Grant stepped in, gesturing for the others to follow. They walked single file, Kane again acting as the rear guard. He listened, but heard nothing but the soft sound of his companions' footsteps and the slow drip of water from somewhere above. The air smelled damp and mildewy.

The passageway ended at a hatch identical to the one they entered. Beveled slits allowed light to peep through from the other side. Grant was unable to see through them. He checked the LCD of the detector and saw nothing on it. Grabbing the release lever, he slowly pulled it up.

The hatchway swung outward, not inward, and the hinges were stiff from rust. When he used his shoulder to push the hatchway open, he stumbled. The bottom edge was a foot above the floor, and he nearly fell.

Regaining his balance quickly, he looked around and saw that he stood in a T junction, at the very center of the intersection. The corridor was clear ahead, but to the left and right he saw nothing but silent, motionless figures in black armor and the hollow, cyclopean eyes of Sin Eater muzzles.

Chapter 19

"One never knows what sort of pest will be found scampering through the walls."

The projected voice was beautifully modulated, mocking and taunting. "The home owner's only recourse is to flush them out and exterminate them."

Grant had never heard Baron Cobalt's voice before, but he knew instinctively it was he who had spoken, probably from the comm-link grids on the walls. Swiftly he made a quick helmet count. There were at least a dozen Magistrates deployed on either side of him, six to the left and six to the right. He was only slightly reassured by the fact that both groups couldn't open fire at once without catching each other in a cross fire.

A voice Grant recognized immediately spoke next. "Get your hands up, Grant. The rest of you come out slowly, hands behind your heads."

As Grant raised his hands, he saw the iron-bearded, grim face of Abrams, who was standing behind the line of Mags on his right. He had never formally met the man, but he had seen the division administrator a number of times and read plenty of his memos.

DeFore stepped out of the passageway first, doing her best to appear calm and unconcerned. A fierce-eyed Domi followed her, and then a very shamed and frightened Salvo stepped down, looking ridiculous in the bullet-holed surgical gown.

"Four fleeing rats," came the baron's amused voice. "But there is one more, is there not? The king rat himself. Come out, Kane. Time to come in now."

Grant heard footfalls on the metal grillwork behind him, then a horrified gasp ripped out of the speakers. He didn't need to see what had evoked the reaction.

Kane held Lakesh out in front of him, left arm crooked around his throat, the barrel of the Sin Eater pressed against his head. He looked around and found the spy-eye lens on the ceiling, almost directly overhead. Staring up at it and imitating Baron Cobalt's mocking cadence, he said, "An interesting problem, Lord Baron. You have us, but we have your favorite pet human. Whatever happens to us will certainly happen to him."

A shriek of frustrated anger filled the corridor, the echoes bouncing off the walls and chasing each other. "This was all your doing, wasn't it, Kane? You and Salvo plotted to kidnap Lakesh and hold him for ransom so I would accede to your treasonous demands."

Kane laughed, the same kind of cold, superior laugh he had subjected the baron to when he'd held him helpless in Dulce. "You've got it all figured out. Not too bad for a dickless freak."

Grant stiffened, fearing Kane would go too far and trigger a fury in Baron Cobalt that would overwhelm his concern for Lakesh.

For a long, tense moment, no sounds issued from the wall speakers. Finally the baron asked a direct question in a flat, unemotional voice. "Name your terms."

"For the moment, they're simple. Let us leave. Later I'll send you a list of demands for Lakesh's release."

"Leave how?"

"How else? The way we came."

"The gateway?"

"Yeah, the gateway."

The baron's voice dropped to a silky whisper. "How did you find out about the one here, may I ask?"

"Does it matter?" countered Kane. "Blame it on the Preservationists."

"Yes, of course. The Preservationists. Very well, I concede."

Baron Cobalt's quick agreement aroused all of their suspicions. Either he had laid another trap or he figured he could trace the gateway's matter-stream frequency to their destination.

"Which way?" Kane whispered into Lakesh's ear.

Lakesh's lips barely moved, and Kane had to strain to hear his answer. "To your left. Twenty paces. Another hidden door."

Grant, Domi, DeFore and Salvo surrounded them as Kane and Lakesh moved into the left branch of the T.

"Let them pass!" Abrams barked, and the line of Magistrates parted.

They went down the corridor, Kane inwardly cursing their slow, clumsy progress. Lakesh was terribly weak, and he walked as if bearing every second of his 250 years. He whispered, "Stop here."

Kane saw only a flat expanse of wall, then his eyes

picked out an almost invisible seam. "How do we get it open? Pressure actuators again?"

"Yes."

A swift over-the-shoulder glance confirmed the Magistrates dogging their heels, pacing slowly, visored eyes and blaster barrels trained on them. "Fuck it," Kane muttered.

He fired his Sin Eater, a booming double-burst that drove bullets into the electronically controlled mechanism. The narrow door swung open on a skewed angle, like the broken wing of a bird.

As he had hoped, the unexpected thunder of his blaster sent the Mags backpedaling for cover, bumping into each other, swearing, feet slipping on the floor. Kane pushed Lakesh through the open panel and into the narrow hall facing the mat-trans chamber. What he had assumed was a dead end was in fact a disguised entrance.

Hustling Lakesh forward, Kane palmed open the control-room door, hearing the others squeeze through the panel. Without looking behind him, he called, "Domi! Discourage our shadows!"

"Gotcha!" she responded eagerly.

Less than five seconds later, a muffled explosion shook the floor and echoed hollowly through the control room. Kane recognized the detonation of a high-ex gren.

At the thunderclap, Lakesh stumbled. His face was white with exhaustion and pain. "Sorry," he gasped.

Kane caught him up, holding him under his arms. "Hang on, old man. We're almost home."

They pelted through the small ready room and piled into the mat-trans chamber. Salvo hesitated only a heartbeat before lunging into it. DeFore punched in the autosequencing code on the standard keypad affixed to the exterior of the door, then the locking sec code. Normally a jumper's destination could be traced by accessing the Last Destination program built into the system. The LD button had been designed as a failsafe device to return mat-trans travelers to their original jump point. Long ago, Lakesh had ensured the LD could not lock in on the transit feed connection to the Cerberus gateway unit.

Grant swung the heavy armaglass door closed, and they waited for the automatic jump initiator to engage and begin the cycle.

Nothing happened.

Everyone cast anxious, fearful glances toward Lakesh. Grimly he said, "I should have known. The baron has interrupted the connection between the initiator and the autosequencer. We're trapped in here."

"Why would he do that?" Grant demanded. "Isn't he afraid we'll chill you?"

"I think he's more afraid I'll fall into the hands of the Preservationists."

Salvo covered his face with quivering hands. "This can't be happening."

"More than likely," Lakesh continued, "he'll transport us to some other unit, probably in Palladiumville, which is the closest, then have all of you apprehended and me rescued while we're disoriented."

"How do you know?" snapped Kane.

Lakesh forced a smile. "It's what I would do." He cleared his throat, a reflex that brought a wince of pain. "All is not lost, however. If one of you had the presence of mind to bring along a Mnemosyne, then we have a chance to unlock the controls.''

Digging into her pouch, Domi brought out a small device shaped like an elongated circle. It was divided down the center by a narrow slit, and several studs protruded from its dull surface. ''Here.''

''Good.'' Lakesh spoke quickly. ''Out in the control room, there is a freestanding operator's console. On it is a manual-override input port. It should be labeled. All you have to it is fasten the Syne to it and press the decrypt setting.''

Domi nodded, slipping the pouch from her shoulder and handing it to DeFore. ''Okay. Gotcha.''

''Hold on,'' protested Grant. ''Let me or Kane do it. We're armored.''

''I'm fastest,'' Domi replied. ''Make smaller target than you two. I go in and out, slick and quick, no problem.''

Grant tried to dispassionately consider her words, realized he couldn't and said, ''Affirm. I'll cover you.''

Levering the door open, he made a sensor sweep of the antechamber and the control room beyond. ''Clean, but it won't last.''

They moved out swiftly, crossing the anteroom and taking up positions on either side of the doorway. Grant whispered to her, ''If you're fired upon, don't waste time returning it. Let me handle the blasting.''

She grinned at him, held up the index finger of her right hand and rushed through the door. Even Grant, who knew she was fast and nimble, was impressed by Domi's display of speed and agility. She bounded through the control room with a feline grace, body curved in a half crouch.

The motion detector beeped a warning at the same time a Sin Eater roared. The heavy-caliber round crashed into the wall beside Grant's partially exposed head. He saw the snout of the blaster projecting through the half-open control-room door. The Mags outside had no idea of what Domi was up to, and choosing to shoot at either an outlander girl or a turncoat Magistrate was no choice at all.

Kicking away from the doorway at an angle, Grant swept his Sin Eater up and out, squeezing the trigger. The first round punched through the door panel, catching the man on the other side of it with a 248-grain hollowpoint round. The impact blew him away from the door.

Grant kept his blaster flaming and thundering, stitching the door with a patchwork pattern of craters. He glimpsed Domi bent beneath a console. She lifted her head just high enough to see over the rim. Her hand jammed the Syne down into the port, making sure the fit was snug, then thumbed the appropriate button on its surface.

She didn't linger over her work. She turned and came toward Grant in a lunging rush. Grant lessened his finger's pressure on the Sin Eater's trigger so she could have a free zone of retreat.

Blasterfire erupted from the door. Enraged Magistrates fired blindly into the control room, hoping one of their slugs would find a target. Domi cried out in shock and pain. Blood sprayed in a thick geyser from her right shoulder, and the fabric of her coverall burst open. She slammed down on the slick floor, skidding on her stomach. She tried to get back up, but her arms and legs wouldn't support her. She collapsed face-down.

Scrambling forward, ducking low beneath the flying bullets that seemed to fill the air, Grant put his armored body between the Magistrates and Domi. He covered the girl's slight frame as slugs ripped through the room, ricocheting away from metal.

Turning her over, Grant slid his hands beneath her shoulders and thighs. In one motion, he hoisted her up like a child, not looking at her face or the scarlet stream pumping from her shoulder. Hot pain thumped into his back, and the jolts of impacting bullets nearly knocked him off his feet.

His vision swam and blurred as he staggered into the anteroom, agony lancing through his torso. He let the sledgehammer blows turn his sprint into a racing dive. When he reached the mat-trans chamber, he tripped on the raised floor plates. DeFore reached out with both arms, relieving him of some of Domi's weight. Kane pulled the door closed as bullets slapped into the armaglass and bounced away.

DeFore laid Domi down, ripping wide the ragged hole in her coverall. Fresh, bright arterial blood gushed out over her hands. White bone chips gleamed in the weltering mess of Domi's shoulder. Clamping her right hand over the wound, DeFore groped with the other for her medical kit.

"She's in shock," she said through gritted teeth. "The axillary artery may be severed, and the coracoid bone is definitely shattered."

A scarlet ribbon crawled over the floor plates, filling the tiny cracks between the individual hexagons.

Lakesh stared at it in horror, struggling madly to free his hands of the cuffs. He wrenched them loose just as the metal disks exuded a silvery shimmer. He fell to his knees beside Domi, touching her white face with palsied fingers.

A wail of fright tore from Salvo's lips as the faint mist appeared in the air, curling up around his feet. "What's happening?"

No one bothered explaining. A distant humming sound grew in volume. Fists and metal blaster butts pounded on the door, muffled voices cursed and threatened. The glass showed the distorted black smears of helmeted heads.

Kane inhaled a deep breath as the vapor swirled around him, feeling grateful for it. At least he could no longer see Domi's blood.

Chapter 20

After two hours of sitting alone in the central control complex, Brigid Baptiste had almost managed to ignore the fear eating away at her nerves like acid. She didn't need to look at the digital wall chron to know three hours and twenty minutes had passed since Kane, Domi, DeFore and Grant entered the jump chamber.

She had forced herself to spend—or waste—that time trying to decipher Lakesh's codes and find the analysis key for the interphaser's memory disk. She had run it through a dozen different decryption programs, but not a single one pointed toward the direction of the Omega Path.

Creating that file name was one thing she had accomplished over the past couple of hours. It made perfect sense, inasmuch as whatever quantum pathway opened by the interphaser led, figuratively, to the end, at least as far as she was concerned.

The solution to the turmoil of the present and the mysteries of the future lay in the dark past, where the horrors that birthed the nukecaust, the skydark and the baronies first took root.

She heard footsteps from the entrance and the faint squeak of rubber wheels. She turned to see Auerbach pushing a gurney ahead of him, a medical kit on top of it.

A new knife of fear stabbed through her. "You've received bad biolink transponder signals." It wasn't a question, but rather a statement.

The big man nodded glumly.

"Lakesh?"

"No," he answered. "His vitals signs stabilized, though they're still off model."

"Kane?"

"Domi. Her readings show a marked degree of trauma, which indicates hemorrhaging. Her blood pressure and brain-wave activity spiked and dropped. We lost her signature."

When he saw the stricken look on Brigid's face, Auerbach added hastily, "We lost everybody's signature about two minutes ago. We're hoping they made the jump."

Auerbach pushed the gurney into the room adjacent to the gateway unit and opened the medical kit, standing by silently.

Brigid swept her gaze over the bank of power gauges and indicator lights. They held steady and dark. She didn't mention that two minutes should have seen the materialization of the team in the chamber.

On occasion, traversing the quantum pathways resulted in minor temporal anomalies, like arriving at a destination three seconds before the jump initiator had actually engaged, according to wrist chrons. She brought up this oddity to Lakesh once, and he replied that time could not be measured or accurately perceived in the quantum stream.

Hypothetically, he said, constant jumpers might find themselves physically rejuvenated, the toll of age erased if enough "backward time" was accumulated in their metabolisms.

Or conversely jumpers might find themselves prematurely aged if the quantum stream bumped them further into the future with each journey.

Brigid ran an impatient hand through her hair. Theories, everything was theories. She understood why Kane lost his temper so easily due to the near-endless theorizing, hypothesizing and surmising in which Lakesh loved to indulge.

Turning back to the console of gauges, she willed them to register something, anything, even an electron that had lost its way.

Suddenly lights flashed and needles wavered.

Brigid leaped from her chair as the humming tone vibrated from the gateway chamber. She ran through the anteroom, past Auerbach, and came to a stop facing the armaglass door. Bright flares, like bursts of distant heat lightning, arced on the other side. The droning hum climbed to a hurricane wail, then dropped down to inaudiblity.

Grabbing the handle, she wrenched up on it. She was nearly bowled off her feet when the door flew open violently, pushed by Grant's shoulder. He rushed out cradling a slack-limbed, red-spattered broken doll in his arms. Blood streaked her limp right hand, and dripped from her fingers to splatter on the floor.

As Grant laid Domi gently down on the gurney, DeFore hurried a trifle unsteadily out of the door, snapping orders at Auerbach to apply a pressure bandage. Kane came out next, wreaths of mist about his ankles. He didn't say anything or even acknowledge her presence with so much as a nod as he moved to the side of the gurney.

It was barely controlled chaos for a moment, so Brigid didn't immediately notice the emaciated figure stepping out of the chamber. Only when he stumbled did she look toward Lakesh. She took a firm grip on his arm, sickened by his wasted appearance and smell and hoping it didn't show on her face.

"Dear Brigid," he murmured breathlessly. "I fear circumstances did not permit me to make myself presentable for the company of ladies."

"Don't know of any in this place," she replied, striving for but failing to achieve a bantering tone. "Good to see you."

"Grant!" DeFore said sharply. "Get Lakesh to the dispensary. Auerbach, go with him, begin the standard rehydration procedure. I'll be along as soon as I get Domi's bleeding under control."

Grant didn't argue. He grabbed Lakesh around the waist, placed one of his arms over his shoulders and said, "Lean on me. Let me do the walking."

As he half carried, half dragged Lakesh out of the center, Brigid cast anxious eyes toward Kane. "Are you all right?"

"Tolerable. Better than Lakesh and Domi."

He tugged off his helmet. Behind him, in the mat-trans chamber, a slow-moving figure in white caught her eye. She squinted. "Who's that?"

Kane smiled wryly and spoke toward the door. "Come on out and meet the Cerberus welcoming committee. We'll do whatever we can to make you feel right at home."

Tentatively Salvo stepped to the door, looked

around and entered the anteroom. Brigid stared at him with hard jade eyes, no expression on her face, not even a fleeting flicker of surprise.

Kane pulled Salvo forward by the front of his smock. "I'm sure you remember Brigid Baptiste, keeper of the archives. Except you called her something else, as I recall. What was it, Baptiste? You have the photographic memory."

Quietly Brigid stated, "He called me, and I quote, 'you whore, you bitch, you rebel, you insurgent.'"

She hit him with a short, swift and perfectly aimed uppercut. Her left fist caught Salvo on the chin and dropped him to the floor without a murmur of surprise or pain. He forced himself to his elbows and gaped at her in a mixture of astonishment and fright.

"Better send for another gurney," Kane said to DeFore.

The medic either didn't hear him or didn't have the inclination to respond. One hand pressing on the thick white bandage over Domi's shoulder, she trotted out of the room, wheeling the gurney before her.

Brigid glared down at Salvo, eyes sparking with emerald glints of hatred. "Where did you find him?"

"With his ass in a sling—literally."

"What?"

By the time Kane completed his terse explanation, Salvo had pushed himself to a sitting position and was massaging his chin and glaring balefully at Brigid.

"So one of your deceptions backfired on you," she said, voice so full of loathing she might as well have been addressing a mutie borer beetle. She glanced toward Kane. "Why didn't you just leave him hanging there?"

"Tell her, Salvo," suggested Kane. "Tell her what you told me."

Salvo snorted and pushed himself to his feet. His face was stamped with his old arrogance. "I won't be questioned by the likes of that turncoat bitch, Kane. She may be your whore, but I'll fucking chill her if she ever—"

The toe of Kane's right boot clubbed into Salvo's jaw, knocking him down and backward against the armaglass. He cried out, clutching at his mouth, blood squirting between his fingers.

Kane reached down, wrestled the man to his feet, grabbed the back of his head and smashed his face into the tabletop. By the collar of his gown, he yanked Salvo upright. Twin streams of scarlet gushed from his nostrils. As he opened his mouth to gasp for air, Kane jacked his left knee into his midriff. Salvo doubled over, emitting a grunt. Kane's right knee connected against Salvo's forehead, driving him to a staggering, half-standing posture.

Brigid was too astonished to move. She had never seen such an expression of undiluted, homicidal fury as the one that contorted Kane's face. The punishment he had meted out to Salvo already seemed only to further arouse his blood lust.

She watched as Kane jabbed a right fist against the side of Salvo's jaw, following up with a smashing roundhouse punch. Salvo reeled backward, a denture plate flying from his mouth, riding a liquid tendril of blood. He fetched up hard against the wall, and Kane followed him, pistoning his fists in a flurry of lefts and rights into his body. Salvo never landed a blow or even tried to launch one. Closing one gloved hand around Salvo's throat, Kane pounded his head against the wall.

"Kane!" shouted Brigid. *"Kane!"*

He stopped pummeling Salvo's midsection, and turned his face toward her with a wild, bright, demented look in his eyes. He was completely lost in his fury.

"Kane!" Brigid said again, afraid to move toward him, thinking she might have to call for Grant to pull him off Salvo. "Enough."

After a moment, Kane slowly stepped away, allowing Salvo to slide to the floor. He stood, catching his breath, glaring down at the semiconscious man, at the frothy blood bubbling from his nostrils. The kill-rage drained out of him, leaving him weary. He leaned his hip against the table edge.

Quietly Brigid asked, "Is that why you brought him here, so you could beat him to death in front of me? Did you think I wanted to see that?"

Kane ran a hand through his hair, not saying anything.

"I don't need you to defend my honor, Kane. You were hoping he'd insult me so you'd have an excuse to take him apart."

Kane, still panting, did not dispute it.

Brigid moved toward the control complex. "I'll fetch a gurney."

"No," Kane said. "I'll take him to the dispensary myself. After we make a little stop."

"He needs treatment now."

"Goddammit, I'll take care of it!" Kane barked.

"You're not a medic," she argued.

Pushing out, then pulling in a long, deep breath, he said thoughtfully, "No, but I am his brother."

He didn't need to see the expression on Brigid's face to know she was shocked into speechlessness. He knelt down in front of Salvo, slapping him quickly on both sides of his face. When the older man moaned, Kane dragged him into a sitting position. Rivulets of blood dripped from his split lips and trickled down the front of the smock. His eyes popped open, blanching when he saw Kane, and he tried desperately to back away.

Kane wouldn't let him, gathering a fistful of gown. "Come on, Salvo," he crooned. "Can't you take it anymore? This is nothing compared to what you did to Lakesh, and he's still up and around."

"What—what..." he sputtered, eyes glassy.

Kane cuffed him, causing his head to wobble. "I want you awake. I want you to take notice."

He jerked him savagely to his feet. Salvo staggered, leaning on the table for support. Brigid looked away from his face. One eye was but a bruised, swollen slit, his lower lip red pulp and he bled profusely from a misshapen nose.

"What did you mean?" she demanded. "That you're his brother?"

Kane pulled Salvo away from the table, hustling him toward the doorway. "Ask Lakesh. He seemed to know something about it. Hell, he probably knows *all* about it."

She made a motion as if to follow him, but she read his eyes and the warning gleaming in them. "Where are you taking him?"

Kane smiled coldly. "At least once in the life of a

lap dog, he should have the chance to lick his master's ass.''

BANKS WAS BORED, which was not an unusual state for him.

He paced the holding facility, looking for something to do, even if it didn't hold his interest more than ten seconds. He had already double-checked the environmental console, made a few exceptionally minor temperature and humidity adjustments, made sure the four computer terminals were functioning, and rearranged the complicated network of glass tubes, retorts and chemical-filtration systems covering the pair of trestle tables.

Since he was accustomed to the acrid odor of diluted peroxide and cattle blood, even grousing about the stench wasn't much of a pastime. Banks was also used to the constant, feathery vibration deep in his head, like a fly buzzing beneath several layers of cotton wadding.

The vibration was always there while he was in the facility, and over three years he had learned the trick of focusing past it, so it was a barely noticeable stimulus on the fringes of his awareness. Only a couple of other Cerberus personnel were adept at tuning out Balam's telepathic touch, so the entity's containment area rarely entertained casual visitors.

Banks walked over to the glass-enclosed left wall. Behind the condensation-beaded pane, he detected no movement in the deeply recessed room. The overhead light strip cast a dim, reddish glow. He saw nothing but the reflection of a tall, thin black man with a boyish, sincere face. He had been told his grin was infectious, but he had nothing to grin about now. Even if Balam cared to respond to his presence, he certainly wouldn't return the grin.

Banks heard the electronic tones of the combination to the door lock being punched into the keypad. He crossed the room when the confirmation circuit chimed. The exterior of the door had no knob, only the keypad device. He turned the handle and pulled the door open, hoping it was Wegmann wanting to play a fast hand of Battleships.

A bloody stranger stumbled over the threshold, propelled by a hard shove from Kane. Banks stepped aside, feeling wonder and anxiety replace his boredom. He didn't know Kane very well and, for that matter, was a bit afraid of him. His black Magistrate's armor made him look grim, formidable and dangerous, as did the icy, fixed expression in his pale eyes.

Respectfully Banks inquired, "Who's this, sir?"

"Take a coffee break, Banks," Kane replied, manhandling the stranger toward Balam's cell.

Banks hesitated before saying, "I'm a tea drinker, sir. And you know the sec protocols clearly state that only myself and Lakesh are allowed to be alone in—"

Kane snapped his head toward him. "Do you have hearing problems, kid?"

Banks swallowed and answered quickly, "No, sir. But I must remind you that we don't know the extent of Balam's mental influence on the human mind. I'd be remiss in my duties if I left you alone."

"Fine," Kane growled. "Stay, then. But it won't be pretty."

Mystified, Banks watched Kane march the stranger

over to the glass front of the cell. Banks jumped when Kane slammed the man's body against it.

Kane held Salvo tightly in place, mashing the side of his captive's face against the pane. In a husky whisper, he said, "You sold out the human race to this thing. Look at it. Look and then dare call me the traitor. Look, you son of a bitch. *Look.*"

Like a swirl of seething mist, a shape shifted in the hell-hued gloom, a darkness within a darkness. For a fraction of a microsecond, an unnaturally slim figure, small and compact, appeared. There was only the briefest, most inchoate impression of a long, pale head and a high, hairless cranium. The mist whirled, blotting out the face. A pair of inhumanly huge, tip-tilted jet-black eyes flamed in the murk, red light glinting from them in burning pinpoints.

Salvo didn't struggle, but a low, bestial moaning drooled from his bloody lips. Kane waited, and the nonvoice insinuated itself into his brain, into Salvo's. The voice was neither male nor female, young nor old, neither high nor deep.

We are old. When your race was wild and bloody and young, we were already ancient. Your tribe has passed, and we are invincible. All of the achievements of man are dust, they are forgotten.

Kane had heard the doctrine before and he was able to ward off the primal terror it instilled. Salvo croaked inarticulately, fighting frenziedly against the strong hands pressing his face against the glass.

We stand, we know, we are. We stalked above man ere we raised him from the ape. Long was the earth ours, and now we have reclaimed it. We shall still reign when man is reduced to the ape again.

Kane sensed the remote, malignant intelligence, feeling the hate emanate from it in almost tangible waves. A choked scream tried to force its way past Salvo's lips, but it came out as a protracted gurgle.

We stand, we know, we are.

The mist faded, seeming to be swallowed up by the red-tinted interior of the cell. The cold, haughty words left Kane's brain. Salvo sagged in Kane's hands and sank down to the floor, eyes blinking frantically as if he were trying to rid the retinas of the image impressed into them. His head rolled as if in agony.

Kane prodded him with a foot, and his dark eyes looked full at him. There was no light of intelligence in them; they were blank, the eyes of a terrified, terrorized animal. He slumped over, hanging his head, palms flat against the floor. His shoulders shook as he dry-heaved.

"That," Kane said, "is an Archon, Balam by name. He's been around a very long time. He's probably responsible for a lot of history. He's who you work for. He and others like him are the masters of the barons and the masters of you. Two centuries ago, they—and greedy bastards just like you—flash-blasted the Earth."

Salvo mumbled, and Kane had to lean down to hear what he was saying. "True...it's all true...it's true...."

"Yeah, it's all true," said Kane bitterly. "And the truth will set you free."

"How could I have known?" Salvo breathed. "How could I have known about that...*thing?*"

Salvo's eyes swam with a raw, soul-deep horror, his face paper white beneath the mask of blood.

"Those things are turning humans into...*themselves?*"

"More or less," Kane answered quietly. "Hybrids to inherit the Earth. And you've been helping them."

Salvo laughed suddenly, a hollow braying of pain. "Finish what you started, Kane. Chill me."

Kane shook his head, pulling Salvo to his feet.

"Chill me," he repeated, a beseeching note in his voice.

"You're not getting off that easy, Salvo, brother, enemy, traitor to humanity. You're going to live with this like the rest of us."

Salvo looked toward Banks, reached for him in a pleading gesture. Then he began sobbing like a brokenhearted child.

Chapter 21

Brigid entered the dispensary and for a couple of seconds had difficulty locating Domi. The girl's marble whiteness blended in with the stark bedsheets. She had barely survived the gateway transition, and it had taken DeFore several hours to stabilize her condition. Still, it was guarded and her prognosis was equally so.

The nick to the artery had been sutured, but the shattered bone required extensive reconstructive surgery involving artificial replacement parts. DeFore had the training to perform the operation, but not the experience, and she wanted to postpone it until Domi was stronger.

A heavy bandage and dressing encased the girl's right shoulder. An IV bag hung to the left of the bed, dripping slowly into a shunt on her arm. Diagnostic scanners hummed purposefully, monitoring her heartbeat and respiration. Domi's sedated sleep was fitful, and she murmured and twitched.

Lakesh occupied the far bed, inside a screened partition. He also had an IV drip, but he was awake, staring at the wall as though it were a window. Some of the color had returned to his face, but he still looked terribly haggard. Tears formed pools with a pale blue bottom in his eye sockets. He blinked when

Brigid stepped inside the screen, and the tears ran down his seamed cheeks. He tried to smile at her.

Disconcerted by the sight of the tears, she said only, "You look better."

Lakesh nodded and reached for a water cup on a bedside table. He couldn't quite touch it, and Brigid stepped closer to get it for him. He drank slowly.

"DeFore wants me to drink a half liter of fluids every hour," he said in a weak voice.

"You're dehydrated," Brigid told him inanely.

Lakesh replaced the cup on the table. "Physically and emotionally."

From a pocket of her bodysuit, Brigid took out his spare pair of glasses with the hearing aid attached to the right earpiece. Handing them to him, she said, "I thought you might want them in case you feel like reading while you convalesce."

He accepted them but didn't put them on. "Where is Salvo?"

"In the third-floor cell, the one with padded walls. Good thing this place has them."

Lakesh closed his eyes. "Cerberus was a military installation, after all."

"I wanted to put him under a suicide watch, but Kane countermanded it. He said if Salvo could figure out a way to chill himself in the cell, he was welcome to do it."

Lakesh didn't reply, and kept his eyes closed.

Brigid gazed at him, thinking sadly how Lakesh looked more like an apparition from a past age than ever before. Only a few of his injuries required treatment other than antiseptic and small bandages, and DeFore had put him on a strict regimen of antibiotics for his pre-pneumonic condition. His true wounds couldn't be treated with medicines or bandages. More tears trickled from beneath Lakesh's closed lids.

She asked, "Why are you crying?"

He didn't answer immediately. After a long period of silence, he said in a thick, flat voice, "I weep for you, for Domi, for everyone in the villes and the Outlands. I weep for the lost souls of humanity. And I weep most of all, and I cannot help it, for myself."

Brigid felt the pain radiating from the roots of his soul, and tears stung her own eyes. She took his hand, noting absently how cold it felt, perhaps a carry over from the century he had spent in cryogenic freeze.

"I sacrificed everything to serve the god of science," he said, "to break down all the barriers between the known and the unknown. When I allowed myself to think of them at all, I convinced myself humankind would only benefit in the long run. Now we've reached the finish line of that long run. There is no hope, no future. I lied, manipulated and deceived so I could bring about a new hope, a new future. All that's left are the falsehoods and deceptions."

Lakesh rolled his head on the pillow. "Kane was right, you know. I *am* a self-deluded egomaniac, no different than the barons. Worse, actually. But I tried, goddammit, I really tried to change things."

He opened his eyes, then squeezed them shut again. Softly he added, "But I failed."

Brigid didn't speak for a moment, wondering if he could be suffering a complete breakdown. She tightened her grip on his hand. "Maybe you didn't fail. Did anyone brief you on our mission to Ireland?"

"No," he intoned. "DeFore commented that you returned from there in a rather unorthodox manner."

Brigid forced herself to chuckle. "She has a gift for understatement. We used your interphaser to get back."

At first Lakesh seemed determined not to consider the implications of her statement. But he was a scientist first, a self-pitying victim second, so he opened his eyes. Interest and skepticism glinted in them.

"It wasn't designed to do that," he said. "You took a very big risk. You could have been trapped in the quantum flow, lost in the fabric of hyperdimensional space-time."

"We very nearly were." She said no more, but watched closely to gauge his reaction.

It wasn't long in coming. He raised his head from the pillow, squinted at her and demanded, "Explain."

She did as best she could, straightforwardly telling everything that had happened to her, Kane, Grant and Domi between the time the interphaser was activated in Newgrange until their arrival back in Cerberus.

At the end of ten minutes, Lakesh was sitting up, twirling his eyeglasses around by the earpiece and very nearly bouncing up and down in delighted fascination. He clapped his hands and almost pulled the IV shunt from his arm.

"Goddamn!" he exclaimed. "*Goddamn!* This is extraordinary! More than extraordinary! I don't have a word to describe it. Do you know what this means?"

Without waiting for her reply, he blurted, "Strongbow's so-called Singularity was like a rotating black hole, creating both an inner and outer event horizon.

The interphaser's field adjusted to its geometrics and created a *double* event horizon! Whereas the Cerberus mat-trans network are gateways to instantaneous travel through linear space rather than time, I always knew you cannot have one without factoring in the other.''

His lips drew down in a frown. "You say you had to leave the interphaser behind in England."

She nodded. "But I pulled its memory disk. We won't know if it's intact until you decrypt it."

Lakesh began worrying at the IV drip. He lifted his voice in a shout. "DeFore! Unhook me! Brigid, be the dear I know you are and fetch the doctor or one of her assistants. And while you're at it, please bring me some clothes."

OVER DEFORE'S HEATED and profane protests, Lakesh checked himself out of the dispensary. His only concession to his medical condition was the wheelchair in which he allowed Brigid to roll him into the control complex. He paused briefly at Domi's bedside to give her cheek a caress.

Brigid parked him before the master console with its four-foot VGA monitor screen. He took the interphaser's CD-ROM and inserted it into the drive port. Brigid silently watched him work, admiring the way his hands moved rapidly and deftly over the keyboard, as if he were a pianist playing a particularly difficult sonata.

When columns of numbers and formulas scrolled across the screen, he thrust his head forward, muttering under his breath. An array of geometric shapes flashed in dizzying profusion—ellipses, overlapping spirals, curves, and triangles so complex Brigid could make no sense of them.

Lakesh cackled in excitement, like an infant at a surprise birthday party. He crowed, "Unbelievable! Un-*damn*-believable!"

He swung his head in Brigid's direction, a grin splitting his face. "This data bridges the gap between the theoretical and the practical."

He turned back to the screen, fingers clattering madly over the keyboard. He mumbled, "Burr and Spiros Marcuse and the other Operation Chronos scientists proceeded from the assumption that the nature of time is like an ever-rolling river. I always found that approach unsatisfying and limiting—rivers have banks, do they not, branches from the main water course...the very existence of time depends on the presence of space, and space can be measured...."

His words trailed off for a moment, then returned, strong and decisive. "I have very little in the database pertaining to the mechanics of Operation Chronos, but I'm cross-referencing what I do have with the interphaser's memory. Hopefully I'll be able to arrive at sequential field equations. If those check out, the results can be duplicated using the mat-trans unit."

Brigid knew the mat-trans inducers were responsible for the initial Operation Chronos breakthroughs, since both relied on quantum mechanics.

"If the results can be duplicated," she asked, "then what?"

"We should have a temporal dilator—theoretically."

She smiled wryly at his use of the qualifier.

Lakesh continued, "Strongbow built his Singularity along the same principles as my interphaser, and though we both approached the actual construction from different directions, we accidentally wound up in the same place. We were both looking for some form of rapid-transit system along hyperdimensional paths, using naturally occurring quantum vortices.

"The interphaser and the Singularity caused an overlapping of what physicists used to refer to as the third and fourth dimensions—a mingling of spatial and temporal distance. I damn myself for not understanding the energy-interchange ratio."

"I'm sure Strongbow does, too," Brigid remarked.

"Yes," he replied absently. "A pity his device was destroyed."

"I don't think you'll find much agreement on that score." She spoke more harshly than she intended.

He glanced up at her, blinking owlishly in momentary confusion. He cast her a shamed smile. "Forgive me. No, of course, such a device in the hands of an evil creature like Strongbow is unthinkable."

She didn't smile at his touch of melodrama, because it was all too true.

Propping his chin on a fist, Lakesh examined the data racing across the screen. "The laws of physics are immutable in appearance only, due to our own limited perceptions. That was one problem both Project Cerberus and Operation Chronos personnel constantly grappled with. Another was computing the precise temporal transfer points. Cerberus moved things from place to place. Chronos had to deal with moving things from place to place and time to time. You cannot imagine the awesome amount of power and programming that were required."

She took a deep breath. "Perhaps not. But here's another problem you'll have to deal with. Kane."

Distractedly he said, "Once the cross-indexing and correlations are complete, I should be able to satisfactorily answer even his questions."

Brigid shifted uncomfortably. "You'd better be—and not just about Operation Chronos, either."

He tapped a pair of keys as if he hadn't heard. Then his shoulders jerked as if he had just received a blow. He rolled the wheelchair away from the console and looked up at her with strained smile. "About the bio-link transponders?"

"That, and another issue."

"Salvo."

"Yes."

Lakesh nodded regretfully, pursing his lips. "Questions that need to be answered. And if I answer them, he—all of you—might become living examples of the bromide 'Ignorance is bliss.' I suppose there's no putting him off."

"Not this time." She tossed her head. "Kane took a tremendous risk going after you."

"Yes, I know, I'm grateful. With the way the baron hates him—"

"That's not exactly what I mean. He's been through an emotional and physical wringer these last few months, partly due to you. DeFore told me he's showing early symptoms of post-traumatic stress syndrome. You're familiar with it?"

Lakesh's answer was barely audible. "I am."

"He's always been temperamental, with a tendency to brood, but his leadership qualities kept it in check. Now that control is slipping. If he loses it altogether, not even Grant can predict what he'll do. Did you know Kane was catatonic for two days after our return? Though he suffered a mild concussion, De-Fore's opinion is that his coma was due to a strong subconscious desire to escape what has become for him an intolerable life situation.''

Brigid paused for a meaningful moment, then said quietly, ''He only came after you because of the possibility of going back in time and changing things. That's his focus now. But he's tired. He's angry. He's lost his center. He feels you betrayed him.''

''I lied by omission, but I did not betray him.''

''I know that. But you're going to have to give him a reason to trust you. Exploring the possibilities of the Omega Path is one way.''

''Even if I do, and come up with a workable plan, do *you* trust him to do the right thing?''

'''To the gallows-afoot—and after,''' she snapped.

He smiled sadly. ''Kipling, 'The Thousandth Man.' I always prefered Kahlil Gibran and Leonard Cohen myself.''

Lakesh bowed his head. Brigid simply stood and looked at him. For a moment, the only sound in the big room was the whir of hard-drive units.

Sighing, Lakesh ran a hand over his face. ''Go get him and Grant. Best to have this over and done with so we can move on...or not.''

Chapter 22

Kane and Grant did not take seats. Instead, they stood shoulder to shoulder, staring down implacably at Lakesh in his wheelchair. Both of their faces were as hard as if they had been chiseled from granite and teak, as though they had already made up their minds on a matter and dared Lakesh to change them.

Kane's narrowed eyes glittered in a way that made Brigid distinctly uncomfortable. She hadn't spoken to him in the past eight hours, and if anything, his dark mood had blackened. She tried to convince herself that he wouldn't attack Lakesh like he had Salvo, no matter the provocation, but she prayed the old man chose his words carefully. Not just out of consideration for Kane's unstable emotional state, but for his own safety.

Judging by the steely glint in Grant's eyes, neither she nor Lakesh could rely on him to intervene if Kane's rage slipped its leash. Though Grant had not spoken of it, he was angry about Domi, partially placing the blame on Lakesh, but shouldering the rest of it himself.

Lakesh ran a hand over his deeply furrowed forehead and began speaking, quickly and to the point. "I didn't tell you about the biolink transponders because I knew you wouldn't agree to their insertion at such an early stage of our relationship."

"You got that pegged," rumbled Grant.

Lakesh acknowledged the comment with a short nod. "Secondarily I wasn't certain how far I could trust you. Both of you had served as Magistrates for most of your lives. That kind of conditioning is very difficult to overcome. Therefore, I needed to keep track of you, just in case you weakened and returned to Cobaltville to betray Cerberus. I had particularly strong doubts about you, Kane. I misjudged you very badly and I apologize.

"I did not realize that men of honor could still exist in this world. Certainly they were a vanishingly small minority even before the nukecaust."

"Thanks," Kane said sarcastically. "Apology not accepted."

Lakesh coughed into his hand, but the bubbling of fluid in his lungs was no longer as pronounced. "As to why the transponders resemble the insignia of Overproject Excalibur, which is the symbol for the Directorate, that is easy to explain. As I told you, I was revived from cryogenic sleep some fifty years ago to help stablize the unification of the baronies. I had access to the Totality Concept redoubts and I took what I thought I might need from them.

"Inasmuch as the instrument to make the transponders had been created by Excalibur technicians, the emblem's appearance is self-explanatory. Also, that symbol could conceivably buy you time if you were ever apprehended in an Archon-controlled area...as you very nearly were in Dulce. Physical examinations include ultraviolet scans. The Excalibur markings would sow the seeds of confusion, at least for a while."

Neither Grant nor Kane showed any emotion. Hoping to initiate some kind of interaction, Brigid said, "That sounds reasonable."

Kane said, "Deceiving us at the same time you sent us to hell-and-gone to risk our asses is no different than what Salvo did when we were Mags, Lakesh." His lips stretched tight, and his mouth became a grim slash of anger. "Is it because of Salvo you had doubts about me in particular?"

Lakesh nodded. "I told you when you first arrived here your case had already been decided, remember?"

"Yeah. You said I'd been selected to play a role, but you had no idea I'd break my conditioning so quickly. You never did explain what you meant by that."

"I shall do so now, friend Kane."

"Don't call me that." Kane's voice cracked like the sudden snap of a whip. "You're not my friend. In fact, depending on what you say next, you may need that chair for the rest of your life."

Lakesh sighed. "And perhaps I deserve worse. Kane, I knew your grandfather and your father. I knew Salvo's grandfather and father. When I determined to build a resistance movement against the Directorate, some forty years ago, I knew I needed warriors. The Salvo and Kane lines appeared exceptionally promising, so I checked into the genetic records to find the qualifications I deemed necessary."

"What kind of qualifications?" Despite herself, Brigid's question was palpable with suspicion.

"High intelligence, a capacity for independent, resourceful action, courage, compassion. Whether some of those traits are hereditary is debatable, but I still selected genotypes which were the best of the best. I used the Directorate's own fixation with purity control against them.''

Lakesh paused, wetting his cracked lips with the tip of his pale tongue. "Kane, I'm putting my life in your hands telling you this. There's little point in prettying it up, so I will be blunt. You will no doubt think me a low-down schemer and conniver, and I will not presume to debate you on that point. I ask you, though, not to kill me until you've heard me out.''

Folding his arms over his chest, Kane said tersely, "Get on with it.''

Lakesh cleared his throat. "I decided to play God, at least on a modest scale. After analyzing the DNA data in the files, I harvested genetic material from your father and Salvo's father.''

"Why them?'' demanded Kane. "Why not our grandfathers?''

"They were both killed putting down a Pit uprising.''

Kane's eyebrows lifted slightly. "I knew that about my own grandfather, but it's news to me about Salvo's.''

"Yes, that's a bond you two could have shared. Among others. Alas, it was not meant to be.''

"Leather the violins. Go on.''

"In predark days, fertility drugs were administered to cause women to ovulate as many as six to eight eggs per menstrual cycle. Overproject Excalibur subdivisions developed a technique to reproduce multiple copies of a given egg-and-sperm sample.''

"What's that got to do with me?" Kane demanded impatiently.

"Hear me out," Lakesh replied. "I used those techniques to select warriors for my cause. Secretly I ensured that the purity-control testing process and experimentation would take place on the same genetic material each time, thus making evaluation of the procedure much more straightforward."

"You produced embryos like that?" Brigid asked.

"Embryos and fetuses, then infants. The first infant was Salvo. At first, his test results looked very promising, but some unfortunate recessive traits began to show up. Nothing major manifested itself, but as he grew, these traits tended to mitigate the results I desired.

"I learned from him, however, and thawed another embryo, and through early gene therapy managed to suppress the traits I did not want, while simultaneously enhancing those I required."

Lakesh looked levelly into Kane's eyes. "You were that embryo, Kane. You and Salvo are siblings, brothers, twins springing from the same egg-and-sperm sample, separated by seven years. When you're dealing with in vitro fertilization, that separation of time is irrelevant."

Grant shook his head in frustration. "You said you did this secretly. Surely Salvo's and Kane's fathers were aware of what you were doing."

"Would that they had not. Or least, the elder Salvo had not."

"Why?" asked Kane.

"Obviously I didn't tell them my true aims. After all, I was a physicist cast in the role of an archivist, pretending to be a geneticist, manipulating a political system that was still in a state of flux.

"When Salvo was six years old his undesirable traits manifested themselves, I decided it was time for you to be born, Kane. You needed all the edge I could covertly give you, and that included nurturing."

Kane scowled. "What do you mean by that?"

"In a word," Lakesh answered, "mothering. You do remember your mother, don't you?"

"Of course." Kane felt the brief, sad ache that always arrived in the wake of memories about his mother. They were dim, ghostly. Ville society was based on a patriarchal structure, and motherhood, as well as marriage, was viewed as a strictly temporary arrangement.

"She was one of my agents. I had arranged matters so she would mother Salvo. When I realized he was not working out to my specifications, I arranged it so she left him and became your mother. It was all done very aboveboard, albeit very unethically."

"And cold-blooded as all hell, too," Brigid said quietly.

Lakesh nodded in acceptance of the charge. "Guilty. But in a war, you employ any tactics that may give you a leg up on the enemy."

Kane glared down at him, anger seeming to paralyze his vocal cords. Finally he said, "Experiments. Salvo and I were experiments."

"Except he was the failure. You were the success."

"You took away his mother, took away his father's mate. And he knows why, doesn't he?"

"Yes. The senior Salvo made a formal protest. I

spoke to him in private and told him that his son was really the issue of your father's genes, Kane. In return for his silence, I promised once again to arrange things. I arranged a high position and preferential treatment for the boy. I also promised to arrange far more unpleasant things if he did not cooperate.

"He knew I had the power to do that, so he accepted the situation, but he passed on his anger and shame to young Salvo. As the years grew, he broke his vow of secrecy and told the boy some of what he knew, evidently without bringing my name into it. Regardless, I'm sure it was a tale twisted to fit his own narrow frame of reference.

"He passed on that jealousy, that need for revenge, building a generational enmity where none need have existed. Salvo was damaged at the same time—and with the same impersonal efficiency that you had been nurtured. And it's all my fault."

Lakesh made a vague hand gesture, and his voice sounded resigned. "That's your and Salvo's history Kane, and my part in it."

"How did my father end up here, with you?"

"As you know, he was a member of the Trust. I undertook quite the risk, taking him into my confidence, but for once my judgment of character was sound. He joined me willingly three years ago. He had high hopes you would do the same one day, and I intended to indoctrinate you slowly over a period of years.

"However, I could not predict your actions. You flew in the face of my extrapolations of your psychology. When Salvo recruited you into the Trust, I feared all my work would be undone. I had no idea you would feel such a strong sense of responsibility to Brigid. Truth to tell, I'm still a bit confused by how quickly you threw away everything you had in order to save her life.''

He chuckled bitterly. ''But here you are, just like I planned and hoped. The means were different, but the ultimate result was the same, although at least five years ahead of my original schedule. Obviously I had not factored friend Grant or darling Domi into the master equation. Random elements, but welcome ones, nonetheless.''

No one said anything. They watched Lakesh intently. Finally Brigid broke the silence. ''How many other people's lives have you 'arranged' like this?''

Lakesh turned toward her. ''What you're really asking is if I arranged yours.''

''Yes, that's exactly what I'm asking.''

''What would you say?''

She cast her eyes downward, not answering.

Lakesh heaved a sigh of weariness, of exhaustion. ''You, Kane, Grant and Domi are fierce, unpredictable, wild at times, stubborn and certainly *not* the kind of warriors I had envisioned to oppose the Directorate.

''Despite all of that, or maybe because of it, you're the only human beings I've met in two centuries who have given me any hope. It was because of all of you I didn't break under the torture. I knew none of you would.''

Kane held up a hand. ''All right, Lakesh. Sentiment doesn't become you. I'll accept what you've just told me at face value. It fills in a lot of blank spaces in my own life and conforms with my memories—that is if you haven't 'arranged' my memories like you did my genes.''

"Rest easy on that score. I didn't.''

"So you're not going to chill him?'' Grant asked.

Kane showed his teeth in a hard, humorless grin. "Not today. If he's figured out what happened to us during the interphase transit, maybe not ever, because he can 'arrange' things so he'll never have a reason to scheme and connive.''

Lakesh's expression didn't alter. "My most heartfelt wish, I assure you. Brigid has already related to me her brief visit to the past, and imparted Domi's experiences. Kane, Grant, I need every detail, every impression of your sojourns and what you witnessed.''

His eyes shifted to Grant. "I am particularly interested in your encounter with Colonel C. W. Thrush. That is a name I never thought to hear again.''

NEITHER KANE'S nor Grant's report took very long. Lakesh put sharp questions to them regarding specific times, clothing styles and language. When they were done, Lakesh leaned back in his chair, eyes strangely vacant. His thoughts could not be read.

He murmured, "Spirits on the temporal stream, bouncing from the banks, carried along the currents and eddies.''

"What are you mumbling about?'' Kane asked.

"The four of you were drawn, perhaps *swept* would be more accurate, to four focal points in the time plane. Each event affected not only the future developments of technology but the political landscape, as well. The common, unifying element is the man in black, the so-called Colonel Thrush.''

"You said you'd heard of him?'' inquired Grant.

"Yes, even met him once. His credentials were those of a U.S. Air Force officer, but I knew he was a spook.''

"Spook?'' Brigid eyed him curiously.

Lakesh smiled sourly. "An active member of the intelligence community, like the CIA, the NSA, the DARPA. He was present a number of times at the installation in Dulce, particularly when one of the Overproject Whisper divisions was conducting tests. As I recall, he showed the most interest in Operation Chronos.''

"Hold on,'' Grant objected. "If Domi saw him in Germany in 1945, and I saw him in Washington in 2001, wouldn't he be as old as…well, as old as you? The man I saw couldn't have been much over thirty-five, forty at the outside.''

Lakesh wagged a good-natured, admonishing finger. "You forget the matters with which we deal, friend Grant. It's patently obvious Colonel Thrush was a chrononaut, dispatched back in time to begin the process of altering certain events to ensure the ultimate victory of the Archon Directorate.

"I informed you months ago that the Archons— through human intermediaries—had allied themselves with the Third Reich, allowing German scientists to begin work on what evolved into the Totality Concept. By killing Hitler, they silenced the one man who could have revealed the Archons' presence to the world.

"He might not have been believed, but had he lived

long enough to stand trial, Hitler would have supplied enough verifiable testimony to set a concerted opposition in motion. There may not have been a Cold War, perhaps America and Russia would have remained allies.''

Lakesh shrugged his shoulders and smiled whimsically. ''So it goes. The presence of C. W. Thrush at the Roswell incident doesn't surprise me, since that was such a flashpoint in U.S. government–Archon relations. Brigid claimed Thrush dictated terms to Admiral Roscoe Hillenkoetter, director of the CIA from 1947 to 1950. Regarding the UFO phenomenon, he was quoted as saying, 'It is time for the truth to be brought out.' As you know, it never was.''

The smile on Lakesh's face faltered, then vanished. ''I always suspected the Directorate played an active role in the assassination of President Kennedy, not simply because he presented a danger to the furtherance of their plans, but because his brutal murder inflicted such incalculable trauma to the collective American psyche. The bullets which killed John F. Kennedy also put an end to the national identity of America. The country never became a unified whole again.''

Lakesh stopped speaking, his eyes distant and clouded. After a moment, he straightened up in the wheelchair. ''Friend Grant, your tale of Colonel Thrush in the Russian embassy is the most interesting. I find what he said to you about all the scattered threads of time being sewn together in a Gordian knot particularly intriguing, as well as his reference to 'time squared.'''

''Why?'' asked Kane.

"Do you know what a Gordian knot is?"

Crisply Brigid stated, "Gordius, an ancient king of Phrygia, tied a knot that was so fiendishly complicated, it could not be untied. According to prophecy, it was to be undone only by the man who should rule Asia. Alexander the Great, unable to work out the knot, simply cut it in two with his sword."

"In other words," Lakesh said, "a Gordian knot refers to a difficulty that can be overcome only by bold or unorthodox measures. At any rate, Colonel Thrush's suspicion that all of you were the same entity, perhaps even chrononauts like himself, dispatched by Operation Chronos, shows he is not infallible."

"You think he's an Archon agent?" Grant asked.

"What else could he be? He appeared at pivotal points in twentieth-century history, branches of the time river, and made the revisions that changed the course into one of many parallel paths—and brought us to this final, dreadful result."

"I don't get this," rasped Grant in irritation. "You said Chronos had only one success with transporting living matter from the past."

"One *recorded* success," Lakesh replied smoothly. "Remember, after that initial success, Operation Chronos personnel and equipment were moved out of Dulce to new quarters. Chicago, I think. Besides, Colonel Thrush was injected *into* the past, not trawled from it."

"The question still remains," Brigid argued. "He still had to be retrieved from the past, didn't he, and reinserted into the different time periods? He hadn't appeared to have aged between 1945 and 2001. Living matter ages.''

"Perhaps Colonel Thrush is not living matter as we understand it," Lakesh said.

Kane made a grunting sound of impatience. "You've lost me."

"I'm simply speculating out loud, friend Kane. Is it all right if I call you that again?"

Rolling his eyes ceilingward, Kane demanded, "Let's get to the goddamn point. Can we or can't we go back in time? And if we can, will we be ghosts like we were before?"

"You weren't ghosts, not in the accepted definition of the word," Lakesh declared. "As Brigid already assumed, your noncorporeal condition was the result of the interphase field. Evidently the field temporarily amplified the power of the electromagnetic energy of the brain, what we call the mind. Presumably your minds were able to break free of the synaptic structure of the brain and bypassed the four dimensions.

"Truly, the phenomenon wasn't that much different than the transition you undergo during a normal mat-trans jump, except in this instance the cohesion field that held your individual patterns was not quite as strong. In the parlance of Project Cerberus, it's called the 'quincunx effect,' a nanosecond of time when lower dimensional space is phased into a higher-dimensional space along the quantum pathway."

"That doesn't answer my question," said Kane stiffly.

Lakesh turned his chair back to the keyboard console. "I'll try to answer it in very short order."

"How long?" Brigid asked.

Lakesh's lips quirked in his old impish smile. "That," he announced, "only time will tell."

Chapter 23

Within hours, Lakesh had written the Omega Path program. After reviewing it, Bry was very unenthusiastic about the entire concept, particularly because it entailed realigning the gateway's matter-stream modulations.

"The mat-trans unit is designed to pierce three-dimensional space along a curved hypertrajectory," he argued. "The fourth dimension is nonspatial in nature. You can't transmit a matter stream along a nonspatial dimension without losing pattern cohesion."

"Said the novice to the master of the art," Lakesh replied with good-humored disdain.

Bry flushed a bit in embarrassment, but he stuck to his scientific guns. "Without access to Operation Chronos specs, we can't recreate what they accomplished."

"I don't intend to," retorted Lakesh, pointing to the shapes, symbols and twenty-digit numerical sequences on the computer screen. "Chronos techs used the fundamentals of the mat-trans inducers to break the chronon structure. They sent remote probes down the line into the past, but they did not utilize the quincunx effect to its full potential. That is what we will do, and we will begin work now."

The alterations took only two days, and Kane,

Grant and Brigid stayed out of their way. The primary work involved reprogramming the mainframe with the logarithmic data copied from the interphaser's memory disk.

A new dedicated control console was installed, and since it was built for function, it didn't conform to the streamlined symmetry of the rest of the equipment. It bristled with thousands of tiny electrodes and complexities of naked circuitry, leading to a switchboard containing relays and readout screens. Lakesh commented dryly that it looked like something put together from odds and ends found in Tom Edison's basement. Bry wasn't sure if his work was being praised or criticized.

Lakesh roughly sketched out his idea of a test probe. Rouch and Cotta took his loose specs and built a small vid camera contrivance mounted within a shielded vanadium-alloy shell.

Bry doubted it would work. "Even with the shielding," he argued, "it'll be exposed to enough energy that the electronics in it will freeze up."

Lakesh related how Operation Chronos had sent remote vid probes down the time line during its initial experiments and that they had returned essentially intact.

Frustrated, Bry exclaimed, "How many times do I have to tell you we're not doing the same things they were doing!"

Lakesh only smiled at him patronizingly.

Early in the evening of the second day, Lakesh announced he was ready for the attempt to forge the Omega Path. He summoned Brigid, Kane and Grant so they could witness failure or success or something in between. Bry dourly noted everyone should be prepared for the former and consider themselves lucky if the latter happened.

Although Lakesh was considerably stronger, his color better, he had conceded to DeFore's orders to confine his movements to the wheelchair. He sat in front of the new console, eyes alight with excitement and anticipation. Brigid wondered if he had looked and acted that way right before Project Cerberus made its first successful transport of organic matter.

"The main mat-trans controls have been rerouted through this board," Lakesh explained. "The unit's destination lock has been reset to focus not just on a point in space, but in time."

"Which is where and when?" Kane asked.

Lakesh shrugged, waving a dismissive hand. "I can't be sure of either. The time lock is set for the turn of this century, with a factored-in leeway of five years. The destination lock is open, so the matter stream will home in on whatever gateway was functioning within this hemisphere, ninety-five to a hundred years ago."

"Give or take five years?" Grant's tone was deeply skeptical. "Who would have been operating the mat-trans network that long ago?"

"Perhaps no one," replied Lakesh airily. "Or perhaps someone will receive quite the surprise."

Bry placed the vid probe in the center of the gateway chamber. It was a small dome sheathed in gray alloy. The tiny camera lens protruded from a round opening. A nearby monitor showed the clear image of brown-hued armaglass walls.

Leaving the chamber, he stood by the door and called, "Ready for the autosequence initiator."

Loudly Lakesh responded, "Button her up, Mr. Bry."

Bry pushed the door shut and stepped hastily back. Immediately a soft drone began. Lakesh reached a hand to close switches on the board. Indicator lights flared brilliantly, registering full power. Dancing lines raced across readout screens.

The drone rose, not to a cyclonic shriek, but to a deep, rumbling roar. Brigid shifted her gaze back and forth from the probe's interior view displayed on the monitor to the outside of the chamber. On the vid screen, mist shot through with miniature lightnings billowed up from the floor plates. Through the arma-glass walls, light pulsed, flared, bloomed.

The view on the monitor broke apart in jagged pixels.

"The probe is away!" Lakesh crowed. "To where and when I do not know."

The roar continued from the mat-trans chamber, rising in volume. On the readout screens connected to the switchboard, sine and cosine waves stretched, pulsated, intertwined. Lakesh stared at them. "Interference pattern!"

Bry shouted, "The goddamn thing is still cycling! It should be shutting down!"

At the alarmed, near panicky note in his voice, Grant, Brigid and Kane went to the doorway of the anteroom. Crooked fingers of energy stabbed through the gateway chamber. They watched with awe and dread as thousands of crackling threads of light coalesced in the center of the unit.

Over her shoulder, Brigid called, "What's happening?"

Lakesh hunched over the board, sweat sheening his face. He stammered, "I—I'm not sure. It's almost as if we've intercepted a jet, a stream of electrons—no, that can't be. That would mean someone or something is trying to dilate the temporal continuum from another mat-trans unit. Whatever it is, it's coming into phase."

Gushing lines of energy formed a luminous cloud within the chamber. Almost faster than the eye could perceive, the cloud grew more dense and definite of outline. Through the walls, they vaguely discerned a human figure.

The roar abruptly dropped to a mutter. Bry cried, "It's cycling down, and there's somebody in there!"

"Somebody, maybe," Kane said grimly. "We don't know who or what the hell it is."

Lakesh wheeled himself into the anteroom, breath coming in excited gasps as he circled the big table. "If our matter-stream transfer worked across the fourth dimension, our guest might be from another time plane. Bry! Open the door."

Bry hesitated. "There's still a lot of wild energy in there."

"Do it, goddamn you!"

Bry wrenched the handle of the door with a convulsive movement. He pulled it backward, trembling slightly, ready to slam it shut on its counterbalanced hinges.

Everyone stiffened in amazement at the figure standing in the chamber. Because a faint halo surrounded him, like cobwebs spun of shimmering light, there was an unearthliness about him.

A tall, lean man in a frayed black frock coat stood there, his long gray hair spilling past his shoulders. Cracked and scuffed riding boots rose to just below his knees. He held an ebony cane in both hands, clutching it to his chest. Light sparkled from the silver snarling lion's head topping it.

The blue eyes in the lined face were alive with intelligence, and his slender frame somehow suggested an aristocratic nature, despite his unique, somewhat shabby clothing. Surveying the people standing in the anteroom, he grinned nervously, displaying excellent teeth.

His first words were strange and startling, uttered in a deep, resonant voice. "By the Three Kennedys! Something tells me I'm not in Omaha."

Lakesh wheeled himself closer to the chamber, pushing between Grant and Kane. The man took a cautious half step back, twisting the lion's head on his cane. He pulled a half foot of glittering, razored steel from the ebony sheath, a gesture more of warning than threat.

The distant mutter suddenly climbed to a roar again. The halo dancing around the man's body exuded curling, crackling strings of energy. He looked around swiftly, eyes showing fearful bewilderment.

"It's cycling again," Bry declared, still hanging on to the door. "We've got to seal the chamber."

Lakesh hesitated, squinting as the shimmer around the man built to a blinding borealis.

Bry half shouted, "We don't know the wavelengths

of that radiation! It could be fatal, could contaminate the redoubt if it's not contained!''

Lakesh gestured sharply. ''Do it.''

Bry hurled his weight against the door, and it closed on the glowing, hazy figure. Almost immediately, a star seemed to go nova behind the armaglass, bringing a millisecond of eye-searing brilliance followed by a millisecond of utter silence.

The roar peaked, dropping swiftly to a grating, irregular whine.

Stumbling back a pace, bumping into the table, Grant furiously knuckled his eyes. ''Son of a *bitch!* What's going on?''

The whine wheezed down to faint, distant susurrus of electronic sound. When everyone's overstressed optic nerves recovered, they saw not even a dimmest candlelight flicker within the chamber.

''Open it,'' Lakesh directed Bry.

Blinking and murmuring peevishly under his breath, Bry lifted up the handle, swinging the door open. The little vid remote squatted on a hexagon, wisps of vapor curling around its metal skin.

Entering the chamber, Bry gingerly reached down for it. A tiny spark popped. He recoiled, cursing, shaking his stinging hand. He looked at Lakesh accusingly.

''Static build-up,'' said Lakesh calmly. ''To be expected.''

Bry cast him another sour look, and tentatively tapped the vanadium shell. ''It's cool.''

''Bring it out, please.''

As Bry bent down to pick it up, Brigid said

thoughtfully, "That man who appeared in the chamber—" She broke off, shaking her head.

"Yes?" Lakesh inquired.

"You've read the *Wyeth Codex,* haven't you?"

"Of course. I was the one responsible for disseminating it through the Historical Divisions of the villes. But unlike you, I didn't memorize it."

The *Wyeth Codex* purported to be the journal of one Dr. Mildred Wyeth, a woman who had been in cryogenic suspension during the nukecaust. Revived a century later, she roamed Deathlands in the company of the legendary Ryan Cawdor. She made a record of her wanderings, as well as her thoughts, observations and speculations regarding the postskydark world. She was particularly suspicious of the redoubts and the Totality Concept.

The manuscript had been found and secretly spread among the archivists of the ville network as an example of the kinds of truth the barons wanted buried.

"One of her companions," said Brigid, "was allegedly the only recorded success of Operation Chronos. A Dr. T. A. Tanner, trawled from the late nineteenth century."

Understanding dawned in Lakesh's eyes. "Yes, of course. Now I remember. According to the *Codex,* his favorite expression was 'By the Three Kennedys.' A particularly vacuous expletive, in my opinion. But it's not possible we intercepted the Chronos matter stream. Tanner was trawled up the line in 1998. Our time lock was set for only a hundred or so years ago."

"After spending a couple of years in the twentieth century, Tanner was bumped a hundred years into the future," Brigid stated. "Maybe we intercepted that carrier wave."

Lakesh's face acquired new creases of concentration. "Or perhaps Tanner stumbled over time-dilation technology in some abandoned redoubt. Wasn't there a reference to an event like that in the *Codex?*"

"Brief and undetailed. Something relating to Chronos found in Puerto Rico. Wyeth really wasn't much for providing straight narratives."

Kane voiced an exasperated sigh. "Who cares? The only puzzle we should be trying to work out is if the Omega Path can take us back in time."

Lakesh nodded in quick agreement, smiling abashedly. "Very true, friend Kane. Let's find out what sights our little probe recorded."

Chapter 24

As it turned out, nothing but variegated streaks of light showed up on the tape, indicating exposure to high levels of electromagnetic radiation.

Bry couldn't resist a smug "I figured as much."

Lakesh was disappointed but not discouraged. "Regardless of the video record, all our instruments showed we bridged the abyss between this temporal plane and another."

"We don't know that for sure," Kane said. "We could've intercepted a carrier wave from another gateway unit."

Lakesh stabbed a finger toward the big Mercator-relief map spanning the wall. "If that was the case, the origin point would be registered there. No, we did it, all right."

"What next?" asked Grant. "Send us back to January 19, 2001, to the Russian embassy?"

"No, that's not the way. Security would never let you past the reception desk. Injecting any of you into the past strictly to undo what Colonel Thrush might have done is too risky, on a number of counts."

"I thought *un*doing is the whole point of the Omega Path," Brigid said.

"Your thinking is correct, as far as it extends." Lakesh steepled his fingers under his chin. "But the ways of achieving an objective are many, and often they are found by traveling *away* from the objective.''

He swept his gaze over the three of them. ''The next step in the process requires a great deal of contemplation and research. I'll let you know when I've reached a conclusion. Mr. Bry, remain here with me, please. There are technical matters to discuss.''

Although annoyed by the abrupt dismissal, Grant, Brigid and Kane were just as glad to be left out of a no-doubt heated exchange spoken in technobabble. Grant went to the dispensary to check on Domi. Brigid walked with Kane along the corridor as far as the elevator.

''Are you headed for the cafeteria?'' she asked.

''No.''

''Salvo?''

''Yes.''

''You finally decided to tell him what Lakesh told you,'' she declared. ''Do you think it'll make a damn bit of difference to him?''

Kane paused before pushing the button to open the door panel. ''I couldn't say.''

''He may have been victimized by Lakesh's schemes,'' Brigid said reasonably, ''but he's way past the age of accountability for his own actions. Whether he let his father's anger and resentment poison his own life is immaterial. Whether you're his brother is irrelevant. He's a petty, sadistic, vicious, evil man. Revenge for you being born is his guiding passion.''

Kane punched the button, and the door rolled aside. ''Tell me something I don't know. But I thought you believed in redemption.''

''I don't know what gave you that impression. Just

because I didn't care to watch you murder him in front of me doesn't mean I think there's anything worth salvaging there.''

He stepped into the elevator, smiling wryly. "Maybe not. I'm new at this. I never had a brother before.''

Tonelessly she said, "Just your luck it has to be him.''

As the elevator dropped him to the third floor, he wondered why he hadn't told her about his dream, about what his father had said regarding the Other. Kane realized it wasn't so much he feared she wouldn't understand, but that she would.

Mentally he traced the sequence of events leading up to this moment. Due to a probability wave dysfunction, the world had been consumed by a nuclear firestorm; the Program of Unification had imposed the tyranny of the barons; Lakesh had played God to create opposition; Salvo and Kane had been born and Salvo hated Kane; and now Salvo waited in an underground padded cell for his brother to visit.

Of course, Lakesh had not begun it—it was the Archons who were responsible, though as they'd discovered on their last mission, the origin of the Archons was itself a legitimate question.

Why was it, Kane wondered, they never managed to lay their hands on the real culprits?

The bottom level of Cerberus was some 150 feet below solid, shielded rock. It held the nuclear generators, various maintenance and machine rooms and the air-conditioning core. A semidetached wing contained ten detention cubicles, all of them as nicely appointed as the average flat in the Cobaltville Enclaves.

Kane tapped in the sec code on the door leading to the wing, walked through a dimly lit corridor that had once been bisected by a wire-mesh security checkpoint and then to Salvo's cell. He looked through the small ob slit before unlocking the door.

The walls and floor were covered by a thick, quilted padding. Water was provided by a soft rubber hose that protruded only half an inch from a socket in the wall. A rimmed depression in a corner served as a toilet.

Salvo lay on his side, face turned toward the wall. A corner of a white bandage stood out brightly in the feeble light of the cubicle. He didn't move, but Kane saw the slow rise and fall of steady respiration. He punched the code into the keypad, and the door hissed aside.

Salvo slowly roused as Kane stepped in, stiffly pushing himself to a sitting position. He wore one of the Cerberus standard-issue white bodysuits and a non-standard-issue plastic splint on his nose. Both of his eyes were slits surrounded by swollen, bruised flesh. His puffy, discolored lower lip showed the six stitches Auerbach had sewn in it. A purple, banana-shaped swelling, partly covered by a bandage, ran the width of his forehead. Although his dentures had been returned to him, he still looked worse than Lakesh had only a few days before.

Kane leaned against the door. "Nice place, isn't it? Better than the cells on C or E Level."

Salvo grunted. "How long have I been down here?"

Kane made a casual show of checking his wrist chron. "About fifty-two hours, give or take a couple of minutes."

"What do you want?"

"To talk to you. Lakesh told me about me and you and how we were born. He was responsible for it, you know."

Salvo nodded. "Dad never said who it was, just that he was high in the baron's favor. Deep down, I guess I always suspected that bastard was behind it."

"Yeah," said Kane darkly. "Deep down. Why did you do it?"

"Do what?"

"Keep this from me for all these years…punish me for something neither one of us could help."

Salvo couldn't really sneer, but he snorted. "You were supposed to be better than me—smarter, stronger, more adaptable."

"And better looking, too," Kane interjected coldly. "So?"

"So, you're not. I set out to prove that you weren't."

"Prove to who?"

"*Me*, you dumb shit!" Salvo slapped his chest. "To my dad. And to you!"

"Pretty one-sided competition, since you didn't let me know I was on the playing field."

Salvo spread his hands in an expansive gesture. "Hey, I didn't say it was fair. That was the beauty of it, Kane. I turned and twisted and double-screwed you so many times, and you never knew why."

"Why did you recruit me into the Trust?"

Salvo opened his mouth to answer, closed it and

shook his head. "The temptation to assign you every filthy, soul-breaking job I could think of was too much to let pass, I guess."

Kane chuckled dryly. "You guess? I don't believe you, Salvo. You probably don't know yourself."

Salvo's slitted eyes bored into his own. "And you do?"

"I can make a pretty good guess." Kane's lips molded themselves into a tight, thin smile. "You hated me, but you couldn't live without me. If you'd actually just wanted me dead, you could've figured out how to do that many times over the years."

Salvo didn't react. He sat and stared unblinkingly.

Kane's smiled broadened, showing an edge of teeth. "The truth you could never accept is that you need me. The true target of all your hatred is fate, for having made you such a buggering monster of a man, but you couldn't punish fate. You could only punish me, and if you chilled me, you could no longer punish me. And then you'd be alone with that big empty hole inside of you, with nothing left to fill it."

Salvo blinked, casting his eyes floorward. Bitterly he said, "You're full of shit, Kane. You don't know anything."

"Maybe not." Slowly Kane eased down to a squat. "But I know this—you're the one who begged me to chill you. You're the one in a cell. You're the one sitting there with a face I gave you, a face not even our father could love. So, tell me, Salvo—who won the competition without even trying?"

Salvo clenched his hands, the knuckles standing out like ivory knobs, tendons popping. He let his upper lip curl in what passed as a snarl. He just stared at

Kane, hating him, needing him, hating himself because he needed him.

When he spoke, his voice was surprisingly mild and level. "Tell me something, Kane—if you have all the answers, why did you flush your whole life because of that woman?"

For a moment, Kane wasn't sure what he meant. "Baptiste?"

"Yeah, the Preservationist bitch. As an agent of the Trust, you could have had any woman you wanted, *all* the women you wanted. Why her?"

Kane suddenly felt on the defensive and he didn't like it. "In the first place, since there are and never have been any Preservationists, she isn't one of them."

Salvo's mouth gaped, dumbstruck. "What? How can that be?"

"Oh, it be. Lakesh made them up so the Mags and the barons would have some enemy to chase after and divert attention from what he was really up to."

Incredulously Salvo declared, "Do you know how many confessions I got from Preservationists? At least a hundred!"

"After you tortured them, sure, they'd confess to being anything you wanted them to be. But they weren't Preservationists."

"This place, it has to be—"

"The former seat of Project Cerberus, not the headquarters of the Preservationists. Now it's a sanctuary."

Salvo's eyes couldn't widen very far, but they shone with disbelief. His entire world was being dismantled, piece by piece, until he had nothing left but his hatred, and even that was proving to have little foundation.

"In the second place," continued Kane, "I didn't flush my life for Baptiste."

Salvo uttered a scornful chuckle. "The hell you didn't. She was a nobody, Kane. A keypuncher. What hold does she have over you? You lost everything because you couldn't get that dumb bitch out of your guts."

Kane managed to control the sudden, hot flush of anger. "You got me involved in shit, Salvo, and I got her involved, too. I had to *un*involve her."

Salvo chuckled again. "You can't say I didn't try to uninvolve her, too, you know."

"You tried to have her executed."

"I did that for you, Kane. She had to die to protect the secrets and to protect you."

"Why did you figure Grant had to die? I know you tried to have him chilled."

Salvo waved both hands dismissively. "Stay on the subject. Why her?"

Momentary confusion made Kane's tongue feel clumsy. "Because—because I know her."

"You never met her until the night before I arrested her!"

Kane's face was stony. "All right, I'll tell you. Because I need her, I need her like you needed me. But the difference is, I trust her."

Salvo offered an ugly little laugh and shook his head in disgust. "You're fused out, Kane. Over a woman. I never thought to see it."

Kane rose to his feet. Quietly he said, "She's Baptiste.'' He turned toward the door. ''I've had my say and my fill of you.''

''What are you going to do with me?''

Kane turned slowly back around. ''I haven't made up my mind. I sure as hell don't want you, and I sure as hell don't need you. If I don't end up chilling you, Domi will find a way, once she's up and around.''

''I'm not afraid of an Outland slut,'' Salvo retorted angrily.

''Too bad. You should be.'' He paused. Then softly he asked, ''Are you worth the effort, Salvo?''

''What effort?''

''To redeem you.''

Salvo stared at him in puzzlement. ''How can I answer that?''

''You may have to answer it before long. Cerberus doesn't need to strain its resources supporting two prisoners.''

Salvo demanded haughtily, ''Are you making me an offer to join you?''

''Like I said, Cerberus is a sanctuary. All of us here are survivors of some tragedy. In your case, it's being born.''

''I'm a Magistrate,'' Salvo stated. ''I took an oath. I have pride.''

Kane shook his head wearily. ''I'm sick of ideology, Salvo. It never seemed to work for me, only for you. The barons and the Archons watched us crawl around the Outlands, the hellzones, chilling our fellow humans like gardeners ripping up weeds. Then they planted their own crop, laughing at our stupidity because we were sowing the seeds of our extinction.''

Kane waited, but Salvo didn't respond, didn't react,

so he said, "Your Magistrate's oath and your Magistrate's pride were taken away from you, just like they were taken away from me. They don't belong to either of us anymore."

He touched his forehead and his chest. "This and this are the only things that still belong to us, and the Archons tried to corrupt them, too. When they hurt, because of conscience or compassion, we were told we deserved the pain. I'm telling you that we don't deserve it, that we don't have to buy into that bullshit now."

Kane opened the door. "That's your chance for redemption, Salvo. If I were you, I'd take advantage of it."

"Is that a threat or an offer?"

Stepping out the cell, Kane replied, "Right now, I'm not sure. But sooner rather than later, I will be."

Chapter 25

The next morning, Lakesh smiled out of the screen and said cheerily, "Greetings, Mohandas Lakesh Singh, greetings from the future. I should wish you a happy new year, but I know in advance it won't be, so I shan't waste my time with social hypocrisy.

"By my calendar—old style—it is 2198 A.D., a shade under two hundred years since Armageddon. You know it's on its way—in fact, you know it's a little less than three weeks down the road. You think there is nothing you can do about it, so you've been desperately trying to convince yourself it's for the best.

"You know damn well you're lying to yourself. Who better to know this than me—since I am you and you are me?"

Grant gestured impatiently. "Hold on. Stop the tape."

Obligingly Lakesh thumbed a button on the console. His image froze on the screen in an unflattering pose, eyes half-closed, lips stretched in a foolish smile.

Lakesh sat in the same chair at the same desk as that displayed on the screen. Grant, Brigid and Kane faced him across that desk, in his small, sparsely furnished office. Besides the desk and chairs, the only other piece of furniture was a small computer console. Lakesh's head and shoulders filled the screen.

"What is this supposed to be?" Grant asked.

Coolly Lakesh answered, "In my search for the right place in the right time to inject history-altering elements, I considered several people who were instrumental in bringing about our present. Brilliant people who dealt with hitherto unknown scientific laws and who would understand a message from the future. Einstein was one. Clark Savage, Niehls Bohr and Torrance Silas Burr were other candidates. Finally I settled on myself."

"You? That's ridiculous," said Kane.

Brigid's eyes lit up with green glints of amusement. "No, quite the contrary. It makes perfect sense."

Lakesh smiled wryly. "Who better than to convince myself I'm making a horrific mistake than myself—someone who was in the position to know the nature of the Totality Concept projects and their terribly destructive results? If I don't find myself credible, then no one else will, either."

Kane's eyebrows arched. "So to do this, you made a little home vid of yourself yapping away about how bad everything is two hundred years later?"

Lakesh scowled. "I was up all night putting this together. I edited in scenes from the vid library here, security tapes made in the Anthill, made here in Cerberus right after the nuke. I provided a sufficiently visual counterpart to my verbal contentions. Do you want to see it or not?"

"Yeah, sure," said Grant dully.

Lakesh hit the Play button. They were not prepared for the scenes of horror that began flashing across the screen, some of them so repulsive that even Kane and Grant were shaken. Bodies with the flesh seared down to the bone, people dying of fallout contamination screaming to the videographers for help, blue-sheened intestines burst and lying on the ground, cities completely consumed by mile-high flame columns, roaring, white-hot fires that covered thousands of acres.

The images of atrocities seemed to go and on, given an extraghastly fillip by Lakesh's calm narration, his delivery as flat as if he were describing a house-painting contest. Finally Lakesh turned it off.

Quietly he announced, "At the end of the recording, I offer the most convincing bit of evidence—myself, discussing highly personal incidents that I never spoke of with anyone. I put this vid together in order to shock, not to win an Oscar for best documentary."

None of them knew who Oscar was, and they weren't particularly interested at the moment.

"How do you plan to get this message to yourself?" Brigid asked.

"Yeah," said Grant suspiciously. "You claimed you spent nearly thirty years in the Dulce installation, then a couple here, then a century frozen in the Anthill complex. Breaking into the Russian embassy to defuse an A-bomb seems a hell of lot easier than trying to penetrate those places."

"Indeed, yes, they probably would be," Lakesh replied. "However, there was a twenty-four-hour period when I was not in any of those places. From around noon, December 31, 2000 to midmorning of January 1, 2001."

"Where were you?" asked Kane.

"The Big Apple. New York City. I and three other Totality Concept project overseers were brought to Manhattan to ring in the new millennium. Though we were accompanied by security warders, people could have gotten to us if they were determined enough."

"And you intend to confront yourself?" Brigid's tone wasn't exactly skeptical, but it was definitely doubtful.

"No," answered Lakesh firmly. "I can't risk a causal paradox. Suppose I go back to Manhattan and am run down by a taxicab or shot by a mugger or even by my own bodyguards?"

Grant frowned. "What would happen?"

"That's the problem and the paradox—I simply don't know. The principle of causality states that causes must precede effects. If my present self is killed in the past, would I even be born? Would we then have an effect without a cause?"

Kane massaged his temples. "Here we go," he said with cold sarcasm. "Just tell us what you have planned, all right?"

Lakesh looked at him reproachfully, as if he resented being rudely cut off just as he was getting to the interesting part. With forced geniality, he said, "As you wish, friend Kane. Here is what I have planned—my trip to New York wasn't simply a vacation. I toured the mat-trans installations in the region. There were three—a redoubt upstate in the Adirondacks, a unit in the South Bronx and one in Manhattan itself, beneath the Twin Towers."

"Twin Towers?" echoed Grant.

"The World Trade Center. That unit was the smallest and newest of the three, the easiest to install due to construction work being done to repair terrorist bomb damage. Inasmuch as it was not a redoubt like the other two, security was lax. The procedures were designed to prevent people from entering it, not leaving it.''

Lakesh leaned back in his chair. ''I'll provide you with a detailed floor plan, a briefing jacket on the political, socioeconomic and cultural conditions of the time and my itinerary. I suggest, however, the best time to reach me and give me the vid disk is when I'm in the theater.''

''What theater?'' Kane asked.

''New York City Center.'' Lakesh smiled fondly at the memory. ''We went to see a revival of *Guys and Dolls,* a famous musical based on a book by Damon Runyon. It was the first and only time I ever saw a Broadway show.''

''Let me make sure I understand,'' Grant said gruffly. ''You're suggesting you transport us to the very tail end of the twentieth century, to New York, to track down your younger self and somehow slip him—you—a vid disk?''

''Not *somehow,*'' Lakesh corrected. ''*Effectively* is the word.''

Kane began to feel the inner keenness, the anticipatory tingle of nerves that a challenge always excited.

''I'll supply you everything you need,'' continued Lakesh. ''Money, the right kind of clothes, identification. I presume all of you will want to embark on this mission?''

Neither Grant, Kane nor Brigid said anything in response.

Lakesh went on, "Your silence gives your assent. Since I have some last-minute checking of calculations to perform, I will ask you to—"

"Let's not jump to conclusions," Kane interjected.

Lakesh eyed him in surprise. "Friend Kane, I thought you were the most anxious to participate in this undertaking."

"I am. But there's no need for all three of us to be at risk."

Brigid shot him an icy green glare. "You're not cutting me out of this one, Kane. With my historical knowledge, I'm more qualified than you are."

"I won't argue with you about that, even though I could. No, you're definitely a part of the jump team. But I'd feel better if Grant sat this one out."

Grant's dark eyes went wide with astonishment. "Just the two of you?"

"I didn't say that. We'll recruit a third member."

"Like who?" Grant demanded in a harsh tone. "Bry? He's technically adept, but he's an academic. DeFore can't go because she's needed to perform Domi's surgery. That leaves personnel who wouldn't know one end of a blaster from another."

"Except for one," replied Kane. "Salvo."

After a tense, hushed moment, the argument erupted. It was far more intense and impassioned than Kane had imagined. Brigid acted scandalized by the very notion of it.

"What's *wrong* with you?" she cried angrily. "Three days ago, you nearly beat the bastard to death. He hates us both! We could never turn our backs on him!"

Grant filled the small office with a lionlike roar of

outrage. "It's the most fucked-up, fused-out idea you've ever had, Kane, and you've had a lot of them! You can't trust him, he'll sell you out or backshoot you at the first opportunity!"

Lakesh didn't yell quite as loudly, but his tone of voice was no less vehement. "It's mad, hopelessly, stupendously unworkable. You're frightfully underestimating the risk of this proposal."

Kane waited until they paused for breath and calmly asked, "What should we do with him, then? Keep him here indefinitely, a permanent prisoner like Balam in the off chance he'll one day be of some use? Do we let Domi loose on him while we all watch? Take him outside and drop him off the cliff, time how long it takes him to hit bottom? Or do we give him the chance to come to terms with himself, with what he's been and what he's done? The same chance that Grant and I had."

Lakesh shook his head. "The doctrine of redemption. You surprise me, Kane. Admirable sentiments, but this is not the mission on which to test them. This very well could be a one-way trip."

"All the more the reason not to put all three of us on the firing line," Kane countered. "My way at least you'll still have Grant as your enforcement arm and you'll be solving the Salvo problem at the same time."

Brigid declared, "Taking Salvo with us increases the risk factor exponentially."

Anxiously Lakesh said, "In more ways than one. You'll be traveling back in the temporal stream to a pivotal point in history. Taking the wrong action at the wrong moment could create a new, branching probability.''

"Isn't that what you wanted?'' Kane responded.

Lakesh pursed his lips and stared at Kane for a long moment. When they came, his words were bitten off sharply, as though he begrudged each one. "I want to set in motion an alternate event horizon without violating the principle of causality. One already occurred, due to Operation Chronos. My plan is to repair the dysfunction, not trigger another, which may have no bearing on this present. Conversely something may happen that will trap the world in a catastrophe that can turn out to be ten times worse than the nuke-caust.''

"A spatial discontinuity?'' Brigid inquired. "That's what Strongbow's Singularity could have triggered.''

"Worse,'' Lakesh said. "And you may believe me that I'm not being melodramatic.''

Kane said tightly, "You formulate the plan. I'll see to it Salvo abides by it. This is his one chance. If he blows it, or if I simply don't like his attitude, I'll have no compunction about chilling him in his tracks. My word on that.''

Brigid laughed lowly, in resignation. "That's quite the endorsement for somebody's behavior. But I guess, considering who it is, it's the best we can hope for.''

Chapter 26

Time stopped with a painful, choking wrench.

Kane felt himself sinking into whirlpools of dark energy that sucked his blood and bones and soul out through the flesh and blew them in hurricane clouds through eternity.

He spiraled up, then down, through every moment of his life, circling the moment of his birth, sling-shotting around the first girl he ever kissed, the first life he ever took. He hung in the balance between present and past, shuddering on a thin thread as fragile as the memory of a half-forgotten dream. The thread slowly unraveled, twisting itself undone, looping and unlooping, then tying itself into knots of existence. He fell through a sea of images, and no matter how hard he tried to hang on to one thread of existence, it twisted through new ones and slipped away from him in the whirling currents. He thrashed and kicked, but touched nothing.

Then came again a sharp, wrenching, dislocating shock that he felt through every fiber, every cell, every follicle. Time started again.

Kane dimly realized his sensations were again those of the physical. As he understood it, he felt pain crowding through his body. His breath had to be drawn in stages because of the nausea floating high in his throat. His head felt all out of proportion, a mass of hollow pain that had no clearly defined borders. He wanted to sleep, but instead he doubled over in a retching spasm.

He hadn't eaten anything for the twelve hours preceding walking into the gateway, so his stomach had nothing to empty. Tears filled his eyes. He heard the sound of his own harsh gagging, repeated, duplicated on either side of him.

Slowly Kane's nausea ebbed, and he stopped trying to heave up the lining of his stomach. He swiped a coat sleeve over his face, blinked blearily around and his whole body jerked upright in the chair. Through the transparent armaglass, he saw a small chamber, with a control console running the length of the north wall. To his left, a two-yard-high passage, walled with clean, softly gleaming metal, led straight ahead.

He was conscious of a faint humming that seemed to be coming from the hexagonal floor plates. Even as he noticed the sound, it faded away, winding down. Seated on either side of him, Salvo and Brigid uttered sighing moans.

Kane pressed the catch release on the buckle of the straps crisscrossing his chest and stood up, staggering dizzily across the metal floor of the chamber to the door. Peeling back the left cuff of his overcoat, he activated the motion detector and swept it back and forth. The glowing LCD indicated no movement within sensor range.

Hearing the rustle of cloth, he turned back to the three small bucket seats, all of them connected by spot welds on the frames. Brigid unstrapped herself from the restraints and unsteadily rose to her feet.

"How do you feel?" he asked.

"Awfully dizzy. My stomach's on fire, too."

"If it's any consolation," he said with a wry grin, "you look good."

"It's not," she replied curtly. "I feel ridiculous."

Brigid's usually unkempt mane of hair had been elaborately coiffed and crimped, using a two-hundred-year-old pix of a fashion model as a guide. Her tresses caught the indirect light and reflected strands of gold.

Her lips were rouged, her cheekbones highlighted, and her mascaraed green eyes shone brightly behind the round, lightly tinted lenses of rimless spectacles. Though the charcoal-colored, two-piece tweed suit she wore was sensible enough, the skirt was very short and tight. Her long legs, encased in black tights, were shown to full advantage, with black boots laced up to midcalf.

She draped a dark gray overcoat over an arm and held a rakishly brimmed fedora in one hand. The bulge made by the Beretta 93-R in cross-draw slide holster above her left hip was barely discernible. Equally well hidden was the vid disk resting in a hidden, zippered pocket inside of her coat.

Cerberus contained a small collection of twentieth-century artifacts, though certainly not as extensive or as varied as that stored in the Historical Division of Cobaltville. Part of the collection featured articles of clothing, and with a few alterations, Brigid, Kane and Salvo had been properly attired in the fashion of the day.

Kane and Salvo wore similar black overcoats, slacks and sports jackets over dark turtlenecks. Kane wished he had his Kevlar-weave Mag greatcoat, but he had been forced to discard it during the Irish op. The right sleeve of his coat had been restitched to accommodate the holstered Sin Eater.

Salvo stirred in his chair, fumbling clumsily with the buckle of the straps. Kane didn't help him. The man no longer wore the nose splint, but the bruised flesh around his eyes was concealed by a pair of dark glasses.

On Bry's suggestion, the three small chairs with restraints had been built to reduce the risk of the jump team being drawn into separate temporal arteries. Although Lakesh doubted such physical safeguards would be effective in a nonphysical continuum, he hadn't opposed the idea.

Lakesh took advantage of the day it took to construct the chairs to fully brief the team on a seemingly endless number of whys, whats and wherefores. He had talked for so long on topics that seemed so esoteric and irrelevant to the mission that Kane had accused him of trying to make them too nervous to even sneeze in the twentieth century.

Lakesh had instantly pounced on the sarcastic observation, spinning out an appalling scenario of them infecting an entire community with microbes to which they were immune, but could be deadly to anyone not born in postskydark America.

As it was, an hour before the jump, they had been forced to undergo an extremely thorough decam process, where everything but their thoughts was sterilized.

Salvo finally managed to work out the intricacies of the buckle and push himself to his feet. In a hushed, awestruck voice, he asked, "Did we make it? Are we here?"

"We're somewhere," Kane answered. "We're not in Cerberus, at any rate. It's too soon to tell if we're in another time, as well as another place."

Brigid slipped on her coat, put on her hat and declared, "Let's find out."

She made a point of stepping wide around Salvo, not completely turning her back to him.

Kane tried to make eye contact with Salvo, but he evaded his gaze. Convincing the man to join the team hadn't required a great deal of persuasion, since Kane had let him know the alternative was a quick demise. Even the prospect of being in close contact with Baptiste hadn't appeared to color his decision. In fact, he had been civil to her before the jump, if not exactly courteous. Of course, the prospect of another brutal beating if he spoke to her disrespectfully more than likely motivated his rare display of tolerable manners.

Kane had briefed Salvo on the mission, its objectives and its dangers. He hoped to reach some small kernel of decency buried within the man, so he would want the chance to put matters right. Kane had no idea if he reached that kernel or not. He assumed Salvo was cooperating out of the oldest of human drives—fear for his own life. Kane understood that, but he had no patience with it.

When he reached for the door handle, his own fear hit him, suddenly and unexpectedly. The resolve that had pushed him to insist on the mission vanished. An icy flood of fear flowed over and through him, just like the time in Dulce when he saw his father's face, sealed and sleeping forever in a cryonics canister.

His hand gripped the metal handle tightly, but he didn't make a move. A tidal wave of unreality crashed over him, abrading his nerve endings.

He heard himself mutter, "This is crazy. What are we doing? We can't time travel, we can't change history."

Brigid moved to his side, putting a hand to rest on his shoulder. "It's all right."

He brushed her hand away, but she replaced it firmly. Quietly she said, "The fear has hit you, that's all."

"I'm never afraid," he growled between gritted teeth. "I can't be afraid."

"Of course you can. I'm afraid, too. Together we'll master it. We'll put the fear behind us and walk out and do what needs to be done, like we always do. Remember who you are, the man who always beats the odds. One percent, remember?"

With an effort of will, he forced the strength back into himself. He dragged in a deep breath, held it, let it out slowly and turned the handle. He whispered, "You're right."

She smiled. "I usually am. That's why you can barely stand me."

Ever the pointman, Kane stepped out into the dim, suffused light. The overhead light strips produced enough illumination for him to find his way easily. Salvo came last, moving very cautiously. He met Kane's eye, then looked hastily away. Kane wondered what he had thought of the scene between him and Baptiste. He was probably bemused and disgusted, though pleased to see the vulnerability in his brother.

Once again, Kane was glad he hadn't permitted Salvo to carry weapons.

The Sin Eater slid into his hand as he followed the straight line of the corridor. It went on for a hundred feet, then reached a junction point, four passages radiating off like the spokes of a wheel. At the mouth of each corridor, numbers one through four were on the floor in red paint.

Kane stood in the hub and turned slowly, scanning with the motion detector. "This is a different layout than other redoubts we've been to."

"It's not a redoubt, exactly," Brigid replied, peering down each branching corridor. "It's like a rat's maze."

Nothing registered on the sensor. "What would rats do?" He grinned. "Hey, Salvo, that's something you should know."

Salvo only scowled at the floor, hands tucked in the pockets of his coat.

Matching Kane's grin, Brigid said, "Best as I recall, rats habitually choose a right hand-path."

They chose the one to their far right. The corridor was much shorter than the one that led from the mat-trans unit. Beyond a doorless square lay a reception room furnished with armchairs, a couch, a low table scattered with magazines and a coffee machine. A television set supported by a metal framework was positioned in a corner just below the ceiling. A double set of doors marked an elevator shaft.

"No guards," Salvo murmured, pacing around the room restlessly.

"If we're where and when we're supposed to be," Brigid said, "then it's a holiday. Since this little installation doesn't have much strategic importance to the Totality Concept, all the personnel were probably given the night off.''

"It doesn't make sense there wouldn't be *any* security," argued Salvo.

"This isn't Cobaltville," Brigid told him coldly.

Though he begrudged it, Kane found he couldn't disagree with Salvo. His pointman's sixth sense rang an alert. The atmosphere of the place had subtly changed somehow. The motion detector beeped.

Kane skipped around, pivoting on his heel. Gliding into the room, only inches beneath the light strip, came a two-foot-long, segmented object that looked like an insect made of burnished steel. A photoelectric cell glowed dull red where the eye should have been. Fringing the edges of the metal carapace were rows of flexible, pincerlike extruders. They clicked open and shut on tiny joints. The thing reached a point above them, hovering silently. Its eye rotated rapidly in the socket.

"A tracking device," said Brigid a low tone. "It's probably transmitting what it sees to a closed-circuit vid somewhere."

"Lakesh didn't say anything about that," Kane growled.

"He told me similar machines were used in the Anthill complex."

"Can it hurt us?" asked Salvo.

Brigid shook her head. "Unlikely. It's been designed primarily for surveillance."

As soon as she finished speaking, the bug hurtled straight down at her head. She dodged nimbly to one side, and it landed on her left arm, the tiny pincers gripping the sleeve tightly.

A crackling buzz came from it. Brigid convulsed, limbs flailing, a hoarse scream starting up her throat. She staggered the length of the room, falling against the wall.

Instantly Kane understood the device was administering electric voltage, trying to shock her into unconsciousness. With one long-legged bound, he reached her side, leveling the Sin Eater at the thing clinging to her arm. The round, fired at point-blank range, hit the bug square in the side of its glowing red eye.

Fragments of it spun away in a brief, eye-hurting shower of sparks. It clattered to the floor, pincers clicking open and shut for only a second before acrid smoke spurted from every seam and between its metal segments.

Brigid leaned against the wall, vigorously rubbing feeling back into her arm. "I'm okay," she said in a quavery voice.

"Usually right, huh?" said Kane grimly, kicking at the smoldering shell.

"I stand corrected. Let's get out of here before more of those things show up."

The elevator doors were opened by a proximity sensor. They slid apart as soon as Salvo came within a foot of them. The car was large, with polished brass handrails. There were no buttons on the exterior. As soon as the doors slid shut, the car ascended. A bland melody floated out of a speaker grid. Brigid identified the tune as "Auld Lang Syne."

The elevator rose swiftly and smoothly, but only

for a handful of seconds. When it sighed to a stop, the doors opened on a large square room. The floor was thickly carpeted in a muted shade of rose red. The walls were marbled, a black-speckled white in color. Paintings of abstract design hung on the walls. Four high-backed, leather-upholstered chairs were arranged around a varnished table.

They faced a long, broad mahogany desk with two tall vases full of flowers at both ends. Hanging on the wall above it was an ornate, gilt-faced clock. The hands pointed to six forty-five. On the right side of the room, a hallway stretched away, lined on both sides with wooden doors. On their left, they saw a glass-and-chrome door.

Kane crept out of the elevator, sweeping the motion detector back and forth with one hand, his Sin Eater firmly gripped in the other. Brigid and Salvo followed him cautiously as he walked, heel-to-toe, across the lobby to the broad desk.

Behind it stood a swivel chair, positioned inside the curving sweep of a horseshoe-shaped console. Five small vid monitors glowed on it, showing uninteresting black-and-white images of bare, shadowy rooms. The sixth screen displayed, playing it over and over, a high-angle view of the three of them, staring upward. The sequence ended with a blurry shot of Brigid and then dissolved in a pattern of pixeled snow.

"You were right about the closed circuit, at least," Kane said to Brigid. "The bug transmitted what went on to a receiver up here."

"Somebody should have seen it, then," Salvo said quickly. "All sorts of alarms should have gone off. Where's the guard on duty?"

The motion detector beeped once. On the LCD, a small dot pulsed far in its right-hand corner. Kane turned the knob on the monitor screen to blank out the incriminating vid images and turned in the direction of the hallway. Faintly he heard the sound of gushing water, of a toilet flushing, then of a door closing. Footfalls sounded on the carpeted floor.

Kane remained beside the desk, leaning his left elbow casually atop it, hiding his blaster in the folds of his coat. A young, slender man with dusky Latino features sauntered down the stretch of corridor. He wore a starched, pale blue uniform with a badge pinned to the shirtfront and insignia patches sewn onto the sleeves. As he walked, he fiddled with the fly of his trousers.

Kane appraised his movements, judging that it would take him a fatally long time to draw the Colt Python revolver snugged in the black plastic holster at his hip. The guard was so occupied with his zipper he didn't notice Kane until he was nearly to the end of the desk. When he did, his expression of startled dismay was so exaggerated, Kane had to repress a laugh.

The young man's gait faltered, his black eyes widening as he took in the three strangers standing in a place they had no business standing. Before he could recover sufficiently from his surprise to voice demands, Kane slipped his hand into an inner pocket of his coat, came out with a little wallet and flipped it open in a practiced authoritarian motion. The guard saw the logo and credentials of a Defense Intelligence Agency operative and swallowed hard.

"DIA," Kane said laconically, closing the wallet.

He glanced at the young man's name tag pinned to a shirt pocket, "Why weren't you at your post, Hector?"

Hooking a thumb over his shoulder, Hector said, "I had to go to the head, sir."

"You're the only man on duty tonight?"

"Yes, sir. See, I'm the newest, so I—"

Kane interrupted, "Has the Dulce scientific envoy made their inspection yet?"

Hector nodded. "Oh, yes sir. Hours ago, sir."

Kane replaced his identification in his pocket. "Just making sure they're sticking to their schedule. Stand easy, son. We're not here to inspect you."

The guard smiled uneasily and went to his chair behind the desk. He frowned slightly when he noticed one of the monitors was dark.

Crisply Kane said, "Buzz us out, please."

"Yes, sir."

Kane turned to the left, striding purposefully toward the glass-and-chrome door. He didn't look behind him to see if Salvo and Brigid were following. He was too busy hoping Hector wouldn't inquire as to how they got into the office.

He had just reached the door when the young man called out hesitantly, "Uh, sir?"

Kane didn't perceptibly tense, but he lightly rested his index finger on the trigger of the Sin Eater. He turned slightly, Brigid and Salvo moving carefully to either side to give him a clear fire zone.

Calmly he asked, "Yes?"

Hector craned his neck to see above the rim of the desk. "Happy New Year."

Kane nodded. "Same to you, son."

The door lock buzzed, a solenoid snapped aside, Kane pushed open the door and stepped into the subterranean parking garage Lakesh had told them about. The air was very cool and held an oily scent. Kane allowed Brigid to take the lead, since she had memorized the floor plan Lakesh had sketched out.

He resisted the impulse to give the variety of vehicles lining their route more than a cursory glance. Just in case spy-eyes observed them, he didn't want to present the impression of man who had never seen so many wags before—which, of course, he was.

Brigid guided them to wide concrete steps reaching upward. Painted on the wall beside them were the words Exit To Street Level. They climbed the stairs, the temperature dropping from cool to cold, the smells becoming stronger, stranger and unpleasant. Unidentifiable rumbling sounds slapped at their ear drums.

They climbed out onto the paved floor of a darkened, hedge-enclosed courtyard between two mindstaggeringly huge structures. Their sheer walls rose above the courtyard for hundreds of feet. Visible overhead between them was an oddly blurred square of indigo sky. Kane momentarily forgot his tension, awed by the time and effort and expense it must have taken to create such towering monuments.

The rumbling noise resolved into the roar of countless automobile engines, tires rolling over asphalt. Horns blared discordantly. They breathed shallowly against the exhaust fumes produced by the stream of traffic.

"New York, New York," Brigid said, hoarse from incredulity.

"Yeah," said Kane, struggling against a new wave of unreality. "A hell of a town."

Chapter 27

Crowds of people, laughing, talking, arguing, cursing, flowed past in a never ending stream. The lighting adorning shopfronts was a blinking, multicolored kaleidoscope against the man-made canyons that rose to block out the sky. Snatches of raucous music interwove with the din of traffic and voices.

There were more people than Brigid, Salvo or Kane had ever seen in one place. Even the seething alleys and lanes of the Tartarus Pits held only a thousand people, and it seemed like twice that many tramped past the dimly lit courtyard in the few minutes they stood there.

A couple of months earlier, Kane, Grant and Brigid had visited Moscow, and the sheer volume and diversity of humanity there had been unsettling. But postskydark Moscow was a sleepy country ville compared to prenuke Manhattan.

Lakesh had told them approximately ten million people occupied the five boroughs comprising greater New York City. At a very conservative estimate, that was twice the population of the entire continental United States.

Even with his half-healed nose, Salvo smelled the blended mixtures of stench and asked sourly, "This is what you want to save?"

"Shut up," Kane said. He made a deliberately slow

show of returning his Sin Eater to its holster. He asked Brigid, "Do you know the way to the theater?"

She nodded. "I memorized the route. Lakesh said it wasn't a good idea to stand around looking at maps. We could be mugged."

"Mugged?" echoed Salvo.

"Slagjacked," Kane interpreted.

Brigid set her wrist chron. "We've a few hours yet before Lakesh is due to arrive. I guess we should get a look at the place."

She started off across the courtyard toward the sidewalk. As Kane followed her, he had a new attack of serious second thoughts. The notion of joining the mass of humanity milling on the street made him distinctly uncomfortable. What if they were mugged? What if something completely unforeseen happened, trapping them in the past, only twenty-one days away from doomsday? With every step he took, his stomach somersaulted.

Then they joined the throng on the sidewalk, and were jostled, bumped, shouldered aside and ignored as if they were invisible. Kane didn't like it one bit, and he saw by Salvo's bunched jaw muscles he liked it even less.

As Magistrates, they were accustomed to their badges and armor parting a crowd like the prow of a ship parts the sea. Lesser breeds scrambled out of their path; they wouldn't even dream of blocking it.

Brigid walked, or tried to, swiftly and purposefully. Never in their lives had they imagined such a numerous, eclectic morass of humanity. Though Lakesh had briefed them on what to expect, even showed them old vids of New York, the sensory input was almost overwhelming. It was utter shouting, clanging, honking, stinking, overcrowded turmoil.

They passed a preponderance of electronics shops, pizzerias, of discount bookstores and cut-rate jewelry stores. Many of the windows were plastered with signs proclaiming New Year's Eve Specials and One-Time Only Millennium Sale, Everything Must Go!

Every few feet, street vendors waved wristwatches, trinkets, sweaters or fireworks. The smell of baked bread drifting from pretzel stands sharply reminded Kane how long it had been since he'd eaten.

There was a curious tension in the air, and Kane tried to pin down its exact nature. He caught bits and pieces of conversation, some spoken in accents he could not identify or barely comprehend. He overheard references to money, to children, to movies, to New Year's resolutions. Twice he heard fearful mumbles about Judgment Day and the imminent end of the world.

Nape hair tingling, he increased his stride so he was abreast of Brigid. Urgently he said, "Some of these people know what's going to happen."

She cast him a curious glance. "What do you mean?"

He told her what he had heard, and she surprised him by laughing. "They don't know," she said, "not really. I read about this."

"Read about what?"

"A cultural phenomenon called millennium fever. About five or six years ago—counting backward from 2000—when the end of the century was approaching, a form of hysteria about the new millennium manifested. First it was only religious types warning about the end of the world, then it filtered down into the public consciousness. That's what they were talking about. They really don't know what's going happen. They're just afraid something will.''

Kane wasn't reassured, particularly when the keening wail of a fire truck's siren cut through the night. Ahead, flashing red-and-blue lights lined both sides of an intersection. There appeared to have been a minor vehicle accident. He glanced back at Salvo. The man stared fixedly at the lights and commotion and didn't see the girl until she bumped into him. Kane was sure it had been intentional, so he slowed, then stopped.

The girl had long blond hair and a face so thickly caked with cosmetics she looked like an evil doll. She blocked Salvo's way with the provocative thrust of her breasts against the knit fabric of a formfitting blouse.

She said, ''Are you from out of town? Want to ring in the New Year in a real big way? I could rock your world.''

Salvo glanced down at her with contempt. He made a move to step around her. ''I doubt it,'' he said dismissively.

Kane watched, amused, then became aware that the girl wasn't really looking at Salvo, but over his shoulder. Kane's sixth sense warned him, and he took a quick, long step forward. He saw the glint of light on steel even before he fully noted the scrawny black man standing behind Salvo.

He started to call out a warning, but it was unnecessary. Salvo acted instinctively, lunging to one side and kicking out with his right foot, catching the man on the sensitive inside of his left thigh. The leg buck-led, and Salvo's knotted fist swung around in a back-ward arc, thudding into the man's forehead, sending him staggering. He would have fallen if not for a lamppost at his back. A thin-bladed knife clattered on the sidewalk.

The girl clawed for Salvo, but Kane caught her by the hair, wrenching her backward. She screamed in frustrated fury, twisting desperately from his grasp. She dived through the crowd and disappeared, leaving Kane with a blond wig in his fist.

Salvo turned to face his assailant, but the man made a staggering lunge off the curb and into the stream of traffic. He dodged, weaved, leaped and hopped with a skill obviously born of long experience. Reaching the opposite side of the boulevard, he disappeared into the dark mouth of an alley.

The crowd had paused only for a moment, mur-muring about crack-whores, then went on their way, not wanting to know anything more about the incident than they had already witnessed.

The knife still glittered on the sidewalk. Salvo bent down and picked it up. "Slaggers assaulting citi-zens," he growled. He straightened up, looking steadily at Kane. "You expect me to believe a world like this is better than the one we have?"

Kane dropped the wig, not responding to Salvo's questions. Slaggers were confined to the Tartarus Pits, where they could prey on one another without fear of official reprisal. However, they could not prey on the citizenry who lived in the Enclaves because they weren't allowed near them, except in the most menial, service-oriented manner.

Secondarily, if a citizen was ever assaulted by a slagger, retaliatory action undertaken by the Mags would be bloody and brutal and out of all reasonable proportion to the original transgression. That policy of overkill had prevented a major Pit uprising for over a generation. The last one had claimed the lives of Kane's and Salvo's grandfathers.

Jerking his head toward the knife in Salvo's hand, Kane said, "Lose the sticker and let's go."

Reflectively Salvo tested with a thumb the razor-sharp blade. Then, with a snapping motion of his arm, he tossed the knife toward the scummy water flowing sluggishly in the gutter.

Brigid had stepped out of the crowd during the brief struggle, leaning against the plate-glass display window of an electronics store. A dozen television sets, stacked in a ziggurat shape, flashed the same vivid color image of a youngish, well-dressed man with salt-and-pepper hair.

"That was really stupid," she snapped to Salvo. "What if you'd chilled him or caused him to be run down by a wag?"

"What if I had?" Salvo retorted in the same hard tone. "No loss."

"How do you know his son or grandson might not be a great scientist or even president? You could've changed history, you simple bastard!"

Kane glanced at the multiple images of the man on the television sets. He read the caption superimposed over the bottom edge of the screen. For a long moment, he stared uncomprehendingly at the words. Finally he managed to say, in a stunned, husky whisper, "President...this isn't right."

Brigid eyed him with irritation, followed his gaze and turned around to look at the televisions. After a few seconds, she gaped, too, for a very long time, straining to hear what the man identified as the President of the United States was saying.

She blinked, swung her head toward Kane, the dazed, stricken expression on her blood-drained face perfectly matching his own. Her lips worked before she blurted, "That's not the right President!"

Salvo flicked his dark-lensed eyes back and forth between Kane, Brigid and the images on the television screens. He demanded, "What are you talking about?"

Brigid leaned a shoulder against the window, as if all her strength were seeping out through the soles of her feet. She put a hand to her forehead.

"Did Lakesh fuck up?" Kane snarled the question. "Did he send us to the wrong time?"

She shook her head. "No, we're in the right time and place. New York City, December 31, 2000."

Kane jabbed an arm toward the televisions. "Then who is that guy? Lakesh showed us pix of who the President was supposed to be, and that's *not* him!"

Brigid bowed her head. She spoke so quietly and in such a dead monotone that Kane and Salvo had difficulty hearing her over the street noise. "'All the scattered threads of time have been sewn together in a Gordian knot. Time squared.'"

Salvo stepped closer, thrusting his head forward angrily. "Cut out the bullshit. Did we or did we not travel back to the right time?"

"We did," she said in a voice barely above a whisper. With effort, she straightened up. "Right time. Right place. Wrong universe."

Chapter 28

Lakesh had told them about the way it was.

In 1988, President Ronald Reagan was succeeded by his vice president. A crisis in Latin America had grown into a prolonged shooting war during Reagan's two terms in office, due to the Soviet Union and United States supplying the opposing factions with weapons and funds.

Reagan's successor faced the Russian leader, Mikhail Gorbachev, across a bargaining table in Geneva so that their respective governments could step back from the brink of outright hostilities with as much grace as could be mustered.

Despite this foreign-relations victory, the President was not voted back in for a second term. In 1992, the U.S. electorate put in office an aging Democrat, a longtime politician from a dynasty of politicians.

The new but certainly not young President made a series of diplomatic blunders during his four years as leader of the United States, some of them verging on the disastrous. In 1996, the previous Republican President was returned to office in a thundering landslide victory, and became, for only the second time in American history, an ousted President who returned in triumph to the White House.

But this had a negligible effect on the global situation, especially on increasingly hostile relations between the U.S. and the Soviet Union. Gorbachev had died in a plane crash in 1993 and for six months thereafter, Russia was racked by a civil war. The man who tried to bring a degree of order out of his country's chaos was the new premier, Ryzhkov. Still, America and Russia exchanged more threats than promises of goodwill over bargaining tables, especially after Fidel Castro was murdered in 1993. The sphere of old-style communism was definitely shrinking around the planet.

Toward the end of the President's term, in the spring of 1999, there occurred an event that led directly to the nuclear holocaust.

In a spectacular coup, Ryzhkov was assassinated in the corridors of the Kremlin by hardline Stalinist revisionists. The coup had been masterminded by the head of the KGB, V. N. Pritisch. He believed the way to restore his country's former glories was to revive the brutal, yet efficient methods of Joseph Stalin.

Unbeknownst to even Pritisch, a fanatical group of disaffected internal security officers calling themselves the Vesesozhzhenie, or "terrible fire," had determined to redress what they perceived as humiliations heaped upon Russian pride. To this end, they saw to the planting of three nuclear warheads in and around Washington, D.C. They timed the detonations, with an ugly sense of irony, for Presidential Inauguration Saturday.

Less than a minute after the first mushroom cloud appeared over the District of Columbia, Air Force General P. X. "Frag" Frederickson keyed in the proper sequence to launch a retaliatory strike at Russia.

Within the next hour, World War III began and ended. No one knew who had won or lost the war, because no government statisticians remained to conduct body counts. Conservative estimates calculated that over two-thirds of earth's population perished during those first two hours and forty-five minutes. Since, by then, the entire planet was a smoldering cinder, there was no sure way of differentiating between the victors and the vanquished.

Sometime late that afternoon, the nuclear winter, or the skydark, began. Massive quantities of pulverized rubble had been propelled into the atmosphere, clogging the sky for a generation, blanketing the entire planet in a thick cloud of radioactive dust, ash, debris, smoke and fallout. After twenty-five years of endless nights, of freezing temperatures even in subtropical climates, of fallout storms, millions more had perished.

When the survivors and the children born after the nukecaust climbed out of their shelters, their bunkers, their caves, they knew only one dream—to survive.

The old cultures were gone, burned down to their foundations. New societies were formed, with their own laws, their own rules, their own beliefs and even their own dialects.

These only dimly reflected the changes of the planet itself. Most of North America was known as the Deathlands, an aptly named home to mutated forms of animal, vegetable and human life, radioactive hotspots, marauders and scattered settlements of people trying to scratch out an existence in a hostile environment. Human culture in the seething hellzones of the Deathlands existed at its lowest level since the Dark Ages. The people were divided into hundreds of restless tribes, warring among themselves, devoted to regional jealousies.

Shortly after the worst of the skydark was over, some descendants of the original survivors decided they had outlasted the aftermath of global devastation for a reason. These families of survivors knew people would revert to primitive levels, so they determined to force some sort of order on barbarism. They were better educated, better bred and better armed than almost anyone else who shambled across the Deathlands. The families became ruling hierarchies, and they spread out across the ruined face of America.

The territories they conquered became baronies. At first, people retreated into the villes ruled by the barons for protection, then as the decades went by, they remained because they had no choice. Generations of Americans were born into serfdom, slavery in everything but name.

As the twenty-second century edged toward the twenty-third, humanity slowly and painfully overcame the horrors of its environment, adapting to it, conquering it, living with it.

Many of the most powerful, most enduring baronies evolved into city-states, walled fortresses whose influence stretched across the Deathlands for hundreds of miles.

In decades past, the barons had warred against one another, each struggling for control and absolute power over territory. Then they realized or were taught that greater rewards were possible if unity was achieved.

Territories were redefined, treaties struck among the barons, and the city-states became interconnected points in a continent-spanning network. A Program of Unification was ratified and ruthlessly employed. The reconstructed form of government was still basically despotic, but now it was institutionalized and shared by all the former independent baronies.

Nine baronies survived the long wars over territorial expansion and resources. Control of the continent was divided among the nine barons. The pretenders, those who were not part of the original hierarchy but who arrogantly assumed the title to carve out their own little pieces of empire, were overrun, exterminated and their territories absorbed. The hierarchical ruling system remained, and the city-states adopted the name of the titular heads of state.

Technology, most of it based on predark designs, appeared mysteriously and simultaneously with the beginning of the Unification Program. There was much speculation at the time that many previously unknown stockpiles were opened up and their contents distributed evenly among the barons. Though the technologies were restricted for the use of those who held the reins of power, life overall improved for the citizens in and around the villes. Manufacturing industries, totally under the control of the villes, began again.

What was left of human history belonged to the Deathlands, the Outlands, the baronies and the Archon Directorate.

That was the history they knew, the history Lakesh had told them. He had implied that agents of the Archons had been the true architects of much of that history, pulling the strings to trigger coups, assassinations, plane crashes, wars and the overall destablization of the entire world.

Moreover, due to Operation Chronos, the power elite knew exactly what would happen and when and had taken no measures to stop it.

That was the history they knew.

Except now, none of it appeared to be true.

THOUGH LIT ONLY by candles on the tables, the restaurant on a side street off West Fifty-fifth Street was crowded and noisy, full of party-goers and people drinking too much, too quickly.

Kane had found them a table in the rear simply by bulling past people waiting in line to be seated. As yet, no waiter had approached them, which was good because they hadn't even glanced at the menus. All three of them pored over the variety of newspapers, current-affairs periodicals and magazines Brigid had paid too much for at a newsstand.

They thumbed through them, passing them back and forth. None of them had come across even the most oblique reference to a coup in Russia, a major war in Latin America or the man who, according to Lakesh, was supposed to hold the office of President of the United States.

The man who occupied the White House now was a Democrat, not a Republican, and was at the end of his second term. The President-elect, who was to be inaugurated a few weeks hence, was somebody they had never heard of.

The only halfway familiar name Kane found was in an obituary column. General Peter Xavier Fredrickson, USAF, had died two days before at the age of fifty-five after a long battle with leukemia. The obituary did not mention if he had also been known as "Frag."

Most of the publications were devoted to predictions and prophecies for the new year and the coming millennium. A soothsayer called Nostradamus was heavily quoted, though Kane could make no sense out of his statements.

Brigid closed a copy of *U.S. News and World Report*. The cover bore the headline The '90s—A Look Back. Even in the muted lighting, Brigid's pallor was pronounced. She said, "The political conditions are very similar, but not the same as the past of the time plane we're from."

"What are the similarities?" Kane asked.

"Reading between the lines in some of these magazines, Adolf Hitler supposedly committed suicide and John Kennedy was assassinated, just like in our own history. Everything seems pretty much a mirror image until the mid-1980s. That decade is the demarcation point, when our two histories begin to diverge."

"In what ways?"

"For example, the Soviet Union collapsed in the late eighties. The trouble in Latin America was confined to never ending brush wars, revolutions and counterrevolutions. The last major conflict involving world powers was the Gulf War, ten years ago. Russia was America's ally during it.

"This world is undeniably unstable, with plenty of domestic strife and acts of terrorism, but there's nothing I can find that will lead up to what we knew as

World War III, certainly not in the next twenty-one days.''

"What about Archon activity?" asked Kane.

She shrugged. "The usual. UFO sightings, alien-abduction reports, tongue-in-cheek references to Roswell."

"Do you think that means the Archons haven't established a beachhead here?"

Brigid's lips tightened. "I think the exact opposite. The 1980s is when the divergence from our own history begins. That's about the same time the Totality Concept projects kicked into high gear. There's obviously a version of Cerberus in operation, or we wouldn't have even gotten here.

"I can't even hazard a guess about how wide or narrow the divergence is from our own temporal plane. For all we know, the nukecaust is still on schedule for January 20. But even if we managed to put the skids on it, nothing would change in our future, because this is not our past."

Salvo looked up, scowling, from a copy of *Weekly World News.* "How could this happen? How could two time-lines coexist and be so different?"

"Well, there's a theory."

Kane forced a bleak grin. "I just knew there had to be."

Brigid didn't return the grin. "Do you remember what Grant reported Colonel Thrush said, about all the threads of time being sewn together in a knot?"

"Yeah," replied Kane, "but I can't make much of it."

"He may have been referring to the so-called multiverse hypothesis, which postulates an infinite series of alternate and parallel universes, all very similar to one another, but set apart by minor variations in history. Have you ever thrown two pebbles into a pond and watched how the patterns of ripples intersect and interact? What we have here is the same principle, but on a quantum scale.

"Quantum physics suggests that alternate universes split off with every historical decision. Those branching alternate times are the threads, or the ripples."

"Even if that's true," Kane demanded, "how did we end up here? An accident? A mistake in Lakesh's calculations?"

She sighed out a deep breath. "I almost wish it were a mistake because errors can be rectified. No, in my opinion, a shunt was created, a temporal interface between our future and this past."

"Created by who?" demanded Salvo. "And why?"

"The answers to both questions are pretty obvious, when you think about it," she declared. "The shunt is to prevent forces from coming back in time to do what we planned to do, stop the nukecaust and change the future. The Archons used Operation Chronos technology to create a branching-probability universe."

Salvo wagged his head back and forth. "That's crazy."

"It's simple logic. If people had foreknowledge of the nukecaust due to Chronos and access to time travel, why didn't they employ an alternate event horizon to avert it? Obviously some people did try and were shunted off into parallel planes where nothing they did could alter their own future."

"According to Grant," Kane commented, "Colonel Thrush said something about time squared. What does that mean?"

"Aside from making a sophomoric pun," answered Brigid, "I surmise he meant our own particular past and future were boxed inside of a temporal cube that can't be opened or reached through the means we employed."

Salvo folded his newspaper and slapped it down so hard on the table the candleholder rattled. "What do we do now? If there's nothing we can do here, there's no reason for us to stay. Let's go back."

He arched a challenging eyebrow at Brigid. "You *do* know how to get us back, right?"

"Right," she snapped. "But do you think I'd tell you?"

"I don't give a shit if you tell me or not," he retorted imperiously. "Just do it."

Kane glared him into silence. "We're not that sure of our facts. Some things match up with what we know, but others don't. I think we should go ahead to the theater and try to find Lakesh…if he exists here. Who knows, maybe the nukecaust is still in the works, and it's just the window dressing that's different."

Brigid nodded decisively. "I agree. If nothing else, giving Lakesh the vid may help him save this world, if not our own. After all is said and done, that's our mission."

Salvo grunted. "From what I've seen so far, if New York is like the rest of it, this world doesn't deserve to be saved."

"Shut up," Brigid said coldly. "You're more at home here than we could ever be."

A bearded waiter in a red velvet vest suddenly appeared at Kane's elbow. His appearance was so unexpected and silent, Kane nearly drew his Sin Eater. Still, he uttered a startled oath.

The waiter saw the icy gleam in the man's blue gray eyes and quickly offered a tray holding three amber-colored drinks in fluted glasses.

"What the hell is this?" demanded Kane suspiciously.

"Ah, your drinks," the waiter said in a soft, lilting voice.

"We didn't order any drinks," Salvo told him.

The waiter nodded in agreement. "No sir, they are compliments of a gentleman at the bar. They're specialty drinks—he had to tell the bartender how to mix them. He said they were your favorites."

Brigid squinted at the liquor. "Specialty drinks?"

"Yes, ma'am. They're called Sapsuckers."

Brigid's squint deepened until her eyes were mere slits in her face. "Sapsuckers? That's some kind of bird, isn't it?"

The waiter smiled nervously and began placing the glasses down on the table. "Yes, ma'am, that's right. I believe they're a variety of thrush."

Chapter 29

The three men who sat at the mahogany bar were all identically trim, and all were dressed in tailored black business suits. One of them had short hair so blond it was nearly white; another had longish light brown hair pulled into a ponytail at the nape of his neck. The third man Kane and Brigid recognized. In that instant, they felt an indescribable tension, as if lengths of slimy ropes slowly knotted in the pits of their stomachs.

The eyes of Colonel C. W. Thrush were hidden by the dark, curving lenses of sunglasses, but they felt the burning energy of his gaze nonetheless. His startlingly red, nauseatingly pretty mouth stretched in a slow, mocking smile, and he raised his glass to them.

Salvo growled "Who is that?"

Kane side-mouthed to him, "Colonel Thrush, or that's what he called himself when Grant met him...three weeks from now."

Kane didn't bother trying to be surreptitious in his visual inspection of the man. He stared at him hard and unblinkingly, struggling with the impulse to draw his blaster and widen that taunting smile with a 9 mm hollowpoint.

Colonel Thrush looked exactly the same as Kane remembered him, as if he'd stepped right out of his memory and planted himself on the bar stool only a second ago. Even the sharp creases in his trousers were the same.

The color of his face was so flat as to be unnatural. Beneath the neatly groomed, black, lusterless hair was a wide, smooth forehead, tapering to a sharp chin. His thin, straight nose stood out as sharply as a ruled line. All in all, he still gave the impression of a cadaver who had decided to get up and walk around in his funeral finery.

The man gracefully unfolded his lean body from the stool and walked in a measured pace toward them, holding the stem of his glass in an oddly effemininate way, between thumb and forefinger. He stopped abruptly at the edge of the table.

"You haven't tasted your drinks. In this culture, that's considered a gross breach of manners. Quite gauche."

The voice was friendly and impartial, but underscored by a vibration they sensed rather than heard. "Do you mind if I join you?"

Kane pushed out a chair with a foot, glancing past Thrush to his companions. The two men sipped their drinks, making a very apparent show of paying no attention to them.

Thrush sat down easily in the chair, crossing one leg over the other, resting his right ankle on his left knee. He inclined his head toward Brigid. "I believe you and I have met, very briefly, some fifty-five years ago."

Nodding in Kane's direction, he said, "And you, as well."

His black-masked eyes locked with Salvo's own dark lenses. "You I do not know, though I wish I had. Decision, authority, ruthlessness—those are qualities I can see in you.''

Flatly Salvo asked, ''What do you want from us, Colonel?''

Black, straight eyebrows rose above the rims of his sunglasses. They looked painted on. ''Ah, you know me. Then you have a small advantage, which itself is exhiliarating, regardless of its overall insignificance. May I know the names of those to whom I have extended my generosity?'' He glanced toward Brigid. ''Ladies first.''

''Baptiste.''

''Kane.''

''Salvo.''

Thrush nodded politely in turn as each person spoke.

Kane indicated the two men in black seated at the bar. ''And your friends?''

''Names are conveniences, to be discarded when history no longer finds them necessary, but you may refer to them as Sparrow and Starling.''

''Which bird of a feather is which?'' Brigid asked.

''Irrelevant.'' His red lips tightened, making his mouth look like the raw edges of a wound. ''You have acted very cleverly, but I feel it is incumbent upon you to explain your presences here. Operation Chronos is not a travel bureau.''

''What makes you think we're part of Operation Chronos?'' challenged Kane.

C. W. Thrush smiled slightly, as if pleased that his ploy had worked. ''Nothing, actually, but I wanted to hear it from you. However, when you arrived in the gateway, I knew you had crossed more than linear distance."

"How do you know that?" Brigid asked.

Thrush tapped a lens of his glasses. "These," he said pleasantly, "see everything. I've had you under surveillance from the moment you materialized."

"Why?" inquired Kane.

"Curiosity. I am curious to know when you're from. I've adduced you are from the future, but which one is the question."

Brigid smiled. "So you're not omniscient. Then why should we tell you anything?"

"Because your final fates may depend on what you know and how you know it. As it is, I've deduced the future you came from isn't very pleasant."

With an edge of bitter humor in his tone, Salvo said, "That depends on who you ask."

"This time is not a particularly happy one, either," commented Thrush. "The cumulative effects of population growth, pollution and destruction of natural resources are severely reducing the possibility of humanity's survival past the middle of the new century. Urban centers like this one are choking to death on their own filth."

"What's the solution?" Brigid asked. "To bomb it back to the Stone Age, exterminate the useless eaters, hope to start over with a clean slate?"

C. W. Thrush stared at her with his blank, dark lenses. "A few lives to change the course of the planet's destiny are worth the sacrifice."

"A *few* lives?" Kane echoed incredulously.

"Must this meeting be a confrontation? I understand you don't agree with my mission, since it quite naturally outrages your limited conceptions of the value of human life.''

Brigid cocked her head at a quizzical angle. ''Do you know why we're here?''

''Of course,'' Thrush answered in clipped tones. ''To undo what was done, to set history right where you perceive it went wrong. Surely you do not think you are the first to make such an attempt? I assure you that it is impossible.''

As Kane listened to him talk, he felt as if the man's spiel was part of some prerecorded speech. ''Why is it impossible?''

''The explanation is too complex mathematically for the layman to understand, but it is based on the uncertainty principle. May not the universe in some sense be brought into being by the participation of those who observe it? After all, from the universe's point of view, time is simultaneously and permanently present to itself.''

''You're obfuscating,'' Brigid said.

''Fluently,'' retorted Thrush.

Salvo shifted in his chair impatiently. ''What happens now?''

''Why, nothing at all,'' Thrush answered mildly. ''You are free to be on your way.''

Kane chuckled mirthlessly. ''You're full of shit.''

''Why is that, Mr. Kane?''

''We know too much.''

Thrush smiled blandly, condescendingly. ''You know absolutely nothing of any value.''

Behind that smile, Kane suddenly felt the presence of a dreadful, hungry consciousness, consumed and fueled by a hatred for that which was its opposite—

human life. Ever so slightly, he felt his hands begin to tremble.

Colonel Thrush uncoiled his angular body from the chair, placing his glass on the table. "Drink up, take part in the New Year's festivities, then go on your way. Attempt nothing foolhardy, and try not to let time hang heavy on your hands. Au revoir, Miss Baptiste, Mr. Kane, Mr. Salvo. May we never meet again, in the past or the future."

Thrush turned smartly on his heel, gestured to his companions at the bar and all of them marched out of the restaurant so quickly and unobtrusively, it was as if they had never been there at all.

Kane picked up Thrush's glass, revolving it by the stem, eyeing the smear of lipstick on the rim. Thoughtfully he said, "He's a real sweetheart."

Salvo took his own glass, tilted his head back and swallowed the liquor in one gulp. He repressed a shudder, wiped his mouth with the back of a hand and announced, "Let's do as he says."

Brigid uttered a low, scornful laugh. "You didn't believe him, did you?"

"Why shouldn't I?"

"First place, we know the kind of history he's been involved in making. Second place, he's got to be an agent of the Directorate. Perhaps he's even a hybrid, perhaps something worse. And in the third place, I'm keeping in mind something else he said to Grant."

"What was that?" asked Kane.

A hard glint came into her emerald eyes. "He quoted a poem, 'the deception of the thrush.'"

Kane nodded. "He may have an idea of when and

where we're from, even the why we're here, but he doesn't know the who.''

They rose from the table, Salvo tucking the copy of the tabloid newspaper under an arm. They left the restaurant and walked up the side street, toward Fifty-fifth. As before, Brigid took the lead, Kane bringing up a close rear. There were only a few pedestrians on both sidewalks.

From behind them came the tortured screech of tires mingled with the roar of an engine. Kane spun around just as a massive black automobile thundered out of the mouth of an alley. The headlights were out, but the chromed grille caught sparkling neon highlights. All the tinted windows were up, except for the back on the driver's side. It was lowered just enough to permit the snout of a Sionics noise suppressor to protrude.

A spearpoint of orange flame flickered from it, and a sound very much like a rubber mallet pounding repeatedly into concrete bounced back and forth.

Autofire raked the facade of the building. Glass shivered and jangled as a display window collapsed to the sidewalk. Kane bounded forward, pushing Salvo down, grabbing Baptiste and directing her to inadequate cover behind a garbage can. Even as he did, the whispers of silenced shots were drowned out by the screams of terrified pedestrians. Bullets sprayed the brickwork, punching craters in a wavering line, sprinkling Kane with fragments and dust.

The Sin Eater sprang into his palm as the car sped past. He rolled into a crouch, bracing the blaster with both hands as he tracked for target acquisition. The vehicle roared by full-tilt, careening onto Fifty-fifth

Street and triggering an outraged symphony of car
horns. He ran to the corner and watched as the car
made a rubber-smoking turn at the Sixth Avenue intersection.

He stood there for a moment, angry and frustrated.
Holstering his weapon, he brushed brick shards off
his coat and turned back. Brigid was already on her
feet, moving swiftly toward Salvo, who bent over a
sobbing woman.

As Kane drew closer, he saw she bled from a superficial cut inflicted by flying glass on her cheek. The
woman babbled in near hysteria, her dark hair in disarray. He also saw she was heavily pregnant, at least
seven months along.

"She's all right," Salvo said reassuringly, gesturing with the folded newspaper. "She's just scared.
She should be fine."

Salvo's solicitous words fanned a flame of suspicion in Kane's mind. He stepped closer. Salvo gave
the newspaper a little shake, dropped it, then placed
the edge of the knife against the woman's throat.

"'Should be' is the operative term here," he continued in the same soothing tone. "That's up to you."

He hauled the woman to her feet. Kane and Brigid
stood stock-still. Inwardly, Kane cursed himself for
not making sure Salvo had really thrown away the
knife, instead of palming it. A first-year Mag
wouldn't have fallen for such a transparent sleight of
hand.

"You tried that human-shield shit on Baptiste in
Idaho," Kane said quietly, forcing a calm note into
his voice.

Salvo grinned. "It worked, didn't it?"

The woman started to wail. Salvo clamped a hand over her mouth. "It'll work again, because I have even less to lose."

She reached up to pry away his fingers, but he pressed harder with the blade. "Relax, bitch. I won't cut your throat unless they make me."

Passersby stood in a wary semicircle around them. They were more curious now than frightened, but were all braced to duck or flee if gunfire broke out again.

"What do you want?" asked Brigid.

"To get away from you two. That's not much to ask, is it, especially since this slagger's life depends on it."

"She's not a slagger."

"She might as well be—everybody in this pesthole ville is probably the ancestor of every slagger, roamer and outlander I've ever burned down." He smiled in genuine amusement. "But who knows—the brat this bitch is carrying might be an important person one day, like a president or a doctor, even somebody like me."

He made a sound of mock fear. "You don't want to live with those consequences."

Brigid stated, "You can't get back without us, Salvo. You don't know the activation codes."

"I've got nothing to go back for, remember? My brother saw to that." His smile vanished. "Decide. You can chill me, but I'll take two lives with me on my way down."

At that moment, Kane would have gladly traded in all of his material possessions—which were few and not of great value—just to have Grant on the street beside him for two seconds. He could hip-shoot Salvo's right eye out of his head without even concentrating.

"We can't let you run loose here," Brigid said.

"Why not? I'm supposed to be more at home here than you are."

Brigid said nothing for a long tick of time, then stepped back. "Let him go," she said to Kane.

Kane didn't argue with her, but his holster whined, clicked and slapped his Sin Eater into his hand. "Let him go," she repeated.

Salvo pulled the woman's head up so light flashed briefly on the razor-keen blade. The point pricked the soft flesh just under her jaw. Moans of terror bubbled from behind his fingers.

"Do what your whore tells you to do, Kane," Salvo snapped. "Let me go."

Kane grimaced, then made a short, savage gesture with his left hand. "Go."

Salvo laughed. "Brother mine."

He backed along the street, away from the bright lights and heavy traffic of Fifty-fifth Street, dragging the woman with him. Brigid and Kane watched silently, hearing the nerve-racking, rising and falling of sirens in the distance. They became louder and closer with every second.

When Salvo was about twenty yards away, he shoved the woman in the back, sending her sprawling to her hands and knees. In the same motion, he lunged into the shadows of an alley.

They raced forward, followed at a discreet distance by two men. Brigid tried to help the shrieking woman to her feet, but she slapped her hands away. Kane started into the alley, but Brigid grabbed his arm, hauling him back.

"Don't waste your time," she said. "There's only two places he can go."

Kane glanced over his shoulder and saw flashing blue lights at the corner. "Yeah," he replied, "that's what worries me."

Chapter 30

At the corner of Mott and Pell Streets, in the heart of Chinatown, Brigid and Kane ducked into a doorway to catch their breath. The police officers had not pursued them; dealing with the hysterical pregnant woman and the contradictory reports from the eye-witnesses was about all they could handle on such a night.

"If Thrush was the blasterman," Kane panted, "he was about the lousiest shot I've ever seen."

"I think his marksmanship was intentionally lousy," replied Brigid simply.

"Why?"

"He was trying to scare us back to the gateway. He's no more sure about us than we are about him. We're random elements, and chilling us could bring about another alternate event horizon...maybe even a probability wave dysfunction."

Kane inhaled a whiff of the rancid air and coughed. "He seemed awfully goddamn sure of himself to me. Both times."

"That's the impression he wanted to give. But like the man himself, it seemed a little fake."

They began walking again, up streets lined by restaurants, bazaars, import shops and warehouses. Pagoda roofs with gilded edges topped narrow balconies. They passed a butcher's shop, where an aged

Oriental man with scraggly chin whiskers wielded a cleaver to section up a pig. A dozen smoked ducks hung from their necks like ornaments in the window. They cut through alleys full of gingery, drifting smoke, past open doorways where loud music assaulted their ears.

Half-shouting into Brigid's ear in order to be heard, he asked, "You think Salvo's headed for the theater or the gateway?"

She gestured for him to wait until they reached a spot of comparative quiet so she could answer without yelling. "I'm more concerned about Thrush and his MIB than Salvo at the moment, but yes, I believe he is."

"Because he hopes to find Lakesh before we do?"

She shook her head in frustration, coiffed hair flying. "I don't know what's on his mind, but he might be planning to chill him before we can reach him with the vid."

"Chill him? That doesn't seem reasonable."

"Don't forget who we're talking about."

"How can I?" His tone was venomous. "I was the stupid bastard who wanted to give him a chance to redeem himself."

Brigid looked at him, her gaze intense, riveting itself on Kane's face. "I'm sure this isn't the first time you were a rotten judge of character. Or me, either. I could have made more of a stink, done my damnedest to overrule you. But we're human beings, not hybrids, not Archons, not those droids you told me about.

"Maybe a droid never makes a mistake, but a human being can. We're susceptible to error. If you're guilty of anything, it's wanting to have faith in another human being.''

She lifted her wrist chron to eye level. ''Lakesh recollected he attended the nine-o'clock performance. We've got less than an hour to get there.''

They quickened their pace, backtracking for a couple of blocks until they came out on crowded Fifty-third Street. Kane pointed to bright yellow vehicles wheeling by. ''Let's grab a cab.''

''No,'' she retorted. ''Lakesh claimed the Times Square area will be mobbed, cordoned off for blocks all around.''

''What for?''

''That's where New Yorkers gather to watch the ball drop.''

Kane grunted in irritation. During the briefing, Lakesh had mentioned that peculiar New Year's tradition. It made less sense to him now than before.

They strode briskly down the sidewalk. All around loomed glittering glass-and-steel towers, exciting in their unspoken promise of an equally glittering future. Kane found them cold, soulless and somehow repellent.

The throngs of people increased in number, not to mention the diversity of their clothing, hairstyles and behavior. They saw a large number of proudly deranged people clustered on street corners, exhibiting their emotional disturbances to anyone within their field of vision.

Beer cans and wine bottles littered the sidewalk. Teenagers sat atop car roofs parked at the curbs, CD players blaring different tunes, but somehow they all sounded the same.

Kane didn't like the lustful glances some men directed toward Brigid, and he liked even less the stares directed toward him. The closer they drew to Times Square, the more they had to push their way through a pandemonium of squirming, struggling humanity.

A shabbily dressed man holding a liquor bottle by the neck shambled into Brigid's path, leering at her, touching his crotch in lascivious invitation. Without breaking stride, she jammed a swift elbow into his stomach, doubling him over. Kane shoved him out of the way, though he didn't fall because of the press of the bodies.

Disgust rose in him, primarily because he found himself agreeing with what Salvo had said about the city and its inhabitants, at least in principle. Mayhem and aberrant behaviors ran unchecked, almost as if dogged nonconformity was conformity. The herd mentality the people displayed was paradoxical in their desire to be penned together, jostled and trampled and stepped on. He wondered if they could only truly be themselves in the company of others being themselves.

It was a small consolation, but he couldn't imagine Salvo steeling himself to push through this. At the thought, red anger flashed through him, as well as gray guilt. He had insisted on bringing Salvo on the op, in hopes of capturing something he never had. Instead, he'd lost something, though he wasn't sure what. Confidence in his instincts, certainly, maybe self-respect in the bargain.

Despite Brigid Baptiste's comforting words, Kane was desperately afraid that the next time his instincts faltered, someone close to him would die.

Fortunately the crowd suddenly began to thin out, changing from a seething mob to a fairly orderly group. Their progress became easier and swifter. Lights of a theater marquee blazed ahead and above, and he glimpsed the words Guys And Dolls glowing against the sky.

New York City Center was a multistoried complex illuminated by an electric glare that washed out all shadows in a yards-wide perimeter. On the roof, barely visible from their vantage point, a neon sign wishing Manhattan a Happy New Year blazed against the backdrop of the towering Chrysler Building.

Wooden-sawhorse barricades cordoned off the wide entrance apron, and the crowd had no choice but walk in single file along a narrow path constructed for them.

Brigid and Kane stepped aside and paused near one of the barricades. He automatically checked his watch. Surprisingly their journey, which had felt like hours, had taken only twenty minutes.

A cluster of exceptionally well-dressed men and women passed through glazed double doors. Positioned just outside the zone of bright lights, Brigid scanned their faces.

"Even if Lakesh shows up," Kane said, "it'll be tough to recognize him. He'll be a hell of a lot younger."

"He showed me pix of himself," she murmured distractedly. "I'll recognize him."

They waited in the cold darkness. A snow flurry sprinkled white powder at their feet, which quickly melted down to damp, dirty lumps. Kane kept his senses alert for Salvo, although he doubted the man could have beaten them to the theater. Still, he had something of a head start.

A long black limousine rolled to a stop at the curbside. A man wearing a maroon topcoat and a silk stovepipe hat bustled from the entranceway, waving his white-gloved hands in negation.

The vehicle's curbside doors opened all at once, and three men in dark suits stepped out, moving with machinelike efficiency. They swept their narrowed eyes back and forth. Each one had a transceiver plug nestled in his right ear.

One of them flashed an ID card at the doorman, who instantly backed away, tugging at the brim of his hat, nodding so obsequiously Kane felt like spitting.

Three men and a woman climbed out of the limousine. They looked around, smiling, sharing laughs, craning their necks to look up at the skyscrapers raking the night sky. The men wore tuxedos, the woman a silver lamé evening gown. Though the clothes appeared to be expensive and custom tailored, they didn't seem to be the kind of garb the four people were inclined to wear. Kane thought the clothes wore them, not the other way around.

Brigid stiffened, tensing up beside him. "There he is," she breathed.

Kane looked but didn't see even a faintly familiar face. "Where?"

She pointed. "Second man on the right. See?"

Following her finger, Kane saw a tall, well-built man with thick, glossy black hair brushed back from a high forehead. His olive complexion was clear, his well-fed face split in a toothy, excited grin, his big brown eyes alight. His mustache was neatly trimmed.

When he turned his head and presented his profile, Kane recognized only the long, aquiline nose.

"I didn't expect him to look so young," he muttered.

Brigid chuckled. "He looks about ten years younger than he really he is. He's about forty-seven now, I guess."

"Who are the others?"

"Security escort, bodyguards. Spiros Marcuse is the short man, the scientific liaison between Operation Chronos and Project Cerberus. The Asian is Kuo Liang, the overseer of Project Sigma. The woman is Connaught O'Brien, head of Project Invictus."

Surrounded by the security warders, the four people went into the lobby.

"Now what?" Kane wanted to know. "If we give him the vid of himself and if he doesn't know about anything nasty in the wind, and if there's not going to be anything nasty, won't we be screwing around with the time line?"

She considered his words for a moment. At length, she said, "I don't know. This isn't our time line, so who knows if we're undertaking an action that's supposed to happen or not? He may think he's the victim of a hoax, or the vid may motivate him to investigate all the ramifications of the Totality Concept."

She smiled ruefully. "Why is it you always wait until we're about to make the plunge to start asking good questions?"

"That's a good question, too."

They watched until the limo pulled away from the curb, then approached the entrance. The maroon-garbed doorman crooked an eyebrow at their attire.

The eyebrow rose even higher when they showed him their DIA credentials.

"VIP security," Kane said curtly.

The man's lips twitched as if he tasted something sour. "What is this, a night out at the opera for spooks? How many of you guys are going to show up?"

Brigid leaned toward him. "Explain."

The man made a helpless gesture, unnerved by her stare. "I don't mean no disrespect to you people, but first three guys in black come in, showing NSA ID, then a few minutes later, another DIA man comes along, then this last bunch, now you two."

Without a word, Kane and Brigid pushed past him into the cavernous, chandelier-lit lobby. It looked large enough to hold half of the Cerberus redoubt and was complete with a long bar, benches, overstuffed armchairs and settees. Urns stood about, sprouting waxed greenery.

They took up position near a marble-walled fountain, the gurgling and splashing of water muting their voices. "This is wonderful," Brigid muttered. "Three MIB and one madman added to the equation."

"We don't know for sure it's Thrush's crew and Salvo." Even Kane didn't sound as if he believed a word of it.

"Who else could it be? Colonel Thrush doesn't know why we're here, but he won't take chances knowing that four Totality Concept scientists are accessible to information they shouldn't have. Who the fuck knows what Salvo has in mind?"

Kane felt mild surprise at her use of profanity. That

meant she was upset indeed. She gave him a searching stare.

"You ought to have some idea of what he means to do."

At first Kane felt anger, then realized bleakly he did have an idea but he just hadn't wanted to bring it to the forefront of his mind.

Slowly he said, "He wants to win, he wants to defeat me. The best way to do that is to put the skids on our mission. And the best way to do that is to chill Lakesh."

Lines of strain and consternation appeared on her face. "That won't accomplish anything. This isn't the Lakesh he knows."

"I don't think he cares, Baptiste. He'll do it just to watch the expression on my face. Hell, maybe he hopes that by chilling him, he'll trigger a chain reaction that makes this time line a duplicate of our own."

Brigid looked swiftly around the broad, vaulted lobby. Men and women mingled, drank wine, chatted and generally blocked her view.

"I don't see Lakesh's party," she complained.

"Didn't he say he was in a private viewing box upstairs?"

"He did."

Kane pointed to an arrow on a sign that read To Balcony Seating.

Following the arrow, they crossed the lobby to an arched doorway. A flight of carpeted steps stretched up to the floor above. They climbed the stairs and entered a wide, long hallway with white walls. They walked along it for a few yards, then came to an intersecting corridor. The left-hand wall bore narrow doorways, spaced at regular intervals. The doorways were divided by red velvet ropes with Reserved signs attached to them.

On impulse, Kane went to the nearest door, stepped over the rope and peered into a small alcove holding six empty seats. Beneath and beyond, overhead spotlights illuminated a stage holding a bizarre, two-dimensional rendition of New York City, painted in bright primary colors. Oversize signs emblazoned with The Bowery, The Battery and 42nd Street were placed at cock-eyed angles all over the set.

An orchestra tuned up in a darkened pit. A snare drum trembled, horns, flutes and saxophones sounded low, ominous registers.

When he returned to the corridor, Kane saw people were beginning to walk up the stairway.

Brigid said, "I think we'd have a better chance if we split up. We'll keep our trans-comm frequencies open."

He nodded reluctantly, putting his hand in his coat pocket, closing it around the palm-sized rectangle of metal and plastic. He thumbed on the voice-activation setting and heard the faint hiss of static.

Brigid faced the wall and Kane stood in front of her, blocking her from view while she drew her Beretta, worked the slide to jack a round into the chamber and placed it in her pocket.

"Primed," she said in low voice. "You take that end of the hall—I'll take this one."

They strode off in opposite directions. He checked every door he came to, even the men's rooms. The private booths he peered into were either vacant or occupied by people who regarded him with haughty, suspicious eyes.

As he approached the last pair of viewing cubicles, a man stepped out of the farther one, hooking the red rope back in place. He took up an alert parade-rest position before the door.

As Kane recognized him as one of Lakesh's security escort, he repressed a sigh of relief. He stopped, leaning against the wall, looking out at the man between the spade-shaped leaves of a potted plant. Unpocketing his trans-comm, he lifted it to his lips and whispered, "Baptiste, I've found Lakesh."

After a moment, her response filtered over the receiver. "I'll be right there. Stand by."

Kane tried not to appear too blatantly out of place next to the well-dressed people who walked past him as he waited for Baptiste. Music swelled boisterously in the theater, and he felt the floor vibrate slightly in time with its fast rhythm.

Hazarding a quick peek at the security agent, he saw the man still stood as immobile as a statue, outwardly unmoved by the music.

A figure suddenly emerged from the adjacent doorway, and Kane's breath seized sharply in his lungs. Salvo casually approached the man. Because of the overture, Kane couldn't hear what he was saying, but he saw him flash his forged DIA credentials.

Kane lunged away from the plant, kicking off the floor in a wild, adrenaline-fueled sprint. The security agent caught Kane's abrupt, rushing appearance at the periphery of his vision, and his eyes flicked away from the identification Salvo held up before them.

That instant of distraction was all Salvo needed to slash his throat.

Chapter 31

The knife blade severed the carotid artery, dragged across the windpipe and larynx, then sank into the jugular vein. Scarlet exploded out of the man's throat in a jetting spray, splattering the opposite wall.

As blood cascaded down and drenched the man's shirtfront, Salvo grasped him by the lapels of his jacket, wrestling him around so his spasming body was between him and Kane.

The security agent dragged an automatic pistol from a waistband holster, but his fingers were slick with his own blood and couldn't acquire a grip. Salvo easily wrested the weapon from his hand. He side-stepped through the door, over the rope, allowing the man's body to slump onto it. He hung in a grotesque pose, supported by his neck as the lips of his wound snagged and closed around the red velvet.

Kane's Sin Eater had slid into his palm in sheer reflex action as soon as he began to run. Barely audible over the orchestra's fanfare, he heard a pair of wet-twig cracks, then a woman's voice rising shrilly in a scream. The scream cut off abruptly.

Pressing his back against the wall, he nudged the security agent with a foot. His slit throat slipped from the rope, and his body crumpled in a leg-twisted heap, blood still gushing from a severed artery and a deeply cut vein.

He heard rapid footfalls down the hallway and he swung his head and blaster barrel in that direction. As he hoped, it was Brigid. He returned his attention to the door, not wasting a second to gauge her reaction to the scene.

She leaned against the wall beside him, her respiration stressed and frightened. "What happened?"

"Salvo. He has that poor bastard's blaster. I heard a couple of shots, but I don't know what—"

"Kane!" Salvo spoke in a triumphant shout.

"I'm here," Kane shouted back.

"Good. Move out to where I can see you. Baptiste, too."

Desperately Kane replied, "She's not here. We split up."

"And you trans-commed her as soon as you saw me. If I don't see her, we're not coming out."

Kane closed his eyes, exhaled an agonized "Shit!" then whispered to Brigid, "We've got to do as he says."

Eyes bright with anger, she muttered, "This is getting very old."

Carefully they eased out into the center of the corridor, hearing blood squish beneath their shoes. They faced the doorway, backing up to the crimson-splattered wall.

Lakesh appeared in the doorway, Salvo's left arm crooked around his throat, the muzzle of the Delta Elite autoblaster planted at the hinge of his jaw. There was a welt on the right side of Lakesh's head, which would turn bluish black within the hour if he lived that long. His dark, wide eyes glistened with tears. His hands shook as if with the ague.

In a horror-choked voice, he croaked, "He killed them. He murdered my bodyguards, he hit Connaught—"

"Shut up, pissant," hissed Salvo. "You have more balls when you're two hundred. Unhook that fucking rope."

Lakesh's trembling fingers could barely work the simple clasp. The rope draped over the lap of the dead warder.

"Now what?" Kane asked, deliberately making his voice sound weary. "I wish you'd come up with a new routine."

"Give me a break, Kane," Salvo replied with a grin. "I'm new at this."

"What do you want?" demanded Brigid.

"Come with me and find out."

"Whatever you have in mind, it won't solve the larger problem."

Salvo laughed defiantly. There was a glazed look in his mud-colored eyes, as if he weren't really seeing her. "How the fuck would you know?"

He edged out into the corridor, nodding toward an L bend at the end of the hallway. "You two go ahead. I want you in front of me."

Lakesh blubbered and whimpered. Kane and Brigid marched side by side. They turned the corner just as the doors of an elevator slid apart. Colonel Thrush, Starling and Sparrow stepped out. His two men carried identical Ingram MAC-10 subguns, the blunt noses of the sound suppressors pointed at the floor.

Before they could swing them up, Kane had them covered with his Sin Eater. Everybody stopped and looked at each other in a frozen tableau.

"Move!" Salvo barked from behind them.

"A little problem," Kane called over his shoulder. "New players on the field."

Growling a curse, Salvo pushed Lakesh forward. When he saw Thrush and his men, he came to a halt. Separated by a span of ten feet, the two groups regarded each other silently.

Nodding toward Thrush, Brigid suggested, "I think you should go first."

Thrush didn't smile as he murmured, "Age before beauty, I take it. Very well. I suspected our objectives might be similar, but I certainly did not envision them intertwining in circumstances like this. What are you planning to do with Dr. Lakesh?"

Indicating Salvo with a backward jerk of his head, Kane answered, "What he said—come with him and find out."

Thrush peered past Brigid and Kane. "Might I suggest the roof? It will offer us a modicum of privacy while we sort this matter out."

Salvo chuckled thickly. "My thoughts exactly."

Lakesh whimpered, "Colonel Thrush, we met at Dulce, remember?"

"Very clearly, Doctor. Please cooperate with this man and do not fret. I am here to make certain it all comes out right in the end."

Tightening his arm about his hostage's throat, Salvo ordered, "Tell your birdies to drop their blasters."

Thrush gestured to Starling and Sparrow, who showed no emotion as they placed their Ingrams on the floor and kicked them across the corridor.

"Now you, Colonel."

Thrush unbuttoned his suit coat, opening it wide. "I am unarmed. Though I've employed firearms in the past, I did so reluctantly. Ugly mechanisms, really."

Salvo grunted. "Baptiste—frisk him."

Brigid glanced at him curiously. "What about our own blasters?"

Salvo chuckled again. "I'm not worried about you two. You and Kane are as predictable as bowel movements. But those three are unknown quantities."

Thrush smiled approvingly. "Solid tactical thinking. Yes, you do possess some admirable characteristics, Mr. Salvo."

Brigid stepped forward and gingerly patted Colonel Thrush down, sliding her hands from his armpits down to his ankles. Her flesh crawled as she did so, as if she touched a substance that looked like a human body, superficially felt like one, yet radiated an indefinable, repellent difference.

At Thrush's right calf, just above his ankle, her fingers encountered the hard outline of a small, holstered blaster. She raised her eyes quickly. Thrush's bland smile hadn't changed and she couldn't see his eyes, but he turned his face downward in an almost imperceptible, questioning nod.

"Well?" Salvo asked impatiently.

Brigid straightened up. "He's clean."

He pushed Lakesh forward. "Let's get the show started. The overture has already begun."

The elevator car comfortably fit all seven of them, and the ascent took only a few seconds. The doors opened within a narrow cupola. Salvo and Lakesh stepped out first.

"Slow and easy," he instructed. "Keep together."

The roof of New York City Center was an artificial forest of steel girders and cube-shaped air-conditioning units. A short flight of metal-slatted stairs led up to a superstructure that held a gigantic electric sign, the words Happy New Year blazing in dazzling white letters twenty feet high. The gray monolithic edifice of the Chrysler Building loomed like a gargantuan tombstone above it. The glow from the neon sign suffused the tar-and-gravel surface with multicolored highlights. An icy wind gusted across the rooftop, plucking at hair and setting coattails to flapping.

"Kane, come with us," Salvo announced. "The rest of you stay where you are. If I see one of you so much as scratch an ear, Lakesh is dead."

Walking backward, Salvo dragged a shivering Lakesh toward the stairway. Kane followed slowly. When they were out of earshot, Brigid whispered to Colonel Thrush, "We're going to have to make a move. He'll chill Lakesh."

Calmly he replied, "Perhaps. Probabilities are in a state of flux at this point. However, I have already formulated a plan to stabilize this situation, regardless of the outcome."

While Kane stood at the foot of the stairs, Salvo and Lakesh carefully climbed them. When they reached the top of the superstructure, Kane followed, taking deliberate steps. Salvo pulled Lakesh close to the sign, standing under and between the splayed neon legs of the *R* in Year. The white glare made Salvo's smiling face look like that of a drowned corpse, lips contorted in a death rictus. Despite the cold, perspiration rivered down his sallow cheeks. Pushing the man out at arm's length, Salvo gripped him by the collar of his tuxedo, the bore of the Delta Elite pressed against his right temple.

In a clear, uncompromising tone of authority, Salvo declared, "Kane, you've got a choice to make. My life or his."

Kane said nothing, eyeballing the distance, the trajectory a bullet would have to travel in order to end up in Salvo before he squeezed his own trigger.

"Here's my proposal," Salvo went on. "I want you down on your knees like you had me. I want you to beg my forgiveness. I want you to crawl over here on your belly and beg me to chill you."

Kane tightened his lips so an impulsive, reflexive *Fuck you* wouldn't escape them.

"Or," stated Salvo, "I want you to try and chill me. That's why I let you keep your blaster."

Doing his best to sound unemotional, as if he were puzzling over a fairly simple and uninteresting problem, Kane inquired, "And Lakesh?"

Salvo's smile broadened. "If you choose the latter option, I'll blow the evil prick's brains out. I won't be able to help it, you know. An involuntary contraction of the muscles as soon as a bullet hits me. You'll get me, sure enough. But I'll get him…sure enough."

Lakesh gasped beseechingly, "Please, sir, do as he says."

Salvo chuckled. "He wants to see you humiliate yourself. First time I've ever agreed with him about anything. You've got five seconds to decide. Five…four…three…"

As Salvo counted down to one, Kane dropped to

his knees, ignoring the sharp-edged gravel cutting into his knees, struggling to control his rage.

"How does it feel, Kane?" A laugh throbbed at the back of Salvo's throat. "Every time we've gone head-to-head, I've beaten you. This time you're fucking going to admit who's the superior man."

Dully Kane said, "That's what this is about?"

Salvo glared at him, eyes fixed on his face as if nothing else existed in the world that could ever hold his attention. "You stupid, arrogant bastard. That's what *everything* is about! Why can't you get that simple fact of existence through your head?

"Lakesh bred you to be the best because only the best survive. That's the law of Nature—always has been and always will be. I'm supposed to be your inferior, yet I know that. Why don't you?"

With a rolling jerk of his head, Salvo gestured to the city around them. "Look at this pesthole, where the worst, the dregs, have taken over. It's the rule of anarchy, the tyranny of chaos over law. The survival of the *unfittest*. Even this scheming son of a bitch knows it, and that's why he welded his lips to the ass of the Directorate!"

Faintly Lakesh said, "I don't know what you're talking about, I'm just a scientist, you've mistaken me for somebody else—"

Salvo brayed out a laugh and dug the bore of the blaster hard against the welt on the side of Lakesh's head. He yelped in pain.

"'Just a scientist,'" Salvo mocked, imitating his lilting East Indian accent. "You're more than that, you bastard. You get to sit out the holocaust, safe and snug. You get to come back and fuck with people's lives so you can destroy the order men like my dad died to build!''

''Holocaust?'' whimpered Lakesh. ''What are you talking about?''

Kane snapped, ''He's not the same Lakesh. He's got nothing to do with your life, my life, with anybody's life in our time.''

Confusion momentarily overwhelmed the hatred in Salvo's feverish eyes. He snarled, ''I don't care. *You're* the one who cares. On your belly, Kane. Start crawling.''

Chapter 32

Quietly Kane asked, "Would admitting that you've won again, that you've defeated me again, stop this bullshit and save Lakesh's life?"

Salvo pretended to seriously ponder the query. "I don't know, I really don't. You humiliated me, Kane. You beat me like I was lowest slime-slag in the filthiest squat of Tartarus. I don't know what would stop this bullshit. Maybe if you could give me back my pride, but that's not likely to happen."

"Is that why you want to die, because of your pride? Because I'm the one who kicked your ass, saved it, kicked it again, then showed you that your whole life was wasted as an errand boy to a bunch of big-headed little gray bastards who could give a shit about your years of service?"

Salvo's lips stretched taut over his teeth. A stitch popped loose, and a string of blood oozed out and down over his chin. "Crawl!"

"It's all about me," Kane announced, raising his voice. "God almighty, nothing else matters to you, does it? You need me, you need to hate me like a jolt-walker needs a daily fix. Even when I offered you a chance to stop hating me, to stop *needing* to hate me, you couldn't give it up."

Salvo grated, "You need that hate, too, Kane. You had three chances to chill me, and you couldn't bring yourself to do it. You wanted me alive so you could keep on trying to prove how much better you are than me.''

"I don't need you, Salvo, I don't hate you. You're not my better. You're not even my enemy. You know what you are? You're a fucking roach, swimming in the baron's shit, eating it, breathing and asking for more. I'd step on you if I were wearing shoes I could throw away later.''

As he spoke, Kane's eyes bored into Salvo's own, watching for that microinstant preceding his finger squeezing the automatic's trigger. When that instant came, Kane knew he would have a tenth of a second to raise his Sin Eater and make a shot that would save one life and end another.

That microinstant never arrived. A blasting roar thundered from above them, a blinding blade of light stabbing down to impale Lakesh and Salvo.

The helicopter, a black mass behind the brilliant spotlights, hovered a bare ten feet above the neon sign. The tremendous down wash of the spinning rotaries sucked up the cold air and created a stifling semivacuum, full of swirling bits of trash and loose pieces of gravel.

Salvo's coat billowed up around him, his face screwed up tight against the glare. For a moment, he removed his blaster from Lakesh's head to beat down the cloth flapping in his face.

The boom of Kane's single shot was swallowed up in the deafening roar produced by the helicopter. The bullet punched Salvo in the chest and slammed him backward, arms flailing, feet kicking. The barrel of the Delta Elite crashed into and shattered the thick glass tube forming the straight leg of the *R*.

Like the victim of a clumsily executed crucifixion, Salvo's arm jerked as a concentration of electrical voltage poured through the barrel of the pistol and raged into his body. White sparks spewed in a miniature starburst from the point where the metal of the pistol intersected with the path of the current.

Kane caught only a fragmented glimpse of Lakesh stumbling and falling to his hands and knees before the entire sign shorted out. White-hot tongues of flame jetted from the letters, glass exploding in jangling showers, sparks flashing and arcing down like the flaring tails of comets.

The chopper's engine whined as it strained for altitude, rising above the pyrotechnics erupting from the neon letters. The glare died abruptly, except for tiny, sputtering squirts of sparks.

Kane blinked hard against the rainbow-colored floaters bobbing across his vision, smelling Salvo before he could fully focus on him. The stench of charred clothing, scorched hair and cooked human flesh made his stomach boil with acid.

Salvo stood with his head bowed, his right arm still up-flung. The wind of the helicopter's vanes buffeted him, and slowly he toppled forward. All Kane saw of his face was a parboiled, leaking swatch of blackened skin. Curling tendrils of smoke trailed from his body as it collapsed full-length onto the tarred gravel.

Kane climbed to his feet and stepped over his smoldering body, not bothering to check for a pulse. He found himself hoping his bullet had chilled Salvo before the voltage did, though he wasn't sure why. Dying from electrocution was supposed to be quicker and therefore more merciful than a bullet shattering all the major thoracic bones and rupturing the heart and lungs.

Lakesh cowered away from Kane as he bent over him, gibbering in his own language. He made strangulated noises like a dog trying to cough up a bone.

Kane lifted him upright by his arm. "You're all right, old man. It's another one you owe me. Sort of."

Eyes brimming with tears, Lakesh rasped, "What do you mean? I don't know you!"

Kane guided him toward the steps. "Not yet. Maybe not ever, if you're lucky. But if you're not, and if my history is replayed here, you will. When that happens, keep this incident in mind. It'll save us both a lot of heartache when you start wondering how far you can trust me."

Brigid, Thrush, Starling and Sparrow gathered at the foot of the staircase. Brigid took Lakesh's hand and squeezed it, speaking to him comfortingly.

Kane pointed to the hovering helicopter. "Yours?" he asked Thrush.

The colonel nodded. "Yes. I arranged it to spirit our mutual friend away."

"Away from us?"

"Not necessarily. Dr. Lakesh has exceptionally sensitive information locked up in his head. Specifically his plans are to combine Cerberus and Chronos to construct a trans-dimensional device that functions similarly to a black hole."

Despite the roar of the helicopter, Lakesh and Brigid overheard and swung their heads around, faces registering astonishment.

"A Singularity?" Brigid asked.

Lakesh stared at Thrush in dismay. "How can you know about that? Nothing is on paper. It's simply a theory I've been toying with."

Thrush shrugged. "By the end of the coming year, you'll do more than toy with it. Your theory will become functioning hardware. Working in secret, you will link the Cerberus and Chronos programs. Your first experiment will be your last. It triggers a spatial discontinuity. After that, temporal anomalies erupt throughout the entire space-time continuum. Both the future and the past coexist. For all intents and purposes, Earth is obliterated."

Horror crawled across Lakesh's face like something alive. "How could you know that?"

Thrush smiled patronizingly, almost pityingly. "Come now, Doctor. How do you think I know it?"

Lakesh swallowed very hard. "Chronos?"

"Exactly."

Dark eyes darting between Kane, Brigid and Thrush, Lakesh exclaimed, "You're all from the future! I understand now. Someday Burr figures out how to translate living matter along the temporal stream, and you come back to rescue me from that maniac!"

"We are from *a* future," Thrush admitted. "Quite different ones, I assume. But as far as coming back to rescue you, I'm afraid that is not within my mission parameters."

The little gun that had been hidden in Thrush's hand made a popping sound, no more audible than a distant handclap. Lakesh tried to cry out as he pitched to his knees, mouth open, eyes rolling as if to look at the small round hole in the middle of his forehead. He fell forward on his face.

Brigid screamed in fury, Kane's blaster whipped up, but so did Thrush's. He aimed it at Brigid, centering it on her left eye, less than two feet away.

"No, no, Mr. Kane," he said coldly. "There's been enough violence for one night. What I said about the spatial discontinuity is true. Dr. Lakesh had to die. I was more than willing to let Mr. Salvo do the deed if matters unfolded in such a fashion, but I was always prepared to fulfill the mission objectives myself. Curious how destiny takes care of itself, regardless of the insertion of random elements."

"Why did you do it?" Brigid demanded, teeth clenched as she struggled to hold her emotions in check. "Once you told him what would happen, he would have never built the thing."

"The uncertainty principle again, applied to very unpredictable human beings. My...employers needed to be very sure. Otherwise, their plans could not proceed. If Dr. Lakesh had turned his theory into a reality, Earth would be an exceptionally chaotic place."

"And," intoned Kane, "if there's one thing the Archons hate, it's chaos."

Colonel Thrush gave him a fleeting, appreciative smile. "I wasn't certain how much you knew in your future. I am gratified."

"Why?" Brigid bit out the word.

"It means you resorted to the very dangerous and desperate measure of time travel in order to oppose the Directorate. It means all your other measures failed. And most of all, it means *my* measures were successful."

Kane made a growling noise deep in his chest. "Just who or what are you?"

"What you already suspect—a conspirator. Few conspiracies succeed unless the keynote is simplicity. Even then, they succeed because humans overlook obvious dangers such as a blind man could see. That is why human history is such a morass of inconsistencies."

"More obfuscation," Brigid spat out the words.

"Not this time," Thrush replied. "Think of it this way—over a period of fifty years, your governments were supplied with materials to build the tools we needed. They believed they were constructing wondrous weapons to keep them safe from aggression, and to wage war on whoever they decided was their enemy in any given year.

"They took particular delight in Operation Chronos, envisioning returning in time to murder Lenin, Mao or Hirohito. Or perhaps even Lincoln, while he was still chopping wood in Illinois.

"It never occurred to even the brightest of them that we deliberately set limits on all our projects. For example, Chronos functioned according to our specs. Nor did it ever occur to them that once it was built, we would use it for our purposes, and make doubly certain it could never be employed to undo what we have done. A conspiracy to manipulate a conspiracy."

"Time squared," Brigid said flatly.

"Precisely," retorted Thrush. "I'll have to remember that one."

Kane asked, "Now what? Shoot us down, too?"

Thrush shook his head. "That is not part of the

mission. Inasmuch as you're not from this time plane,
leaving your corpses to be found and examined could
conceivably cause more problems than solve them.
No, you are free to go, once my aides and I have
departed. You'll have no difficulty reentering the
gateway installation. Only young Hector is on duty,
and I've deactivated the drones. Now, please disarm
yourselves."

Sparrow marched over to Kane, holding out his
hand expectantly. Glowering, Kane tugged up his coat
sleeve and unbuckled the straps of his holster. Starling
approached Brigid.

The hovering helicopter dropped, and a rope ladder
snaked down, unrolling as it fell.

"Nice and easy moves, please," Thrush said loudly
over the pounding engine noise.

Sparrow reached out to take the Sin Eater harness
from Kane. The chopper tilted slightly to port, causing the ladder to flip and twist, clattering loudly
against a steel girder. Sparrow's eyes shifted sharply
toward it as his fingers closed over the holster.

In that split second, Kane lifted his left hand, palm
outward, fingers curled, wrist locked. He drove his
hand forward from the shoulder in a fast, flat trajectory. Sparrow detected the blur of movement, took a
half step backward, eyes widening.

The palm of Kane's hand impacted like a battering
ram against the bottom tip of Sparrow's nose. There
was a very faint, mushy crunch of cartilage. Like a
skier catching a low branch under the chin, the man's
head snapped back, his legs flying out from under
him. His crushed nose spewed blood as bone splinters

pushed through his sinus cavities and into his brain. Sparrow was dead before his body settled.

Thrush whirled around, his hand hardly moving from the recoil of the pistol as he snapped off a shot. The steel-jacketed slug struck a blue spark from the metal stairway behind Kane. He dropped flat on his left side, sweeping his right leg out in a slashing kick, catching Thrush just behind the knees. His legs buckled, and he staggered but he didn't fall.

At the same instant Brigid, who had been drawing her Beretta from her coat pocket, found the trigger and squeezed it. The 9 mm parabellum round tore through the fabric and smacked into and through Starling's lower belly.

In the short span of time it took Thrush to recover his balance, Kane had his hands on his Sin Eater and he fired a triburst into the man's head.

Colonel Thrush's sunglasses, hair and part of his scalp floated away, and the flesh on the left side of his face was flayed away as if exposed to a high-speed flensing knife.

He stumbled backward, long legs kicking frantically. His back slammed hard against the sheet-metal surface of an air-conditioning unit. Metal banged loudly. He kept his feet and he didn't die. He got his feet under him and pushed himself up to his full height.

Kane stared, feeling the recycling of an old fear and disgust.

The head of Colonel Thrush was hairless, and the left side of it, beneath shredded scraps of flesh, was burnished metal devoid of another layer of epidermis, blood vessels or ligaments. But his eye, a wet, gelatinous black pit, drooled down his chromed cheek.

He still held the little automatic pistol, which he raised again. Kane triggered another 3-round burst. Thrush's hand seemed to dissolve, his arm jerking up and bobbing almost bonelessly, like a strip of cloth in a high wind. Gun, fingers and patches of shirt cuff flew across the rooftop in different directions.

Rising to his feet, Kane automatically checked the zone, noting Sparrow's slack, blood-drenched face and Starling doubled up and writhing around his belly wound.

"Track the chopper, Baptiste," he ordered.

He strode over to Thrush, who watched him approach with one inhumanly large, inhumanly black eye.

"That's how the Directorate got around the problem of translating living matter through time," he said grimly. "A faux human. You're nothing but a goddamn droid."

The right side of Thrush's mouth curved up in a mild smile. "An oversimplification. I'm not a robot."

"Then you're a cyborg, worse than a hybrid."

"Actually I am a hybrid of organic and inorganic compounds. My brain cells are fused with metal electrodes, tied into a mainframe computer. It's linked with the surveillance drones in the installation. Everything it saw was transmitted to me. That's how I knew of your arrival. My body itself is basically composed of protein molecules, with a highly simplified digestive system and fewer internal organs than you're used to carrying around.

He smiled ruefully at the bloodless, ragged stump

of his wrist. "My epidermis is not tissue at all, as you've probably guessed by now. My bones are bonded with a Teflon-ceramic mixture."

Kane's tone of voice and expression displayed his complete revulsion and loathing. "You're a human being and you allowed the Archons to do that to you?"

Thrush snorted contemptuously. "The idiocies you humans spout never fail to amuse me. Do you think the Archons would entrust one of you creatures with my responsibilities?"

Kane frowned in understanding. "You're a hybrid, aren't you, a hybrid of a hybrid?"

Thrush looked up to the helicopter. "I meant what I said that you were free to go, you know."

"That doesn't mean you are."

"Allow me to point out that the aircraft above you is equipped with a .50-caliber machine gun. I am in constant touch with the pilot and the crew. If I suggest that a demonstration is in order to convince you—"

Tongues of flame spit from the nose of chopper. Even over the noise of the engine and whirling blades, Kane heard the loud, rattling roar of autofire. Gravel and chunks of tar sprang up in geysers, punching a semicircle six feet around Brigid. The burst was brief, only a couple of seconds in duration, but it was convincing.

"So, you see," continued Thrush reasonably, "it is in your best interests to conclude our business as amicably as possible. It really doesn't matter what happens to me. Colonel Thrush is not an individual, but a program. My body is mortal, but the program will simply animate another one like me."

Kane grimaced in frustrated anger, glancing up at the helicopter hovering over them like a bird of prey. "You murdered Lakesh."

"And you belabor the obvious. Besides, I did not harm the Lakesh you know, in your own time plane, merely a version of him. And in ending that life, I saved this planet from a catastrophe of unparalleled proportions."

"You saved it only so the Archons could gut it."

"The distinction escapes me. Make your decision, Mr. Kane, and do not try to engage me any further in hypothetical hair-splitting."

Kane stepped back from him, gesturing to the dangling rope ladder.

Colonel C. W. Thrush nodded graciously. "Thank you. By the way, I shall arrange for the disposal of Mr. Salvo's remains."

Surprised, Kane demanded, "Why?"

"Partly so as not to delay your departure from this time plane. Primarily I like to be neat. Aside from that, as I told him, he possessed certain qualities I admired. Perhaps something of them can be salvaged."

Thrush strode swiftly toward the rope ladder. As he seized the wooden rungs and swung himself up, he looked back at Kane. "At the risk of repeating myself, au revoir."

Kane shook his head and shouted, "Another time, Colonel. Another time."

Colonel Thrush laughed, a grotesque sound exuding from a grotesque face. "Just so. Another time."

The helicopter rose, the spotlight blinking off. The dark shape above it claimed Thrush's figure.

Chapter 33

Tears streaked Brigid's face as she looked down at Lakesh's body. Bitterly she whispered, "The Omega Path. It led only to the end."

Kane didn't reply, but looked toward the slumped shape of Salvo. He felt nothing, not even the ache of a connection being cut forever. Nor did he feel he had gained a part of him, unless it was his maddened determination to die on his own terms.

Despite everything he had learned, despite what Thrush had told him, he was sure his life was in his own hands. He could yield himself up to death, but he wouldn't do it, not yet. There were tasks, missions still to perform.

Brigid moved away from the body. "Only a couple of hours until midnight. A new year, a new millennium."

She walked numbly over to the edge of the roof, leaning on the parapet to stare at the street below. Kane joined her, gazing down at the neon-washed canyons of the city. The voices of the jubilant crowd drifted up to them.

From here, he thought, the city looked like it was supposed to—bright, clean, full of hope for tomorrow.

Brigid said softly, listlessly, "I wish there was something to celebrate in our time...just one tiny part of one year where we can delude ourselves into believing things will be better."

She straightened up, running her fingers through her hair. Due to its heaviness, almost all of the ringlets and coiffed waves had fallen out of it. She noted it with a sad smile.

Turning to face Kane, she said dryly, "We'd better make our New Year's resolutions now. We won't have another chance."

He smiled slightly. "We'll make the chances, Baptiste, even if they're only one percent."

Then he took her in his arms and stared deep into her eyes, which widened in sudden surprise.

"Resolutions be damned," he said roughly, and kissed her.

A violent struggle for survival
in a post-holocaust world

JAMES AXLER
DEATH LANDS®

Freedom Lost

Following up rumors of trouble on his old home ground, Ryan and his band seek shelter inside the walls of what was once the largest shopping mall in the Carolinas. The baron of the fortress gives them no choice but to join his security detail. As outside invaders step up their raids on the mall, Ryan must battle both sides for a chance to save their lives.

Where there's smoke...

THE Destroyer™

#111 Prophet of Doom

Created by
WARREN MURPHY
and RICHARD SAPIR

Everyone with a spare million is lining up at the gates of Ranch Ragnarok, home to Esther Clear Seer's Church of the Absolute and Incontrovertible Truth. Here an evil yellow smoke shrouds an ancient oracle that offers glimpses into the future. But when young virgins start disappearing, CURE smells something more than a scam—and Remo is slated to become a sacrificial vessel....

Look for it in April 1998 wherever Gold Eagle books are sold.

From the creator of

comes a new journey in a world
with little hope...